I0724374

Flynn

The Craigdon Family Dynasty

Book Six

CHRIS TAYLOR

© 2021 Chris Taylor

© 2021 by Chris Taylor

(All Rights Reserved)

Without limiting the rights under copyright(s) reserved below, no part of this publication may be reproduced, stored in or introduced into a retrieval system, or transmitted, in any form, or by any means (electronic, mechanical, photocopying, recording, or otherwise) without the prior permission of the copyright owner.

LCT Productions Pty Ltd
18364 Kamilaroi Highway, Narrabri NSW 2390

ISBN. 978-1-925119-84-8 (Paperback)

Flynn is a work of fiction. Names, characters, places, brands, media and incidents either are the product of the author's imagination or are used fictitiously. Any resemblance to actual persons, living or dead, events, or locales, is entirely coincidental.

Published in the United States of America.

Books by Chris Taylor

THE MUNRO FAMILY SERIES
The Profiler
The Investigator
The Predator
The Betrayal
The Deception
The Negotiator
The Christmas Vigil
The Ransom
The Defendant
The Shooting
The Maker
(Available in Audio)

THE SYDNEY HARBOUR HOSPITAL SERIES
The Perfect Husband
The Body Thief
The Baby Snatchers
The Final Bullet
The Debt Collector
The Lab Test
The Stolen Identity
The Cliff-top Killer
The Likeable Fraudster

THE SYDNEY LEGAL SERIES
An Accidental Murderer
At the Hand of Her Father
A Woman Scorned
Lies and Deception
Ordinary Evil
The Ties That Bind
The Perfect Crime
A Toxic Inheritance
Malicious Love

THE CRAIGDON FAMILY SERIES
Callum
Joel
Isabella
Nicholas
Sophia
Flynn
Noah
Logan
Elizabeth

THE BARRINGTON FAMILY SERIES
Broken Lives
Broken Promises
Broken Bonds
Broken Spirits
Broken Vows
Broken Minds
Broken Dreams
Broken Hearts
Broken Homes

THE FAIRFAX FAMILY SERIES
A Cattleman in Disguise
A Cattleman's Quest
A Cattleman's Daughter
A Cattleman's Secret Baby
To Catch a Cattleman
The Doctor and the Cattleman
To Rescue a Cattleman
A Cattleman's Heart
For the Love of a Cattleman

BACHELORS AND BRIDES SERIES
Matilda
Austin
Farrah

Benjamin
Verity
Denver
Ebony
Tyrone
Willow

Chris Taylor writing as
BELLA CHRISTIAN

THIS IS WHERE IT ENDS SERIES
(in order)
Jessie's Story
Ryan's Story
Holly's Story
Sarah's Story
Veronica's Story

Get a FREE book when you sign up for Chris Taylor's
newsletter at: www.christaylorauthor.com.au

Love Audiobooks? Check out Chris Taylor Books on audio
on Audible.com, Amazon.com and Apple Books.

Join Chris Taylor's Facebook reader group/fan page and be
among the first to receive news of book releases, read and
review books prior to release and other amazing offers. Join
Now at: www.facebook.com/groups/1758023621144744/

Find out more about all of Chris Taylor's books, by visiting her
website at: www.christaylorauthor.com.au

Dedication

This book is dedicated to my sister, Nic. Thank you for all the brainstorming that has helped to make the Craigdon Family series a reality. I hope you're enjoying the final result!

And as always, to my husband, Linden. My best friend, my soul mate. I love you to the moon and back.

Acknowledgments

As usual, no book comes into being without a lot of help and support by my friends and family. A world of thanks must go to my wonderful editor, Pat Thomas. Thank you for everything that you do to make my stories even more amazing than I could ever dare to dream. To former Detective Superintendent Michael Kilfoyle, thank you for lending my story credibility. Any mistakes are wholly my own.

To Mary and all of the team at Miblart, thank you for the fantastic book cover. To my sister, Nicole Guihot and to my friends, Ally Thomson and Sue Ricardo, thank you for your excellent editorial comments, proof reading skills and suggestions. I hope you like the final result.

To Amy Atwell, Kirby and the dedicated team at Author E.M.S. who are so much more than book formatters. Amy, once again, thank you for your magic.

To the fantastic writer organizations such as Romance Writers of Australia, Romance Writers of America and Romance Writers of New Zealand for all the help, support and encouragement they offer new and aspiring writers, including me.

To my readers, thank you for your support and love for my stories. Your encouragement and enjoyment make this journey all worthwhile.

And lastly, to my friends and family, especially my husband and children. Thank you for putting up with late dinners and even later conversations as I've emerged day after day from the sometimes scary but always enthralling world I've created on my computer.

Chapter One

Flynn Craigdon's phone beeped, indicating an incoming message. Checking the screen, he looked at the image and read the accompanying message. He chuckled.

Yes! Everything was going to plan…

It was the day of Callum's buck's night. The lucky groom, his best man and his three groomsmen were at the suit hire shop, having their final fittings. The wedding was only two days away and the tension on Callum's face was testament to that. No matter that he was marrying the love of his life and he'd given up a future in the priesthood to be with her, it was normal for any guy to experience last minute jitters and Callum was certainly not immune.

Flynn sent his cousin a reassuring smile. "Don't look so terrified, Callum. It's going to be fine."

Callum grimaced and looked past the elderly tailor who hovered close, adjusting this and that on Callum's morning suit. He'd gone for a pale gray coat and tails. The color contrasted nicely with Callum's dark blond hair and blue eyes and the cut and quality of the cloth was in keeping with the shop's atmosphere of exclusivity. The store was lined from floor to ceiling with dark, rich-colored wood. The lighting was well placed and bright enough to highlight the superb quality of the suits that lined two walls. The thick carpet beneath their feet silenced their footsteps. The full-length mirrors at the back of the shop were edged in gold. It was the kind of shop that screamed quality and no doubt the price tags on the suits matched.

Tucked away between Sydney's Pitt Street Mall and George Street, in the heritage-listed, Victorian-style Strand Arcade, it might not have been Callum's kind of shop, but it was definitely the kind of store people of the standing and reputation of the Craigdon family were expected to conduct their business. Especially for something as important as a high society wedding. As Callum's best man, it was Flynn's job to keep him calm and bring a smile to his rather tense face. And Flynn knew just how to do that.

He looked at the image on his phone again. Angel was a DD cup, size-six blond with legs up to her armpits. Flynn had found her on the Internet and had arranged for her to call on them at Beaches in Balmoral, later that night. The bar was located on a hill above one of Sydney's northern beaches and encapsulated sweeping views of the harbor. Angel had been told to pay particular attention to the groom.

"Hey, Flynn! Put that damn phone down and go and try on your suit!"

Flynn glanced at his cousin again. Callum looked tired and irritated. Flynn could understand why. Apart from the stresses of the upcoming wedding, they'd all agreed to meet at the store at midday. It was now going on for two. Jett had turned up an hour late, apologizing and mumbling something about a call-out to an emergency. Joel had also been running late. As detectives in busy Sydney police stations, Flynn could understand how work sometimes got in the way of other things, but surely they could have called and re-scheduled? It wasn't like he and Nicholas were sitting around with nothing else to do.

As a busy lawyer employed by the highly reputable Sydney Legal law firm, Flynn had juggled appointments and made sure he blocked out the time in his diary to enable him to attend the suit fitting in time. As managing director of Craigdon Enterprises, Nicholas had obviously done the same. Running the day-to-day activities of his late father's billion-dollar business no doubt had its challenges, and yet Nicholas had managed to make it there on time.

Swallowing a sigh, Flynn offered Callum an apologetic smile and slipped into the change room. Tugging off his clothes, he pulled on the wedding garb. Along with the pale gray coat and tails, there was also a pristine white ruffled shirt and a dark-gray bow tie. The combination was the height of young urban male. Flynn wondered if Callum's fiancée, Grace had selected the color and style.

More than likely.

Flynn couldn't imagine Callum taking the time to choose such a sophisticated combination. No matter. The suit looked good and as Flynn pulled the jacket across his shoulders, he was pleased with the fit. He stepped out of the change room and awaited Callum and the tailor's inspection.

"That looks about right," Mr Johnson muttered around the measuring tape in his mouth.

When they arrived, the old tailor had told them that the shop had been in his family for generations. His father and his grandfather had both been tailors. Back in those days, the suits had been made by hand.

Now Flynn stood still while Johnson pulled at, and straightened the suit before standing back to look at the final result. It was obvious the man aimed for perfection. Flynn had no problem with that. He demanded excellence himself.

Callum's oldest brother, Jett sidled close. He spoke in a low voice.

"So, what time are things kicking off tonight?"

"About seven. Does that suit?"

"Yeah. My shift ends at six. I'll change at work and meet you there. Beaches in Balmoral, right?"

Flynn nodded. "Killer views, apparently. So Noah says. He's the one who suggested it."

"Sounds good. Hopefully I won't be called out again," Jett added and then dropped his voice to a conspiratorial whisper. "Did you arrange anything special?"

Flynn grinned and pulled out his phone. He showed Jett the picture of Angel.

Jett whistled under his breath. "She sure looks special. Do you think Callum will go for her?"

Flynn shrugged. "Who knows? It's hard to tell when the guy was once hell-bent on becoming a priest, but I had to do something. If Callum doesn't take her up on her offer, I'm sure someone else will." He gave Jett a pointed look. "We're not *all* spoken for."

Jett laughed. "Don't tell Danielle, but it's times like this I wish I was single!"

Flynn winked and pressed a finger against his lips. "I promise not to breathe a word."

Jett laughed again. They both knew he was jesting. Flynn had never seen a more dedicated husband than his cousin, Jett. He and Danielle had been married nearly five years and had two cute kids. Whenever Flynn saw the couple together, they looked as loved-up as ever.

It was nice. Flynn was happy for them. It almost inspired him to give a more permanent relationship a go. Almost. He enjoyed his freedom and the plain and simple fact was, he loved women. All kinds of women. If someone asked if he had a type, he'd probably respond that blue-eyed blonds had always held a special appeal. Then again, his last girlfriend, Casey, had been a brunette. Maybe that's why she'd only lasted a few weeks.

"Well, everything looks good to me," the tailor said and looked at Callum. "Are you happy with everything, Mr Craigdon?"

Callum nodded and gave the man a smile. "Yes, thank you. You've done well, Mr Johnson. I appreciate the time you've taken to make sure everything fits."

The man inclined his head slightly. "It's our business to make sure everything fits, Mr Craigdon. I'm pleased you're happy with the final result. I wish you all the best with your wedding. I hope it's a splendid day."

Callum managed a tight smile. "Me, too."

Flynn clamped a friendly hand on Callum's shoulder. "It looks like the suits are sorted. What else is on the list?"

Callum sighed. "I think that's about it." He looked around at his brothers. "You all got the memo about the boots?"

Joel rolled his eyes. "Yes, Callum. We got the memo. We're to wear our black RM Williams boots."

"And make sure they're clean," Callum added. His tone conveyed his irritation.

This time it was Nicholas who rolled his eyes. Joel frowned and opened his mouth. Flynn could tell from the dark expression on Joel's face that he was about to let Callum have it. Flynn stepped in to defuse the situation.

"How about we all go and have a beer to celebrate?"

"I thought we were leaving that for later?" Callum grumbled. "Isn't that what buck's nights are for?"

Flynn grinned. "Hey, there's nothing to stop us from getting a head start. Unless you have somewhere else you need to be?"

"Grace wants me back home as soon as we're finished here. Apparently there are still some last-minute decisions to be made. She's worried about the weather."

"Can't do anything about the weather." Flynn grinned. "Don't stress, cuz. It will be fine. Rain, hail or shine. We'll get you to the church on time and make sure you get the deed done. Then all you'll have to worry about is what to wear on your wedding night." He winked.

Joel and Jett and Nicholas all chuckled. Callum merely blushed. It was well known among his family that he'd been a virgin until he met Grace.

"Has anyone heard from Mom?" Callum asked, deftly changing the subject.

Callum's brothers all shook their heads. Callum sighed. "I can't believe she took off like that. I mean, the woman suffered a heart attack only a week ago. What the hell was she thinking, discharging herself from hospital without telling anyone?"

Nicholas compressed his lips and looked grim. "I suspect Isabella knows something about that," he said, referring to their sister. "For all we know, she might have even helped facilitate it."

Joel nodded in agreement. "That makes sense. After all, she's a doctor employed at the same hospital and she was keeping a close eye on Mom."

Callum sighed again. "It's come as a shock to everyone to discover Uncle Archie's Sophia's father, but for heaven's sake, Mom didn't have to run away. Nobody's perfect. We already knew she'd had an affair. It's not like we would have judged her."

Flynn frowned. "That's all right for you to say. You weren't blindsided, like I was. At least you'd had some warning your mother had been unfaithful. I didn't have a clue Dad had been involved with your mother, and all while he was married. And to discover Sophia's my half-sister and not my cousin… It takes some getting used to."

Jett glowered. "Surely you're not blaming our mother?"

Flynn held up his hands in a sign of surrender. "Hey! I didn't say I was blaming anyone. Just that I'm still trying to wrap my head around what happened. It doesn't mean I don't want your mother at the wedding. Of course she should be there. Not only for Callum, but for Grace."

Callum nodded. "Yes. Especially for Grace. With no parents of her own, the only family she'll have there are her children. She and Mom have grown close these past months. I know it would disappoint her greatly if Mom didn't attend."

Nicholas' shoulders slumped. "So who wants to make the phone call? I've tried Mom half a dozen times already. She hasn't returned any of my calls."

"Yeah. Me too," Jett replied.

"What about Isabella?" Flynn asked. "Has anyone spoken to her?"

"Yes, I did," Callum replied. "Almost a week ago, now. Right after Mom disappeared. I had an inkling Issy might have been involved in secreting Mom some place once she got her out of the hospital."

"What did she say?" Flynn asked.

"She was vague on details, but she did say Mom was fine. She needed some time alone, away from the family… To recuperate."

"No doubt she also wanted us to have some time to come to terms with her bombshell about Sophia," Nicholas mumbled.

"Has anyone spoken to Soph?" Callum asked.

"Yes. I visited her in hospital as soon as I found out," Flynn replied. "She was still in shock. Like all of us."

"Along with recovering from that awful beating," Nicholas added, his eyes hard. "She's lucky to be alive."

Both Jett and Joel looked away. Though they were shocked and angered by the cop who'd gone rogue and savagely beaten their sister half to death, they wouldn't speak out against a fellow officer. At least not in public.

"Has she been discharged, yet?" Callum asked, trying to break the tension.

"Yes," Flynn replied. "Jarrod took her home yesterday."

"Good. At least she has someone to take care of her."

"He's a good bloke," Flynn agreed. "Their path to true love might have started out a little rocky, but I think they're meant for each other."

The brothers all agreed. Flynn glanced at his watch. "Well, if no one wants to come for a drink, I guess I'll catch up with you all tonight. Seven o'clock at Beaches." He winked. "Don't be late."

Isabella Craigdon set the kettle to boil and reached up into the cupboard for the teabags. Two days earlier, she'd arrived at the family-owned holiday house in Noosa, in the sunshine state of Queensland, to check on her mother. Though she'd been in constant phone contact, she'd wanted to make sure Elizabeth was doing all right.

The heart attack had come out of nowhere. Though her mother had turned sixty earlier that year, she'd been fit and healthy and always looked after herself. And she looked a decade younger than her age. Still, Isabella knew all too well heart attacks could strike anyone. Sometimes there were none of the usual indicators. She could only put it down to her mother's anxiety over the serious assault Sophia had suffered and the stress around disclosing to her family the truth about her youngest daughter's biological father. Discovering their uncle was in fact Sophia's father had been the biggest shock of all.

Filling the cups with boiling water, Isabella added milk and sugar to her mother's tea. She left hers black. Collecting the cups and setting them on a tray, she added a plate of assorted pastries she'd bought from the bakery down the road earlier that morning. With tray in hand, she crossed the living room and stepped out onto the balcony where her mother sat enjoying the sunshine.

"I made you some tea," Isabella said. She set the tray down on the small table beside her mother's chair.

Elizabeth turned to her and gave her a wan smile. "Thank you, darling. I'm so glad you're here."

Though it had only been a week since the shock announcement, in that short time it seemed like her mother had aged. There were new lines around her mouth. She was pale and her eyes were despondent.

"I wanted to check on how you were doing." Isabella reached for her teacup and took the seat beside her mother. "Everyone's worried about you, Mom."

"How's Sophia? Have you heard from her? I've called her every day, but all I get is her voicemail."

Isabella made a sound of impatience. "What did you expect, Mom?"

At the look of hurt and pain that filled her mother's face, Isabella's anger dissolved. Her shoulders slumped on a sigh and she tried to explain: "She's doing as well as can be expected. She just needs time. As for her wounds, they're healing well. Jarrod took her home yesterday."

Elizabeth offered another sad smile. "Jarrod. I'm so glad they found each other. He loves her, you know."

Isabella grimaced. "Given he's her husband, I assume he loves her."

"Well, it wasn't smooth sailing. Your sister took some convincing, let me tell you."

Isabella chuckled. "Seems like that runs in the family. I think we've all resisted the call of love. Must be something to do with our upbringing."

Her mother immediately looked stricken. "Oh, Isabella! I'm so sorry!"

"It's all right, Mom," Isabella said dismissively. "We all know you and Daddy weren't a love match."

"We were in the beginning," her mother said quietly. Sadness flooded her eyes.

Isabella ignored the twinge of guilt and focused on what was important. "You can't hide out here forever, Mom. And what about Uncle Archie? You walked out on him, too. He's just as shell-shocked as the rest of us. He deserves an explanation. Besides, Callum's getting married in two days. He wants you to be there. We all do. Even Sophia."

Elizabeth looked up. A hopeful expression lit up her face. "You've asked her?"

Isabella grimaced. "No I haven't, but I know she and Jarrod would want you to be there. You're the groom's mother! You need to be there. We all want you to be there."

Her mother sighed. "Poor Sophia! How will she ever forgive me?"

Once again, Isabella curbed her irritation. "Give her time, Mom. At some point she'll realize that by coming forward with that information, you saved her life. She has a rare blood type. If Archie hadn't agreed to give her his blood, she might have died. I'm sure she's still in shock about discovering the man she's always thought was her uncle is actually her father, but once she's had time to get used to the idea, she'll come round. I'm sure of it."

Elizabeth looked at her. Hope warred with anguish on her face. "How can you be so certain?"

Isabella sighed. "Because when everything is said and done, she loves you, Mom. She's not going to hold this against you forever. Trust me. Life's too short for grudges. Look what happened to Daddy? None of us expected him to drop dead so suddenly. We've all learned a lesson from that." She patted her mother's hand. "Like I said, just give her time."

Elizabeth sipped her tea and stared off in the distance. Isabella did the same. The three-bedroom, three-bathroom, luxury beachside apartment had been given to her mother by her husband for her fiftieth birthday. No doubt it was a way of assuaging his guilt over his numerous affairs, but whatever reason had motivated the gift, Isabella was glad for it now. It was a place well away from the day-to-day pressures of life and family and her mother needed this time to rest and recuperate and find the strength to face her family. Because face them she would. Isabella refused to leave there without her mother in tow.

Her teacup was long since empty when her mother finally sighed quietly and turned to her.

"Okay. I'll come back with you. I have to face the music sometime. It might as well be now."

Isabella sat up in her chair. "Will you attend the wedding?"

"Yes. I don't want to let Callum and Grace down."

Isabella was filled with relief. "You're doing the right thing, Mom."

Elizabeth merely regarded her solemnly. "Let's hope you're right."

Chapter Two

Beaches bar sat perched high above Balmoral Beach and was popular with the wealthy, young and beautiful people who populated Sydney's lower north shore. It was one of those places in Balmoral that had been tired and rundown, before being gentrified a decade earlier. Where there had once been red brick, limestone and timber verandahs, now stood walls of charcoal-colored cement render, glass and shiny stainless steel.

It was only a few minutes before seven, but already the place was crowded with cashed up twenty-somethings all letting their hair down for the night. The upmarket bar was booming, with a live band playing loud music in one corner and people yelling at each other over the noise. Flynn had arranged for a private room for the buck's night and now threaded his way through the crowd to the appointed meeting place.

He pushed open the door and was greeted by two of Callum's brothers and a handful of his friends. Flynn's brothers, Noah and Logan, were also there.

"Hey, guys!" Flynn called out over the noise, grinning. "It's good to see you all!"

He was met with a chorus of greetings. A jukebox had been set up in one corner and was playing rock and roll. Jugs of beer lined the table, along with plenty of glasses. The owner of the bar had allocated them their own waitress. No doubt she'd be kept busy as the night wore on.

Flynn glanced at his watch. The strippers were due at eight. He'd managed to persuade Angel to bring along a couple of friends.

"The more the merrier," he'd encouraged when he'd spoken to her over the phone. "I'll make sure it's worth their while."

He spied Joel on the other side of the room and went over to his cousin. "Where's Callum?"

By way of greeting, Joel slapped him on the back. "Jett's collecting him after he finishes work. Callum said he'd be at the soup kitchen, overseeing the final stages of construction. He hopes to open the apartments to the public early next year."

Flynn nodded. He'd been involved in his cousin's dream to provide affordable housing for those in need. Along with Callum's ten-million-dollar inheritance, Flynn had donated a significant sum of his own money toward the project. He'd been more than happy to support Callum and was pleased to see the project had almost come to fruition.

"Here," Joel said and handed him a beer.

The two men clinked glasses and Flynn took a healthy swallow of the cold brew. The door to the room swung open and the crowd of partygoers let out a cheer. Callum stood in the doorway, grinning. Jett was right behind him.

"You're here!" Flynn shouted above the noise.

Callum ducked his head. Of all the Craigdon men, Callum was the most subdued. No doubt it had something to do with the years he'd spent in the seminary, training to be a Catholic priest. Flynn crossed the room and thrust a glass of beer into Callum's hand and thumped him on the back.

"Welcome to the best night of your life, cuz. Let's get this party rolling."

A succession of waitresses entered the room, carrying trays laden with food. Canapés, mini hotdogs, cheese-and-tomato scrolls. Spring rolls, mini pies and quiches, crab sticks, seafood bites, a variety of gourmet cheeses. The platters were spread out across the long table and the guests needed no further urging to eat.

"So, two more nights of bachelorhood. How does it feel?" Flynn asked, grinning at his cousin.

Callum swallowed a mouthful of beer and smiled. "It feels good. I don't think about it as losing something. Instead, I'm gaining a wife and a family. Much more valuable than what I'm giving up. I couldn't be happier."

Flynn pulled a face. "I'll have to take your word for it."

Callum laughed. "Hey, don't disregard the possibility. A year ago, I couldn't have imagined any of this. I thought my destiny lay in the priesthood. Now I'm about to commit myself to a woman for the rest of my life. A woman who comes with a ready-made family. Even better, she's more than willing to add to the brood." This time it was Callum who winked.

Flynn grinned. Callum moved away to greet some of the other guests. Flynn stood back and watched. He had to admit, for a man about to tie himself down to one woman for the rest of his life, Callum sure looked happy about it. Flynn, on the other hand, shuddered at the thought.

Someone turned up the music and the throbbing beat reverberated against his chest. The drinks flowed, along with bursts of loud laughter and conversation. It looked like everyone was having a good time. Then the door behind him swung open once again. The newcomers were met with a series of loud cheers. This time, there were catcalls thrown in.

Flynn turned and spied three strippers. Two blonds and a brunette. One of the blonds he recognized as Angel. Pushing away from the wall, Flynn made his way over to her.

Dressed in a white-gold, sparkly bikini that barely covered the essentials, Angel looked every bit as appetizing in real life as she had in her online photos. Her double D breasts were almost bursting out of her shimmering top and emphasized the tiny span of her waist.

"Angel! Thank you for coming. I'm Flynn Craigdon. We spoke on the phone."

Angel's answering grin was wide and toothy. She gave him a slow once-over. "It's nice to meet you, Flynn Craigdon."

Her voice was deep and throaty. His cock immediately responded to the blatant invitation in her eyes. He reached out and ran a finger across her breast. Her bare skin was warm beneath his touch.

"Later," he promised. "Right now, this all about my cousin. Callum Craigdon, the bridegroom. He's standing over there in the corner, talking to those two men. Callum's the one in the white shirt."

Angel gave Flynn another simmering look before sauntering off in Callum's direction. Flynn stood by and watched. He knew the instant Callum became aware of her. His cousin blushed crimson and then spun around and set his accusing gaze on Flynn. Callum shook his head slowly from side to side, but his initial surprise and anger morphed into a wry grin.

Flynn breathed out a sigh of relief. He'd made a fair assumption his cousin wasn't into strippers, but what was a buck's night without a bit of fun? He was pleased his cousin had taken it in the spirit it was intended.

And then someone changed the music to something with a throbbing beat and the strippers began to entertain the guests. Moving their lithe, barely clothed bodies to the rhythm, it wasn't long before all three of the women had removed all but their panties and gyrated semi-naked around the men. Callum sat in the seat of honor at the head of the table, trying to avoid everyone's gaze as Angel gave him a lap dance.

Flynn grinned at the embarrassment on Callum's face. No doubt this was the first time his cousin had experienced some one-on-one time with a stripper. He best enjoy it. Once he was married, there would be no more lap dances, or anything else with a woman who wasn't his wife. Yet another reason to avoid the institution.

The brunette stripper moved away from the group of partygoers and walked up to where Flynn stood. She brushed her bare breasts against him and fluttered her false eyelashes. She was young and attractive and quite obviously willing. Once again, Flynn's body stirred. He smiled at the woman and reached out and playfully squeezed one of her bouncing breasts. She looked up at him and slowly licked her lips. Her teeth were white and even. He smelled peppermint on her breath. Then with a teasing smile, she spun away from him and headed toward one of the other men.

Flynn let her go. Watching the women work their wiles on the crowd, he was reminded of how long it had been since he'd had sex. A week at least. After the playful exchange with the stripper, his cock was hard and his balls were full and tight. It was just as well he wasn't spoken for. There was nothing stopping him from taking one of the women home for the night.

As the music played and the drinks flowed, Flynn and Logan and some of Callum's mates made the most of the entertainment. As usual, Flynn's brother, Noah, held himself back from the frivolity. It wasn't that Noah didn't like women. He was just shy. Almost painfully so. Even worse than Nicholas. Although ever since Nick had met and fallen in love with Harper Wyburn, he'd come out of himself and was far more outgoing than he used to be. It was nice when a woman had such a positive effect. Flynn hoped for Nick's sake Harper intended to hang around.

Flynn finished another beer. Though he could hold his

alcohol better than most, he'd lost count of the number of glasses he'd consumed. Quite a lot, if the buzz he had going on was any indication. He looked at Callum, who was now surrounded by the girls. To Flynn's relief, his cousin appeared to be taking the attention in good stride.

"Great party, Flynn."

Flynn turned as Noah moved up beside him. "Thanks, bro. Can I get you a beer? It looks like you could do with a bit of loosening up."

Noah shook his head and pushed his glasses further up his nose. "No, thanks. I don't need to be drunk in order to have a good time."

"But are you? Having a good time, I mean?"

Noah smiled, but Flynn saw the strain behind his eyes. "Of course."

Flynn leaned in closer. "I'll let you in on a little secret. There are three hot women in this room all looking to make you happy. Why don't you relax and have a bit of fun?"

"I'm fine." Noah paused. "Hey, it looks like we could do with some refills. How about I grab some fresh jugs of beer from the bar?"

Flynn shrugged. If his brother would rather put in an order for a fresh round of drinks than get up close and dirty with a warm and willing, half-naked woman, that was up to him.

Noah turned away and disappeared through the open doorway, closing the door behind him. Flynn focused his attention once again on the girls. He normally went for the blonds, but there was nothing wrong with the hot little brunette. Right now she was on top of the table showing them some interesting moves. Flynn had no idea someone could be that flexible. Once again, his cock hardened in response.

Then the two blonds joined in and mimicked graphic sexual moves as a threesome, setting every hot-blooded male's pulse racing. Most of them openly ogled the women. Callum looked mildly amused.

Wondering what was taking Noah so long, Flynn let himself out of the room and strode over to the bar. He looked down the length of the shiny wooden surface and saw his brother chatting to a black-haired beauty with striking blue eyes and high cheekbones. He frowned in surprise. It wasn't like Noah to chat up any woman, let alone a barmaid.

Still, he could see the appeal. The woman wore a tight black T-shirt that emphasized her large breasts. The word "Beaches" was painted in white across the fabric. Her lips were full and red. She stood behind the bar with a dishcloth in her hand, listening while Noah spoke. And then she threw her head back and laughed at something he said. Full-throated, husky and sexy as hell. Flynn watched, intrigued. His brother turned red.

No wonder Noah hasn't shown any interest in the strippers. His attention's elsewhere… Like on this hot little barmaid…

He wondered who she was. It was apparent she and Noah knew each other from the easy way he interacted with her. It was just as obvious how much his brother liked her. Noah had always shied away from women and even though he was a cop, he'd chosen a job in internal affairs, where he spent most of his time behind a desk where his interaction with the general public was limited.

But here it looked very much like he was flirting with the barmaid and though she wasn't exactly fluttering her long eyelashes at him, she certainly wasn't rebuffing his attention. And then Flynn's curiosity got the better of him. He moved down the bar toward them and came to stop beside his brother.

"Noah. When's the beer coming? We're getting thirsty back there."

Noah blushed and ducked his head, avoiding Flynn's gaze. "I-I'll be right there."

Flynn shot a disarming grin in the barmaid's direction. "It looks like my brother here's been distracted from his work."

The woman arched a shapely dark eyebrow. "Oh?"

She was even more beautiful up close. Thick, dark lashes swept upward as she gave him an assessing look. Tiny flecks of navy dotted the clear blue of her eyes. Her olive complexion complemented her tanned skin.

"Flynn Craigdon," he said, holding out his hand. He offered her his most charming smile.

She shook his hand. Her grip was surprisingly firm. "Jayde. Jayde Hassad."

"It's nice to meet you, Jayde Hassad."

"And you, Flynn Craigdon." She said it matter-of-factly, without a hint of flirtatiousness. It was obvious she was far more interested in his brother. Flynn tamped down his disappointment.

"Well, anyway. I just wanted to see what was keeping Noah."

The woman moved away and filled two jugs with beer. She brought them to Flynn and set them down in front of him.

"This should keep you for a little while. Noah will bring more directly." There was dismissal in her tone.

"Thanks," Flynn said and picked up the jugs. "I'll catch you in a bit, Noah."

His brother made a non-committal sound and once again avoided his gaze. Feeling a little out of sorts, Flynn turned away with the beer and headed back to the party. He wasn't used to being overlooked by a woman. Even more disconcerting was that he'd been overlooked in favor of his shy and awkward brother. He must be losing his touch.

It was late when the party wound down. As the guests filed out, along with Callum and his brothers, Flynn found himself alone with Angel. He fished in his back pocket for his wallet and peeled out several hundred-dollar notes. "One thousand upfront and one thousand at the end of the night, right?" he said.

Angel smiled and nodded. She put out her hand and he pressed the money into it. She closed her hand over his fingers.

"It seems to me you've earned some special attention," she murmured. She tucked the money into a beaded handbag and then began to nuzzle his neck. "Are you ready to have some fun?"

His body instantly reacted and blood rushed into his loins. He took a moment to close and lock the door and sauntered back to her. With his hands on either side of her hips, he drew her toward him and kissed her. And then she was on her knees in front of him and reaching for his belt. Leaning against the wall for support, he closed his eyes at the same time her lips closed around his cock.

"*Ahhh.*"

His thoughts went immediately to the black-haired beauty on the other side of the door and he cursed softly. With a conscious effort, he focused his attention on Angel. Her lips and hands were skillful and it wasn't long before he climaxed in her mouth. As he tucked himself back into his boxers and did up his pants, he reached once again for his wallet. She stayed him with her hand.

"That was a thank you for a great night," she said, coming to her feet. "The girls and I never know what kind of crowd we're going to get at one of these things, but you guys were great. Polite. Respectful. We appreciate that."

Flynn nodded. "Of course. You're entitled to be treated well, just like anyone else."

Angel gave him a wry grin. "Not everyone sees it like that."

He waited while she pulled a loose cotton dress over her bikini and then he opened the door for her. As they crossed the main room, he couldn't help but glance toward the bar. Noah's barmaid was busy wiping down glasses. He almost called out to her to bid her goodnight, but then decided against it. She barely glanced in Flynn's direction as he left.

He stood with Angel on the footpath outside the bar until a cab finally pulled up. Closing the car door behind her, he lifted his hand in a brief wave of farewell. Then he turned and began to walk in the direction of home, keeping an eye out for another taxi. When one finally appeared, he flagged it down and climbed gratefully into the back seat.

He gave the driver his address in Manly and then leaned back and closed his eyes. Images of the barmaid were interspersed with Angel's blond head. It wasn't the first time he'd had sex with a random stranger, even if it was only a BJ, but for the first time he felt jaded and wondered if there were more to life than this.

Most of his cousins had found their soulmates and were now blissfully in love. They were planning engagements, weddings…babies. The very thought of all that domesticity scared him half to death. But their happiness was obvious. Surely they all couldn't be wrong about how good it was to think they'd found their one and only?

One and only? What the hell am I thinking? I must be drunker than I thought…

There was no way he wanted to be tied down to just one woman, to have to confer with someone every time he made a decision. Worse still…babies. He shuddered. Sleepless nights, dirty nappies, spitting up all over the place. No, the single life was the one he preferred. No one to answer to, quiz him on his movements, make him feel guilty about drinking and partying or staying out all night. Why would he want that hassle?

But his thoughts kept circling back to Callum and how happy he was to be marrying Grace. She already had two children, but Callum had talked about wanting more and sounding so happy about it. It seemed his cousin couldn't wait to be part of one big happy family.

But what about all those marriages that didn't work out? Like his aunt and uncle, his father? Though they'd remained married to their various spouses, no one could convince him they were happy. People didn't cheat on each other if all was rosy.

With a weary sigh, Flynn entered his quiet apartment and showered and climbed naked into his bed. He relaxed against the cool sheets and was grateful for the silence. No snoring spouse, no crying babies. Just pure peace and quiet. Still… some time during the early hours of the morning when he woke to use the bathroom and then returned to his empty bed, he wondered if there was more to it than living the life of a bachelor. What would it be like to share his days with a woman he loved above all others?

Chapter Three

The day of Callum and Grace's wedding dawned bright and sunny. It was one of those perfect spring mornings in Sydney that made Flynn glad to be alive. He wasn't one to waste time on flowery prose or extravagant descriptions, but the clear blue sky, gentle harbor breeze and balmy air reminded him he lived in the best city in the world. He grabbed a coffee on the way and arrived at the hotel suites five minutes ahead of schedule. Now all he had to do was to get Callum to the church on time and for them all to get through the next few hours.

"Where are my boots? Has anyone seen them?" Callum asked, his expression tense.

Flynn found the boots on the floor near the bed. He kicked aside the scattered clothing, picked them up and handed them to the groom.

"Here you go."

Callum muttered his thanks and sat down on the bed to pull them on. The hotel room was crowded with the wedding party. Along with Flynn, Callum's groomsmen—his brothers—Jett, Joel and Nicholas—were also in various stages of getting dressed. Flynn glanced at his watch.

"We have about ten minutes before the photographer arrives, fellas. Those of you who are still swanning around in your underwear need to get a move on."

Joel gave him a jaunty salute. "Yes, boss."

Nick took a swig from his beer before setting it down and attending to the buttons on his shirt. At least Jett was mostly dressed. He stood on the far side of the room in front of the mirror, fiddling with his bow tie.

Flynn went over to him and brushed away his hands. "Here. Let me." Within moments the tie was set in place.

"How come you're so good at that?" Jett grumbled.

Flynn chuckled. "I've had a lot of practice."

"Where's my boutonniere?" Callum cried, his voice edged with panic.

Flynn picked up the corsage that lay in the florist box and calmly pinned the white rose to Callum's lapel. He took his cousin by the shoulders and gave him a slight shake.

"Relax, Callum. You're getting married. This is the happiest day of your life."

Callum managed a tight smile. "Of course it is. You're right. Today I'm marrying the love of my life."

"Atta boy." Flynn looked around. "Now, who isn't ready?"

"I still need a corsage," Nicholas said.

"Me, too." This from Joel.

Flynn handed out the remaining corsages and made sure the men pinned them in the right place. When he was satisfied they all looked as good as they could, he glanced around for his coffee. It was nowhere to be seen so he popped the tab on a fresh can of beer, perched on the edge of the bed and sighed.

"All right, fellas. Let's go and get married!"

There was a chorus of cheers and chugging of beers. They were interrupted by a knock on the door. Flynn opened it to reveal the photographer. A dour older man stood there laden with photographic equipment. Behind him was a good-looking, leggy blond, presumably the man's assistant. Flynn gave her a saucy wink.

"Welcome to the wedding of the century. Let's get this show on the road!"

To Flynn's relief, the moment Callum set eyes on his bride walking down the aisle of St Monica's toward him, he visibly relaxed. The color that had leached from his face earlier, returned. By the time Grace stood at Callum's side, offering him a nervous smile through the gauze of her white veil, Callum's usual strength and calm had returned to him. He took Grace's hand and drew her closer. He bent and whispered some words of reassurance in her ear. The smile she gave him in response was full of tenderness. Callum's face lit up with love.

Flynn swallowed past a lump of emotion. He was surprised at his reaction. He wasn't one to get all mushy at a wedding, even when the bridegroom was his close cousin. He must be going soft in his old age.

As the bridesmaids took their positions beside the radiant bride, Flynn took a moment to survey the crowd that had gathered in the church to bear witness to the wedding vows. The seats on the Craigdon side of the church were full to bursting. It seemed every Craigdon in the land was there, including the groom's mother. Elizabeth looked pale and drawn, but at least she'd made it to the celebration. Callum had fretted all week that she might not.

She sat in the second row next to Isabella and Raine. Danielle, Sheridan and Harper were also there. Sophia and Jarrod sat two seats further back. Neither Sophia nor her mother looked at each other. Flynn suppressed a sigh.

His gaze moved a few rows past them. He spied his father sitting alone. Archie's face was drawn and tired. Flynn hadn't spoken to him since the shocking discovery Sophia was Archie's daughter. Flynn's half-sister. There was a lot to come to terms with and with the stresses of the upcoming wedding, he just hadn't found the time. No, scrap that. He hadn't *wanted* to find the time. He still didn't know what to say. What did he have to say to his father who'd cheated on Flynn's mother and sired another child?

There were far fewer guests on the Gunning side. Grace was an orphan. Her only brother had been killed in a car accident earlier in the year. There were her children, of course: Seth and Alyssa. Seth was the page and Alyssa the flower girl. They were now seated in the front row and looked kind of cute in clothes that matched those of the bridal party. A sky-blue silk organza dress for Alyssa and for Seth a child's version of the pale gray suits worn by the groomsmen, complete with boutonniere, tails and bow tie.

There were also a handful of friends and work colleagues who filled the first few seats. Flynn recognized Sister Mary Catherine from Jennifer's soup kitchen, along with a couple of other regular volunteers. It was nice to see them there, offering their love and support.

The priest called the crowd to order and the ceremony began. Callum needed no prompting to say his vows, his voice firm and confident as he spoke the words which, in the eyes of God, would bind him to Grace for life. Grace's words to Callum were spoken in a voice that was equally sure and strong. Flynn couldn't help but feel, for this couple at least, their marriage just might last the distance.

And then it was time for the exchange of rings. After a brief moment of panic when Flynn put his hand into his jacket pocket and came up empty, he remembered he'd put them inside his pants pocket right after Seth had handed them over to him. His fingers closed around the gold bands with relief. He handed over the rings to the priest who blessed them before offering one first to Callum and then to Grace. The happy couple smiled at each other, their gazes tender and loving, as they exchanged the rings, the symbol that bound them together as husband and wife.

It was all so sappy and beautiful. More than one person in the crowd dabbed at tears. As the bride and groom shared their first kiss as a married couple, the congregation broke into a cheer. The white-haired pianist and equally elderly violinist started playing Pachelbel's Canon in D.

Flynn shook Callum's hand and pecked Grace on the cheek. "Congratulations, you two. You did it!"

Callum grinned from ear to ear. Flynn wondered if it were possible for a man to look happier. It certainly appeared that Callum was looking forward to spending the rest of his life with Grace.

Despite the love that was heavy in the air, Flynn suppressed a shudder.

Hours later, and after posing for more photos than Flynn could count, the wedding party arrived via stretch limousine at Craigdon Manor. Flynn's lips hurt from all the smiling and if someone asked for him to pose for another photo, he thought he might very well strangle them. Why photographers insisted on shot after shot, moving from one location to another and another and another when everyone knew one or two photos were all that ever made it out on display, he'd never know. No doubt the photographer had fleeced the happy couple of a hefty sum, all tied up in a neat bow labeled "the wedding package" and had to earn his keep.

The formal gardens of Craigdon Manor looked even more stunning than usual. Thousands of fairy lights adorned the trees. Large paper lanterns in blue and silver and white hung from the branches. Round tables that seated ten apiece were dressed in crisp white linen tablecloths. They dotted the manicured lawn. Napkins the exact shade of blue as the bridesmaids' dresses, along with silverware and shiny silver candlesticks were set in place on each table.

Aunt Elizabeth and her army of decorators had outdone themselves.

Spying a makeshift bar that had been set up underneath an ancient Moreton Bay fig tree, Flynn made his way toward it through the crowd of wedding guests. Nodding greetings to people he recognized, his gaze caught on a familiar black-haired beauty. She was dressed from shoulders to mid-thigh in sparkly silver lycra. It was the woman from Beaches. Noah's girl.

Jayde Hassad.

She looked even more beautiful in the daylight. The silver threads in her dress caught the light until her body seemed to shimmer. Her long slim legs were shapely and tanned. Her breasts filled the bodice of her dress to overflowing. His body tightened reflexively. He wondered how she came to be there. Unless she was part of the bar staff…?

Then Noah moved into Flynn's line of vision. His brother said something to Jayde. They both laughed. Noah threw an arm around her shoulders and pulled her in for a casual hug. She went willingly.

So… That's how it is… Of course… She's here with Noah…

Flynn felt a grudging respect for his little brother. It seemed Noah had found the courage to invite the delectable Jayde Hassad along as his guest to Callum's wedding. Flynn swallowed a surge of disappointment. She sure was a looker. Still, there was no way he'd muscle in on his brother's date. He knew what it had taken Noah to ask her. His brother must surely have fallen hard for the woman. He only hoped she appreciated the effort Noah had gone to in order to have her there by his side, and more importantly, that she felt the same way.

Determined to steer clear of her, he deliberately averted his gaze and continued toward the bar. A stiff drink was exactly what he needed to distract himself. Besides, no doubt there were plenty of other beautiful and more importantly, available women present who he could while away the time with. He didn't need to stoop so low as to make a move on his brother's date.

Right on cue, the sound of girlish laughter drew his attention. Two twenty-something young women, both blond, both cute, stood not far away. They eyed him with interest. He sauntered over and introduced himself with a smile.

"We're friends of the bride," the one with the larger breasts said.

"We volunteer at the soup kitchen," the other one added.

"What do you do when you're not helping out there?" Flynn asked, already slightly bored.

"We both go to university," large breasts replied.

"I'm studying psychology," her friend said.

"And I'm halfway through law," large breasts added.

Flynn hid his surprise. Neither girl looked like they were capable of studying anything.

"What do you do?" large breasts asked.

"I'm a lawyer," Flynn replied and gave her a tight smile.

Large breasts cooed in delight. "A lawyer! Fancy that! Do you work in one of those swanky law firms in the city?"

Flynn nodded and looked around for an escape. The bar seemed an interminable distance away.

Large breasts looked at him with an increased air of enthusiasm. She grabbed hold of his arm.

"Do you think you could get me a clerkship? Or even a summer job? It's so hard to get a start in some of those law firms, especially if you don't have the right connections. They only take the cream of the crop."

Flynn managed another strained smile and shrugged off her hold. How he'd thought either women could distract him from Jayde now seemed laughable. He couldn't wait to get rid of them.

"I'm afraid I don't have any influence over employment offers," he lied. "You'll have to contact our human resources department and go through the usual channels. If you're good enough, I'm sure they'll offer you a place."

Large breasts looked disappointed.

Before she could respond, he bid them both farewell and quickly took his leave. As he walked away from them, he breathed a sigh of relief. Neither woman held a candle to Jayde—not in looks or intelligence. If this was any indication of the quality of the single women at the wedding, he was in for a long night.

Detective Constable Jayde Hassad tugged self-consciously at the hem of her dress and wished she'd worn something a little less conspicuous. Though she was far from indecent, standing among the glamorous wedding guests, all dressed in the latest designer clothes, shoes and jewelry, she felt awkward and out of place. She'd grown up in a working-class family, a lifetime away from the inner circle of these people, some of whom were regularly featured in Sydney's social pages.

What am I doing here?

And then she forced herself to remember. It wasn't everyday that someone like her got the opportunity to observe the Craigdon family up close. At a wedding, no less. A time for love and joy and family celebration. A time many people let down their guard. It was the perfect opportunity to gather intelligence about a family the police had been most interested in for some time. Henry Craigdon's death hadn't changed that.

Jayde had stumbled across Noah Craigdon quite by accident when he turned up with a group of rowdy friends at her father's bar a few months earlier. Of course, she'd known right away who he was, including that he was a cop, but it wouldn't be the first time one of their own had turned bad.

After that initial chance meeting, Noah had become a regular at Beaches. Jayde knew full well what drew him there. His interest in her was obvious. Though she didn't return his feelings, it helped her cause to encourage him.

Despite the fact the patriarch of the Craigdon family had been dead ten months, the rumors of Henry's involvement in the illegal drug trade hadn't faded with his passing. It had been interesting to discover the ownership of his company had been signed over to his nephew, Logan Craigdon, and the day-to-day running to Henry's son, Nicholas. On the surface, neither man appeared suspicious, but as an undercover detective with the Drug Enforcement Agency, Jayde knew firsthand how much appearances could deceive.

There were investigators with a much higher pay grade than hers who'd long suspected Henry had been laundering drug money through his company. Jayde had been given the task of getting to the bottom of it. And that meant befriending Noah Craigdon. He was her ticket to getting closer to the Craigdon family and, in particular, to the men who now owned and ran Craigdon Enterprises.

With his glasses and cute smile, Noah was sweet and sexy in a slightly awkward way. She took care not to give him too much encouragement, but at the same time, she needed to keep him coming back. She just had to make sure she didn't rouse his suspicions. He was a cop, after all.

The invitation to attend his brother's wedding had come as an unexpected, but pleasant surprise. Jayde had been thrilled to pass on the information to her handler. Getting up close and personal with the Craigdons *en masse,* in their own environment, was an opportunity she hadn't anticipated. Especially so early into her investigation.

Her gaze scanned the crowd and landed on Noah's older brother. He stood by the bar with a drink in his hand. Tall, commanding, at ease. Thick dark-blond hair, brown eyes. He looked gorgeous in his wedding finery.

Flynn Craigdon.

She'd made it her business to study all of the members of Henry's family, including his nephews. She'd gathered a dossier of information on each of them. Flynn was a thirty-year-old lawyer who specialized in family law. Unmarried. No children. At least, none that she'd discovered.

Confident, charismatic, sexy as all hell. So different from his brother. She'd felt the force of attraction the very first moment Flynn had spoken to her, but she'd been determined to keep him at arm's length. Though he could be just as valuable to her investigation as Noah, her instant attraction to him made trying to get closer to him, impossible. There was no way she could befriend him, pretend to flirt with him, encourage him to take her into his confidence, when all the time she'd be fighting to overcome her very real desire to get to know him better. Much better.

She could tell right off he was a womanizer. Okay, he might not be sleazy about it and the fact he was single meant he could sleep with any woman he pleased, but her research had indicated he was a love 'em and leave 'em kind of guy who'd left behind a string of broken hearts and she wasn't interested in being another notch on his belt.

Besides, she'd come there with Noah. He was her priority. She needed him to believe she was as interested in him as he so obviously was in her. Under normal circumstances, she'd feel guilty about using someone so blatantly, even running the risk she might break his heart, but these weren't normal circumstances and she wasn't there for the fun. She was part of a serious investigation and she needed to play her part. Her team relied on her for a breakthrough. She wouldn't let them down.

"Can I get you a drink?" Noah asked.

Jayde offered him a warm smile. "Thanks. That would be lovely."

"Champagne?"

"Sounds good to me." She smiled again and watched as Noah disappeared into the crowd.

She took the time to survey some of the other wedding guests. The current Lord Mayor of Sydney, with her short, spiky dark hair and wearing a trademark designer suit in stunning deep purple, laughed uproariously at something said by someone in her entourage. The state premier was also there. On her arm was a man half her age. Jayde recognized him as one of her staffers.

"Here you go."

Jayde looked around in time to see Noah handing her a champagne glass. She murmured her thanks and then took a tentative sip. The champagne was cold and tart and slid easily down her throat. Too easily. It was like no other champagne she'd ever tasted. No doubt it was French and cost a fortune. Only the best for a Craigdon wedding. She took another sip and then silently reminded herself to take it easy. After all, she was on the job.

Noah touched his glass to hers. "Here's cheers. I hope you're having a good time."

She smiled. "Of course. The ceremony was lovely."

"It was," Noah agreed. He scanned the crowd and his face broke into a smile. He turned back to Jayde. "Let me introduce you to my younger brother."

Jayde watched on with interest as Noah caught the attention of another man. "Logan!" he yelled. "Come over and meet Jayde."

A bleached-blond surfer dude turned to face her and gave her a polite smile. In his black tuxedo and matching bow tie, he was every bit as good looking as the other Craigdon men, but there was something distant about his demeanor, like he had other more weighty issues on his mind. Logan Craigdon had inherited his uncle's company, but had handed the reins to someone else. Jayde couldn't help but wonder why.

"It's nice to meet you Logan," she said and offered him her hand.

He shook it briefly and mumbled a response. A moment later, he excused himself. Noah's face flushed with embarrassment.

"I'm sorry about Logan. He's out of sorts."

She shot Noah a look of encouragement. "Oh?"

"Yes, he…um… He has a lot going on."

"I see. He seems a bit morose for someone who's supposed to be celebrating his cousin's wedding," she prodded.

Noah grimaced and took a gulp from his beer. "I think that's the problem." His voice lowered to a conspiratorial whisper. "Logan's nursing a broken heart. He was supposed to get married last year. It was a big, fancy affair. Then his bride-to-be jilted him at the altar. That kind of humiliation takes some getting over."

"Oh no!" Jayde replied, genuinely upset for Noah's brother. She hadn't come across that tidbit during her research.

"Yes. He also had a bad accident a few years ago that ended his career as a professional sailor," Noah added. "He's still trying to adjust."

Jayde nodded in understanding and remained silent. She knew all about the boating accident. It had been widely covered by the media. She took another sip of her champagne.

Noah took her by the elbow and led her away from the crowd. Finding a vacant bench beneath a flowering crepe myrtle tree, they sat down with their drinks. A number of guests wandered past, some pausing to chat. The men greeted Noah with friendly handshakes. The women offered him smiles.

And then another Craigdon came by and Noah got to his feet.

"Nick. It's good to see you. This is Jayde."

Jayde stood and held out her hand to the man who by all accounts was now managing director of his late father's company. She gave him a quick assessing look, missing nothing. Tall and handsome, like the other Craigdon men, his blond hair was about the same shade as his cousins'. His blue eyes were friendly and full of intelligence, but there was none of the confidence and arrogance of Flynn, nor the adorable eagerness she found in Noah. Nicholas held her eyes for only a moment, before he shyly dipped his gaze. And then he introduced her to the stunning redhead who stood beside him.

"It's nice to meet you, Jayde. This is my fiancée, Harper Wyburn."

Noah's gaze went wide. "Fiancée? Wow! Congratulations! No one told me."

Nicholas pulled a face and leaned in closer. He lowered his voice. "That's because no one knows, yet. Not even my mother. I proposed to Harper a couple of days ago. I couldn't wait any longer. But we didn't want to steal the limelight. This is Callum and Grace's special day. Our news can wait. We'd appreciate it if you kept it to yourselves for a bit longer."

"Of course," Noah readily agreed.

Jayde merely nodded. Before her stood another example of a man who appeared to be as normal and grounded as could be, but there were persistent rumors of illegal activity. She couldn't help but wonder if Nicholas was involved.

Since February, he'd been in charge of the day-to-day operations of a billion dollar company. He had easy access to all of his late father's business contacts. It wouldn't be impossible for him to have taken up where his father left off.

Yes, Nicholas Craigdon certainly bore closer investigation, as did the rest of the Craigdon clan.

Chapter Four

Flynn took another mouthful of beer and tried his best to get into the party spirit. Laughter and conversation and the soothing sounds of a harp surrounded him and yet he couldn't shake off the doldrums. Of course his bad mood had everything to do with Noah and his delectable date, and that irritated Flynn no end.

What he needed to do was stay the hell away from her. She wasn't the only woman at the party. Okay, so she was the sexiest woman he'd laid eyes on in a long time—maybe ever— but she was his brother's date. Totally off limits.

The trouble was, every time he tried to engage another woman in conversation, his gaze strayed toward Jayde. He found himself standing taller, looking over other people's heads, searching for her in the crowd. He strained to hear her throaty laughter, or even a husky giggle. It was proving incredibly distracting and was quietly driving him mad.

As a result, his customary good humor had deserted him. He'd been snapping at anyone who stopped to chat. His brusqueness had left his father looking bewildered. Too late Flynn remembered the turmoil Archie had also suffered of late. Flynn hadn't even taken the time to ask him how he'd been coping with the shock.

The fact his father had been unfaithful to Flynn's mother

was something he'd yet to come to terms with. Flynn remembered his mother as sweet and quiet and loving. He was only twenty when his mother had been tragically killed in a car accident. The whole sorry incident had been made worse by the fact his Uncle Henry had been behind the wheel at the time of the crash. Flynn missed her gentle smile and her love.

With a sigh, he forced the sad thoughts away and made his way back over to the bar.

"What can I get for you?" the young barman asked.

"I'll have another beer, thanks."

By the time he'd been served, Noah had joined him. Clinking their glasses together, they turned and leaned against the bar and surveyed the crowd. Callum and Grace stood with their arms around each other, laughing and talking to their guests. They both looked more than happy. Isabella and Raine were seated at a table, kissing. Jett and Danielle were out on the lawn, playing a game with their kids. It seemed Flynn was the only one not enjoying himself.

"Did you hear Nick's news?" Noah asked.

"No."

"Don't tell anyone, but he and Harper are engaged."

Flynn groaned. "Oh, hell. Not another one. Soon we'll be the only bachelors in the family!" Flynn grabbed his brother's arm in mock panic. "Promise me, Noah. Promise me you'll never be tempted to go down that path."

Noah shrugged off Flynn's hold. His gaze returned to the crowd. Like a heat-seeking missile, Flynn spied Jayde across the lawn. Noah spied her a few seconds later.

"So, brother. Tell me about Jayde," Flynn asked, keeping his tone conversational.

"There's not much to tell. She's twenty-seven. Single. She works in the bar owned by her father."

Flynn shot him a knowing grin. "Ah, yes. Beaches. Now I know why you were so keen to hold the buck's night there."

Noah flushed. "I wasn't keen. I merely suggested we go there. It's a happening place with a great vibe and even better views. You can see clear across the harbor from there."

Flynn winked and then returned his gaze to Jayde. "You're right about the views."

"Stay the hell away from her, Flynn! She's mine."

The ferocity of Noah's reaction took Flynn aback. He held up his hands in surrender. "Hey, mate. Steady on. I'm kidding. I didn't realize she was so important to you."

"Of course she's important! Why do you think I invited her?"

"How long have you known her?"

"A few months. What does it matter?"

"It doesn't. I'm just surprised you feel so strongly about her when you haven't known her for long."

"I know all I need to. She's smart and kind and funny. I'm… I'm in love with her."

Flynn choked on his beer. "In love with her? Oh, Noah! You barely know her! Have you even taken her out for dinner? Had sex? Met her friends? Her family?"

"I already told you. Her mother's dead. The only family she has left is her father and he's never around." A determined look came across Noah's face. He looked past the crowd to where Jayde stood, chatting to the groom's mother. His expression turned fierce.

"I love her, Flynn. I don't care what you think. She's the one. The amount of time I've known her is immaterial. One day, you'll know what I'm talking about."

Flynn took another swallow of beer and remained silent. Despite his best efforts, his gaze was once again drawn to the woman who had Noah tied up in knots. He understood all too well the attraction. He just wished to God he didn't feel the same.

Christopher Barrington was bored witless. He usually avoided big society dos like this, but his step-mother had insisted. Given that she'd recently recovered from a heart attack, he thought turning up to her son's wedding was the least he could do. After all, Elizabeth Craigdon had always shown him kindness and acceptance, regardless of the bad blood that had stood between him and her late husband.

As the guests mingled on the front lawn that was decorated with all sorts of frivolities, he noticed Noah and Flynn standing shoulder to shoulder, staring grimly in the same direction. He followed the line of their gazes and saw a black-haired beauty with long legs and a skimpy outfit that only emphasized her shapely figure. She appeared to be engrossed in conversation with another guest.

And then he recognized her.

The barmaid from Beaches. What's she doing at a fancy do like this?

Regardless of who had brought her, it was obvious his cousins were enthralled. Both men had their gazes fixed on her, as if oblivious to everything and everyone around them. Noah, in particular, looked like a lovesick puppy.

Interesting…

Christopher had made it a point to notice things around him, especially circumstances that might later work to his advantage. One never knew when one might need a favor. He worked hard to ensure there were as many people as possible in his debt. He wondered which one of them was in the race to win the woman's heart.

His money was on Flynn. Everyone knew Flynn's penchant for beautiful women. A modern day Lothario, he went through women like some people went through underwear. Though Flynn would object to the analogy, as far as Christopher was concerned, it suited him perfectly.

Noah, on the other hand, had never had a serious girlfriend. At least not to Christopher's knowledge. He'd always been quiet and shy and serious. Christopher had been surprised when Noah had joined the police force, but then the decision made sense when, instead of walking the beat and arresting criminals, Noah chose to investigate his own. Internal Affairs. Typical.

Christopher looked back at Jayde and couldn't help but smile. Though she continued to be engaged in conversation with those around her, he noticed how every now and then she stole a glance in Noah and Flynn's direction. It was obvious she was interested in the men.

The question is, which one?

Yes, watching this play out between the brothers would no doubt provide hours of entertainment. Especially if Christopher took the opportunity to fan the flames. With that thought in mind, he wove his way through the crowd of wedding guests until he'd made it to Jayde's side. Sensing his presence, she turned to him. Her eyes went wide with surprise.

"Christopher! How nice to see you!"

Jayde didn't try to hide her surprise. Christopher was a regular at her father's bar. As a loosely related member of the Craigdon family, she'd researched him along with all the others, but as far as Christopher was aware, she only knew him as a Beaches customer. It was important she act accordingly to avoid raising suspicion.

She'd spent the previous little while talking to as many guests as possible. It was important to gather as much information about the Craigdons as she could. There was no telling if she'd ever get another opportunity to get up close and personal with them and their associates. She'd even managed to corner the matriarch of the family for a few moments.

Elizabeth Craigdon looked every bit as rich and regal as she did in her media photos. What Jayde hadn't expected was to discover the woman was so approachable. There was no attitude, no arrogance—nothing but pleasant conversation. Despite the fact the woman was recovering from a recent heart attack, she'd taken the time to welcome Jayde as Noah's guest and urged her to enjoy the party.

"I didn't realize you knew the Craigdons," Christopher mused, drawing her attention back to him. "Or are you a guest of the bride?"

She forced a nonchalant shrug. "I could ask you the same thing."

"Me? Well, that's easy. The late great Henry Craigdon was my father."

She acted convincingly shocked. "Henry Craigdon was your father? But…?" She shook her head, pretending confusion.

Christopher laughed. "It's okay. I was the product of an affair. Though Henry was single at the time, he didn't offer to marry my mother. She raised me on her own until she had the good fortune to catch the eye of Frank Barrington. He adopted me when I was twelve."

Jayde nodded slowly in mock comprehension. "Hence the name Barrington."

Christopher's answering smile was more like a grimace. "Yes. Good old Henry didn't see fit to recognize me as his biological son."

Jayde felt a moment of compassion. Despite Christopher's offhand manner, she heard the bitterness in his tone. It seemed time hadn't healed the wounds of his father's rejection. She knew how that kind of pain felt.

"Now it's your turn," Christopher said, interrupting her thoughts. "Are you a friend of the bride or the groom?"

Jayde forced a smile. "Neither. I'm here as Noah's guest."

Christopher's eyebrows rose in surprise. "Noah? I see. I had no idea you two knew each other."

"I met him at Beaches. The same place I met you."

Christopher winked. "If I'd known you were on the lookout for a date, I'd have asked you myself."

Given the frequency of Christopher's visits to the bar, she'd wondered if he was an undercover cop. It wasn't out of the question. The Craigdons weren't the only people under surveillance, after all. Jayde's father was well known to the police. Like Henry, John Hassad was suspected of dealing in drugs. But given Christopher's connection to the Craigdons, it was also necessary to consider the possibility he might be working for the other side. He had a sly air about him that made Jayde uneasy.

Is he a goody, or a baddie? She needed to find out. There was no time like a family wedding to pump him for information. Hopefully his guard was down.

With that thought in mind, she sidled closer. She deliberately let the side of her breast brush against his arm. He quirked an eyebrow at her, his eyes filled with a mixture of surprise and curiosity. She merely lowered her gaze and smiled, then calmly took another sip of champagne.

"So, what do you do for a living, Christopher? I take it you don't work for Craigdon Enterprises?"

He looked at her in mock horror and gave an exaggerated shudder. "Hell, no. My father couldn't stand the sight of me. With that going on, do you think he would have deigned to offer me a job in his beloved company?"

Jayde shrugged. "I wasn't sure how deep the discontent ran."

Christopher's lip curled up with derision. "Oh, it ran deep, all right. Far too deep for you to possibly fathom. The old prick even left me out of his will. Not a single mention. A billion-dollar estate and I didn't get a penny. Are you getting the picture?"

She took a sip of her champagne. "Ouch."

"Yes, ouch. My dearly departed father. Do you blame me for suing the estate?"

She concealed her surprise. "You're suing the estate?"

"Wouldn't you?"

"Yes," she replied honestly. "Given what you've told me, I think I would. You're his biological son. I assume there was no dispute about that?"

"Of course not."

"Then you have as much claim to his estate as the rest of his children. Good on you for having the courage. It can't have been easy."

His expression softened. "You barely know me and yet you understand me so well. Who are you, Jayde Hassad? Where did you come from?"

She laughed a little self-consciously and surreptitiously put some distance between them. It wouldn't do to lay it on too thick. She needed information, not a boyfriend.

"You already know all there is to know about me. I work in my father's bar in Balmoral. Every day I listen to stories, offer sage advice and pour beers. Plain simple, and quite boring, really. That's my life. There's nothing else to know."

Christopher moved closer and his gaze zeroed in on her lips. He reached out and ran a fingertip down her cheek. "There's nothing plain or boring about you, Jayde Hassad."

Jayde tensed, but forced herself to play along. She managed a tight smile. "You're too kind. I'm a barmaid. That's it."

He leaned in close. For a horrible moment, she thought he was going to kiss her. Swallowing a gasp, she moved her head away. At the same time, she deliberately jiggled her glass.

"Oh, I'm so sorry! I've spilled my drink all over you!" Grabbing a napkin off a nearby table, she dabbed at the liquid that now stained his shirt.

Christopher's face flooded with irritation, but he stilled her hand. "It's all right. Don't worry about it. I'm sure it will dry in no time."

"Are you sure? Please, send me the dry cleaning bill. I insist."

He waved away her offer and gave her a strained smile. "Think nothing of it. It was an accident."

She continued the charade. "I'm so embarrassed. You're being very gracious. Tell you what, next time you're at Beaches, the drinks are on me." With that, she made her escape.

From his perch on a stool beside the makeshift bar, Flynn watched the exchange between Jayde and his half-brother with increasing tension. It was obvious Christopher was flirting with the woman. Hell, he was practically on top of her. Even more irritating, she seemed to be enjoying the attention.

Flynn chanced a glance in Noah's direction. The ferocious scowl that darkened his brother's face told Flynn all he needed to know. Noah hadn't been exaggerating when he'd claimed to be in love with Jayde. It was obvious he'd fallen hard. And he'd also just seen Christopher in action.

Flynn suppressed a sigh and took a gulp of beer. It looked like both of them had been passed over for another man. What galled him most was that the man she'd chosen was his half-brother. Christopher Barrington was completely undeserving.

Flynn glanced at Noah again. "You all right, mate?' he asked quietly.

Noah's shoulders slumped. "Yeah."

Flynn nudged his brother. "Hey, don't take it too hard. There are plenty more fish in the sea." He managed to dig up a smile, but he needn't have bothered. Noah continued to look glum.

"I really liked her, Flynn. I thought she liked me, too."

Flynn tried to think of something to cheer his brother up. "Don't be too quick to judge her. This might not be what it looks like. You know Christopher. He's always up to no good. Maybe he found out she was here with you and he wanted to cause trouble. Maybe he couldn't stand the thought that you had a hot girl by your side and he didn't. He might have been putting on a show for your sake. To make you think she's now his."

Noah looked at him, a hopeful look on his face. "Do you think so?"

"I wouldn't put it past him. And look, she's moving away from him and he doesn't appear too happy about it."

Noah glanced in the direction where Jayde and Christopher had been seated and nodded. "You're right. She's left him standing there all alone. Look at the scowl on his face!"

Flynn smiled, glad to see his brother was looking more upbeat. "See? I told you. She's still your girl. I'm sure of it. Why don't you go and find her? Take her a fresh glass of champagne. I think we're all about to be seated for the meal. I'm sure you'll be seated together. She's your date, after all. You'll have a chance to wow her with your charm and brilliant conversation."

Noah immediately looked nervous, but shot him a grateful look. "Thanks, Flynn. I tell you, for a while there, I thought *you* were the one I had to worry about. I was sure as hell you had a thing for her. I'm sorry I misjudged you. It's Christopher who's the prick."

Flynn's smile became strained and he fought off a surge of guilt. It was followed by another wave of disappointment. His earlier lustful thoughts about Jayde would remain just that— fantasies that would never see the light of day. And that's the way it had to be. Women would come and go from his life. Noah was his brother forever.

Chapter Five

$\mathcal{E}$lizabeth did her best to relax and enjoy her son's wedding celebration, but it was difficult after recently being forced to share secrets she'd hoped to take to her grave. Accompanied by Isabella, she'd arrived back in Sydney late the night before and had gone straight to Craigdon Manor. All morning, she'd purposefully avoided the rest of her family. But she couldn't avoid them forever and that knowledge had her on edge.

The place settings had been arranged weeks before and now she was forced to sit beside Archie. No one had known at the time that he was Sophia's father. They still didn't know the affair was long term. Had been ongoing for twenty-two years. The thought of telling her children about that sent a fresh wave of panic rushing through her.

She must have made a sound of distress, although she was unaware of doing so. Seated across from her, Isabella shot her a look of concern.

"Is everything all right, Mom?"

Elizabeth clenched her hands beneath the table and managed a nod. "Yes, honey. I think it's the heat," she lied. "Is anyone else feeling it?"

There were polite murmurs of agreement from the others seated around the table. Raine sat next to Isabella. Then came

Sheridan, Harper and Danielle. All three of their significant others were seated at the main table, along with the rest of the bridal party. Two aunts and an uncle completed the group. She couldn't remember where Sophia and Jarrod had been seated.

At least I've been spared all the curious glances and unending questions from my family… Except for Archie.

He still hadn't spoken to her. He'd barely even looked at her. She'd hurt him dreadfully by keeping the news of Sophia from him all these years, but she genuinely believed she'd had no other choice. Unable to stand his icy silence, she reached for his hand.

"I'm sorry, Archie. I'm so sorry."

His frown was ferocious, his words succinct. "Not. Here." He pulled his hand out of her grasp.

Though her heart stuttered at the anger and hurt that filled his eyes, she was grateful for the reprieve. Later, after the wedding celebrations were over, would be soon enough to deal with her family and answer their questions. No doubt there would be many.

Looking across the expanse of tables, her gaze finally landed on her youngest daughter. Sophia looked drawn and pale. It had only a week since the terrible assault that had nearly taken her life. Shadows of pain still clouded her beautiful blue eyes.

A wave of guilt washed over Elizabeth and she bowed her head under the weight of it. In some distant part of her mind, she'd braced herself for the time she'd be forced to face up to the consequences of her decision. She'd put it off for a long time—more than twenty-one years—and she'd managed to convince herself it was best for everyone. But after witnessing the shock and hurt and anger on the faces of her family as they realized the enormity of the secret she'd held all these years…

Now she wasn't at all certain she'd made the right choice.

Jayde found herself seated beside Noah. Logan had taken the seat opposite. He looked just as morose and distant as he had earlier and one look at him told her this wasn't the time or place to engage him in lighthearted conversation. She'd have to wait for another time and hope she got such an opportunity again.

She looked around expectantly, hoping Flynn might also be seated with his brothers. Then she spied him at the bridal table. *Of course…he's part of the bridal party…*

Her spirits plummeted. She was immediately irritated by her reaction. Flynn might be a good source of information, but as far as anything personal went, he was off-limits. She could barely think straight when he was around, let alone have the wherewithal to probe him for family secrets without giving herself away.

He was a lawyer, sharp-eyed and keen of mind, with a gaze that was so direct she was sure he could see right through her. The last thing she needed was to rouse his suspicions and have him wondering about her curiosity in the Craigdon family. After all, as far as he knew, she was nothing more than a barmaid his brother had asked to the wedding.

No, the best thing to do was to steer well clear of Flynn Craigdon. She could concentrate instead on his brothers. Particularly Noah who'd been glued to her side since they'd sat down.

"Can I get you another drink?" Noah asked.

Jayde shook her head. "No, thank you. I'm driving."

Noah shot her a sideways glance and then shyly looked away. "We could always catch a cab back together to the city. I live on the same side of town."

She blinked. "How do you know where I live, Noah Craigdon? Have you been following me?"

He blushed adorably. "N-no! Of course not!"

She looked at him in mock alarm. "Don't tell me you're a cop? No. Not a cop. One of those private investigators. Yes. Like they show on TV. Is that how you know where I live?"

Noah's embarrassment ravaged his face. Jayde almost felt sorry for him. She wondered if he'd tell her what he did for a living. When he spoke again, she had her answer.

"Actually," he began hesitantly. "This might sound weird, but I *am* a cop."

She widened her eyes in mock surprise. "I knew it! Have you been looking me up in your cop database? Getting all the juicy details on me?"

Poor Noah shook his head vehemently from side to side, almost beside himself. It was an offense for a cop to do any such thing without reasonable cause and would result in an immediate suspension, followed by disciplinary proceedings. She was sure Noah knew the rules as well as she did.

His expression turned earnest. "No, Jayde. Please, you misunderstand. I'd never do something like that. It's illegal. The thing is, I only guessed you live on the northern beaches because you work over that way. The truth is, I don't have a clue where you live."

He gave her an apologetic look that was so sincere, she had to fight back a surge of sympathy. Poor Noah. He had no idea. She patted his arm.

"It's okay, Noah. I'm sure you're not a stalker. For a moment I was feeling flattered you might have cared enough to want to find out. No matter. It's all good. And you're right. I do live on the north side."

His face lit up. "You do?"

"Yes. I live in Balmoral. Above the bar."

Noah smiled. "Of course. And why wouldn't you? Your father owns the place."

She scowled reflexively at the mention of her father and

then quickly smoothed out her expression. She reached out again and touched Noah on the arm, letting her hand linger there.

"So, tell me where you live, Noah?"

"I live at Manly."

"On the beach?"

He nodded self-consciously. "Yes."

"On your own?"

This time, he blushed. "Yes."

She smiled and squeezed his arm. "I see."

"Would you like to see it sometime?" he asked in a rush.

She smiled again and withdrew her hand. It was time to take a step back. "That sounds like fun."

"How about tomorrow?" he blurted.

She bit her lip and then shook her head. "I'm sorry. I'm working tomorrow. Maybe some other time."

His face fell, but there was nothing she could do about it. While she needed to keep him close in order to pump him for information, she didn't want to take things to the point where things got awkward.

Deliberately turning away from him, she engaged his brother in polite conversation. Though it was hard work, after several flirtatious exchanges, Jayde finally got Logan to smile. Though he couldn't match the charm and charisma of his oldest brother, he was a heartthrob just the same. She wondered briefly about the fiancée who'd left him at the altar and then dismissed the thought from her mind. Logan Craigdon was the CEO of Craigdon Enterprises. He was the one who was in her sights, along with his brothers and cousins. Who he dated or fell in love with was none of her concern.

The speeches were over; the cake had been cut. The newlyweds had danced their first dance as husband and wife.

As the night wore on, the crowd slowly dispersed until there was no one but family remaining. Standing off to one side, Flynn saw Noah leave with Jayde. His gut clenched involuntarily in silent protest and he cursed under his breath.

If Jayde chose to spend the night with his brother then all the better for Noah. If it were with any other woman than Jayde, Flynn would have been thrilled for his brother. As it was, he had to fight off a stab of jealousy. But a few minutes later, he saw Noah return. He was alone. Flynn met his brother halfway across the lawn.

"What happened to Jayde?" he asked, keeping his tone light.

Noah grimaced and averted his gaze. "She called it a night. She has to work in the morning."

Flynn merely nodded, but inside he rejoiced. Almost immediately he was filled with shame.

"Too bad," he managed and then gave his brother a reassuring slap on the back. "I'll see you inside," he added and then turned away.

From not far away, Flynn heard Elizabeth heave a heavy sigh and then saw her slowly turn to make her way into the house. All of a sudden, she looked old and frail, two words he'd never before associated with her. He moved up beside her and gently touched her arm.

"Are you all right, Aunt Elizabeth?" he asked in concern.

She stopped and turned and nodded briefly in his direction, looking pale and grim. Then she slowly moved forward again.

The makeshift bar had been disbanded, the dance floor all packed up. The only people milling around were the staff from the hire companies who were waiting to pack up the chairs and tables. Flynn followed the rest of the family inside. Elizabeth made it known to them earlier that she'd deal with their questions after the wedding. That time had come.

When Flynn entered the formal dining room, he noticed she was already seated at the head of the table. Her hands were clasped tightly in front of her. Her mouth was set in a thin line. She looked like she was about to face her executioner. No doubt for her, that's how it felt. Flynn had a few questions of his own, but his would be directed at his father. Elizabeth wasn't the only one who had some explaining to do.

The family filed in and took their places at the table, all of them looking grim. Archie, who usually sat on Elizabeth's left, now took the seat at the opposite end of the table. None of them failed to notice it was as far away from her as he could get. Sophia and Jarrod also chose seats distant from her mother. Nick and Harper walked in holding hands. Of all those present, they looked the happiest. They took seats close to Elizabeth. Isabella and Raine did the same.

Jett and Danielle, Joel and Sheridan, Noah, Logan and lastly, Flynn all took seats at the table. Only Christopher and the newlyweds were missing.

Elizabeth regarded them solemnly, her gaze moving slowly around the table. "Where are the children?" she asked.

Jett cleared his throat. "Our two are upstairs, asleep in bed. I believe Alyssa and Seth are, too. There's a nanny up there with them."

Elizabeth nodded. "Good."

There was another moment of silence. Everyone held their breath. Flynn glanced at his aunt. She stared down at the table. Her hands clenched and unclenched. It was obvious she was trying to hold on to her courage. He felt a flash of sympathy. He couldn't imagine how difficult this was for her. None of them were perfect. Although he had a number of questions, it wasn't his place to judge.

Before Elizabeth could speak again, Nick pushed back his chair. Reaching for Harper's hand, he looked around the room and gave them all a cautious, nervous smile.

"Um, this probably isn't the best time, but I'm pretty sure once Mom has finished no one will be in the mood for my—*our*—news."

He looked down at Harper and grinned. She gave him a tender smile. It was all Flynn could do not to roll his eyes.

Am I the only one who breaks out in hives at the thought of chaining myself to one woman for life…?

Nick cleared his throat. "You see, me and Harper… That is, I've asked Harper to marry me. And she said yes! She's going to be my wife!"

The final words fell out in a rush. Nick beamed from ear to ear. Harper stood and threw her arms around him. Everyone cheered and then offered the happy couple congratulations. Flynn glanced around the room. The tension had been broken. Everyone appeared a little more relaxed, including Elizabeth. And then she drew in a deep breath.

"Let me offer you my sincere congratulations, Nick and Harper. I'm so happy for you both. All I ask of God is for my children to find their perfect life partners and to be happy." She looked around at them and gave them a shaky smile. "So far, my prayers have been answered."

She paused a moment and drew in another breath. "Now, I want to apologize for disappearing last week the way I did. I know you've all been worried about me—I still can't believe I suffered a heart attack! But I want you to know I'm feeling perfectly well. I just… I needed to get away for a while. I'm tired and I had a lot on my mind."

"You could have at least told us where you were," Jett grumbled. "We were all worried sick."

"Yes, of course. And I'm sorry. All I can say is, I wasn't in the right frame of mind to be calling any of you and telling you of my plans. The truth is, I didn't have a plan. The only thing in my mind was to get away from everything." She shot an apologetic look toward Archie.

"I'm sorry, Archie. That included you."

Flynn's father merely stared hard at the table. An angry flush stained his cheeks. Elizabeth bit her lip and continued.

"I asked Isabella to help me get out of the hospital. She kindly did what was necessary to allow me to leave. It's not that I wanted to worry you, or that I had no intention of offering you an explanation. I just needed time. I was so upset about Sophia. She could have died!"

Elizabeth shot an earnest look filled with distress in the direction of her youngest daughter, but Sophia's gaze remained fixed firmly at her lap. Her lips were compressed, her expression taut. Flynn caught the glint of tears in her eyes.

"I never meant for my secret to come out like that," Elizabeth continued in a shaky voice. "When it did, when it had to, in order to save Sophia's life, I didn't know what to do. I had no time to think about the consequences or how shocked you all would be. My only thought was to save Sophia. And Archie was the only one who could do that."

"You should have told me years ago!" Archie cried. He banged the table with his fist. "She's my daughter! I had a right to know!"

Elizabeth visibly recoiled from the hurt and anger on Archie's face. Once again, the air was filled with tension. Flynn made an effort to lighten the mood.

"I guess now we all know why Soph was dealt such a harsh hand under Uncle Henry's will. I take it he knew Sophia wasn't his child?"

Elizabeth nodded. "Yes. He put the question to me and I never lied to him."

"You didn't feel any such compunction with me!" Archie cried.

Elizabeth's expression filled with remorse. "We were both still married, Archie. I did what I thought was right. For everyone."

"You had no right, Elizabeth! She was my daughter, too."

Archie's voice cracked on a sob. Tears filled his eyes. Flynn grimaced, uncomfortable at the sight of his father's pain. Everyone found somewhere else to look.

"You'll never know how sorry I am, Archie," Elizabeth said quietly, her face a picture of distress.

Archie glared at her. "Sorry isn't going to cut it, Elizabeth."

Sophia pushed back from the table. She stood with her hands on her hips and glared at her mother.

"Okay, so I wasn't Henry's daughter. Thanks for telling me. What about Nick? He was overlooked for Craigdon Enterprises. Does he belong to someone else, too?

"No!" Elizabeth cried, aghast.

"How do we know you're telling the truth?" Sophia shouted. "After all, you lied to me all these years!"

Elizabeth leaned forward and implored them. "Nicholas *is* Henry's child. The truth is, Henry always believed differently. There was nothing I could say to change his mind." She turned and stared at Nick. "Please, Nicholas. You must believe me. You're Henry's biological son."

Nick stared down at the table, but gave a brief nod of acknowledgement. It seemed to Flynn as if Nick had already had time to process the information. Flynn looked around the table and his gaze fell on Logan. His stomach slowly filled with dread.

"While we're revealing old secrets and making confessions, what about Logan? Would someone care to explain why my brother was left such a generous inheritance by his *uncle*? Unless..." Flynn narrowed his gaze at his father. After a moment, he deliberately shifted his gaze to Logan.

Archie stood and pushed his chair away from the table with such force it fell over. "No way!" he cried. "You've gone too far, Flynn. How *dare* you besmirch your mother's memory!

She would *never* have cheated on me! We… We loved each other, right to the very end."

"Oh, of course. That's why you had an affair with Aunt Elizabeth," Flynn responded dryly.

Noah shot Flynn a look of warning and then turned to his father. "No one's accusing Mom of anything," he said in a calm voice. "Flynn's talking nonsense, Dad. He's been drinking all afternoon. Don't pay any attention to him."

Flynn opened his mouth to object, but what Noah said was true. He'd probably consumed more than his fair share of alcohol, mostly in an effort to distract himself from one very desirable and completely unavailable barmaid.

Pushing away from the table, Flynn ignored the chorus of protests and left. He needed to get away from there. He needed to clear his head.

Chapter Six

Flynn stumbled down the wide stone steps and paused to catch his breath. The balmy night air was heavily scented with honeysuckle. A warm breeze lifted his hair. His keys jangled in his pocket, but he was in no fit state to drive. Leaving behind his Ferrari, he began walking down the long paved driveway that led out onto the main road. He pulled his phone out of his pocket and booked an Uber.

The ride into the city was uneventful. Traffic had thinned and the driver made it across the northern suburbs to Balmoral in record time. He'd hardly been aware of giving the Uber driver the address, but forty-five minutes after leaving Craigdon Manor, he found himself outside Beaches bar.

It was late. The carpark was nearly empty. Only a couple of BMWs and a Mercedes sedan. The faint sounds of the jukebox could be heard from inside.

What am I doing here? She was just at the wedding. There's no way she's here now...

But something inside him needed to make sure. Refusing to analyze the yearning, he only knew he had to see Jayde again. He pushed open the door and stepped inside. The place was dim and deserted. Two men sat on stools at the bar, both well into their cups. A third sat alone in a booth, his gaze fixed on the flat screen TV in one corner that was replaying a cricket match.

Flynn glanced over toward the bar. A solitary man with short gray hair and a moustache stood behind the counter, wiping glasses.

She's not here…

Filled with disappointment, Flynn shouldered open the door and stumbled back outside. The Uber had already left. Unmindful of his expensive wedding suit, he sank down on the top step and leaned against a post. His head thumped with the effects of the alcohol that still coursed through his blood. He was tired. It had been a long day. He ought to call up another Uber and go home.

I shouldn't be here! I hardly know the woman! Why the hell am I so disappointed? It's bullshit. She's Noah's girl. He fancies himself in love with her. There's no way I'll interfere with that…

It was like he'd told himself already: It was the best thing for everyone if he stayed the hell away.

From her vantage point in front of the upstairs window above the bar, Jayde saw a car pull up in the darkened parking lot and watched as Flynn Craigdon climbed out and went inside. A short time later, he came out again. She wondered if he was looking for her and then told herself not to be stupid. They barely knew each other.

Then another, more troubling thought occurred to her. Was Flynn there for something else, something far less savory…? It was no secret to those in the know that her father supplied drugs to whoever wanted them. Was Flynn there to score? Was that the reason behind his late-night visit to the bar?

Though the police had long suspected her father's involvement in illegal activity, they hadn't gathered enough evidence to make an arrest. That was the reason Jayde had been brought in to help. With her years of experience in the

Drug Enforcement Agency, the DEA, and her relationship to John Hassad, she was an obvious choice.

Though she'd initially resisted the call to arms, the death of her brother from a drug overdose had changed everything. Now she was all in and determined to gather enough intelligence to put her father away for life.

As his daughter, she was the last person he'd suspect. Though it turned her stomach to do so, she played the part of doting daughter to the hilt. Every day she worked there, was another day she gained his trust. He'd had nothing to do with her since he'd walked out on his family when she was seven. He didn't have a clue she was an undercover cop. It made this assignment all the more amusing. The day they arrested him would be the happiest day of her life.

If Flynn was there to score drugs, she'd have nothing more to do with him. As far as she was concerned, it was her father's involvement in the drug industry that had destroyed her life— and the life of her brother.

But Flynn continued to sit there and it looked like he might have fallen asleep. She stared at him, unable to look away. His eyes were closed. His mouth was slack. He looked so vulnerable in the dim light. In sleep, he looked much more like Noah.

She smiled slightly at the thought. Flynn might look similar to Noah, but they were polar opposites in personality. Noah was sweet and gentle. Flynn was all charm and confidence and charisma, his manner bordering on arrogant. An alpha male in every sense. He gave off a dangerous vibe. Dangerous to her sensibilities. He was exactly the kind of man she normally avoided.

So what am I doing, watching him through the window, wanting to talk to him again?

It irked her to admit she was attracted to all that maleness. She lived and worked in a male-dominated world. She ought to be sick of that kind of man. It would be much more sensible to be attracted to a gentler one, a man like Noah.

If only it were that easy...

Jayde sighed and turned away from the window in an attempt to dismiss Flynn from her mind. She needed to keep her guard up against him. At this point she had no idea about the extent of Henry's involvement in the drug industry, or how much that involvement included other members of the Craidgon family. Until she knew where everyone stood, she best keep her fantasies about Henry's nephew to herself. It didn't make sense to go down and talk to him. There were too many crucial unanswered questions... She drew the curtains and turned away.

She walked into her bedroom and peeled off her clothes. She turned on the shower and stood under the warm spray. It was the first anniversary of her mother's death. All day, she'd worked hard to keep the sad memories at bay. But now, after a long and eventful day, it caught up with her. As the water cascaded over her shoulders, she let the tears fall.

The family meeting had ended on an unsatisfactory note. The fact that her affair with Archie was now out in the open provided Elizabeth with a level of relief, but the family was far from accepting of it. Flynn had left in a huff. Sophia had stormed out not long after. And Elizabeth still hadn't told them the affair was ongoing. How were they going to react to that? All she could hope was that time would heal things, but right now she didn't feel too confident of that.

At least the wedding had gone off without a hitch. After all the preparations, it was wonderful to see the happy couple so at ease with each other and so much in love. It was such a turnaround from the life Elizabeth had foreseen for her son, but one she was completely in agreement with. Callum was meant to be a husband and father. The life of the church wasn't for him.

It had also been pleasing to see Noah there with a date. Elizabeth's nephew had long caused anguish for his father. Archie often despaired Noah might never find a mate. He was painfully shy around woman and had never had a girlfriend. And yet he'd brought Jayde to the wedding. Elizabeth had spent a few moments in conversation with the woman and had been pleased with what she saw. Hopefully whatever there was between them would last.

She sighed. It was way past late. The house was quiet and still. The last of the guests had left hours earlier. The few family members staying at the manor overnight had long since retired. Only she and Archie remained awake, both too overwrought to sleep. They were in the music room, well away from the bedrooms upstairs. Though Elizabeth had offered Archie a drink, he'd declined. Instead, he paced the carpet, his agitation clear for her to see.

"I still don't understand why you told Henry and not me!" Archie cried.

She saw the hurt on his face and hated that she was responsible for putting it there. She'd been hurt many times herself by her husband, a man she'd once loved with all her heart. It pained her to know she'd brought that kind of distress upon Archie.

In an effort to deflect his anger, she kept her voice low and calm. "I didn't tell him."

"Then how did he know?"

Elizabeth swallowed a sigh and did her best to explain. "He guessed. We were estranged at the time. He was seeing other women. I was…seeing you. Henry and I hadn't been intimate for months. It wasn't hard for him to work out the baby wasn't his. And of course, he knew how you felt about me. How we felt about each other. Remember that time he caught us kissing?"

Archie nodded reluctantly.

"That's why he suspected the same of Nick, but the irony is, I was still faithful to him back when Nick was conceived. Nick *is* Henry's son and yet Henry refused to believe it. Flynn guessed correctly. That's exactly why Henry overlooked Nick when it came to handing over the company."

"You knew that all along?"

"I had no idea about the contents of Henry's will, but when it was read, I understood right away why he acted as he had."

Archie's face twisted into a grimace. "Okay, so Henry was a prick. He thought we were together long before we were. That kiss he witnessed was a one-off, but he had no way of knowing that. I still don't understand why you didn't tell me about Sophia. And why you're still refusing to tell the rest of the family about us. You've already told them about the affair. What difference does it make if they know we're still together?"

Once again, the pain and anger on his face tore at Elizabeth's heart, but she remained stubbornly tight-lipped. The irony was, she still didn't fully understand herself why she was so reluctant to give her family the unadulterated truth. It wasn't as though she had any thought of leaving Archie. She loved him.

She guessed it probably had something to do with the fact her family had been through so much upheaval that year. First, Henry's unexpected death, followed by the shocking terms of his will. Then being told she'd had an affair, and lastly, their discovery about Sophia. It was a lot to take in and she didn't want to add to their anguish. At least, that's what she told herself.

At her continued silence, Archie's face grew red with anger. "What? You have nothing to say? This isn't the first time we've argued about this, Elizabeth. For Pete's sake! Henry's been dead more than ten months! How long are you going to wait?"

"This isn't the right time," she said quietly. "I want to give the children time to adjust to the new turmoil in their lives. They've been through so much already."

"What about me?" Archie cried. "Don't I matter? You seem to be taking everyone else's feelings into account. Why aren't mine important? I've loved you most of my life. Even when you were married to my brother. I hated that you were his. You and I were meant to be together. We knew it then; we know it now. Please, Elizabeth. I love you! I want to call you my wife. Before it's too late."

She risked a glance in Archie's direction. His expression was still filled with hurt and now despair clouded his eyes. She felt a pang of guilt, but held firm. Instead, she changed the subject.

"I can't stop thinking about what Flynn said. There's one thing I can't figure out: Why did Henry give his company to Logan? I have nothing against your son, but Logan's never been interested in Craigdon Enterprises. Even before his accident. It doesn't make sense. Unless…?"

Archie looked at her wearily. "Unless what?

"Unless what Flynn suggested was true…"

She left the words hanging there. It wasn't the first time the possibility had crossed her mind, but out of respect for Archie and his sons and their late mother, Janelle, Elizabeth had remained silent about it. She didn't have to wait long for Archie's reaction.

An angry flush stained his cheeks. "Janelle was a saint! She'd never have been unfaithful to me!"

Elizabeth ignored the twinge of jealousy his words caused her and stared calmly back at him. "How can you be so sure? You were unfaithful to her."

Archie's gaze shifted away. "Yes, but she never knew that. I made sure I was discreet and I *never* gave her cause to question me."

Elizabeth frowned as the full import of his words hit her. "So you mean to say you were still sleeping with her the whole time we were together?"

Archie set his jaw at a defiant angle. "Yes."

"You bastard!"

Archie threw his arms up in the air. "What did you expect me to do? You weren't prepared to leave Henry. Even if I'd walked out on Janelle, you were never going to be mine. Besides, I was a father to three young boys. I had no choice but to maintain the status quo."

"And Janelle believed you loved her all that time?"

"Yes."

Elizabeth scoffed. "You're lying to yourself, Archie. There's no way your wife wouldn't have been able to tell. Why do you think Henry thought Nick belonged to someone else?" Not waiting for him to respond, she continued. "It was because I'd lost interest in having sex with him. Naturally he thought I must be getting it somewhere else." Her lip curled up in disgust. "Typical male."

Archie shook his head back and forth. "That doesn't mean Janelle was having an affair with Henry."

Elizabeth blew her breath out impatiently. "Think about it, Archie. Henry cut Nick out of his will. He gave his most valuable asset to his nephew. The only thing that makes sense is that Henry thought Logan was his son."

Archie's expression turned stubborn. "No. I refuse to believe that."

Elizabeth closed her eyes briefly. Her shoulders slumped on a weary sigh. She'd learned from experience when Archie took a firm stand on something like this, there was nothing more to be said...for now.

The week following the wedding, Flynn arrived at the Cammeray Tennis Club for his weekly game with Steven Walker. It was a club on the lower north shore not too far from Flynn's beachside apartment in Manly. Steven was a work colleague and a mate. While Flynn earned his keep by performing in the Family Court, Steven specialized in defending high-profile criminal cases.

Ever since the wedding, Flynn had been finding it hard to concentrate. The problem was Jayde. He couldn't get her off his mind. Given the additional distractions of the Christmas season that was well and truly upon them, and his patience was razor thin. He served the ball and sent it stinging over the net, acing the shot and barely missing his opponent in the meantime.

"Hey!" Steven protested. "I thought this was supposed to be a friendly game."

"Sorry," Flynn mumbled and got ready to serve another. Once again, he sent a cracker of a shot flying in Steven's direction. Another ace.

"What's got you so riled up?" Steven complained. "This late in the year, I can't imagine you have a big hearing coming up. Have you forgotten the courts close for the Christmas break at the end of the week?"

Flynn merely grunted in response. There's no way he'd mention Jayde to his friend. Steven would never let him hear the end of it.

"How are you doing with the Frank Romano case?" Flynn said, deflecting attention to Steven's high-profile drug dealer trial that was due to be heard in February.

"We're getting there. Facing the usual challenges. Plenty of character witnesses, but when it comes down to going on the record, no one wants to talk. With Romano's bail refused, he's somewhat limited in reaching out to his people."

"I wouldn't think Romano would have any trouble getting people to come out in support of him. They'd be too scared not to. After all, if he wins his case he's going to be back out on the streets. I'm sure he'll remember his friends…and those who deserted him."

"Yeah, you'd think so. I know which side I'd rather be on."

Flynn grinned. "You'd just better make sure you win."

Feeling some of his tension ease, Flynn served another shot. The two of them got into a decent rally before Flynn finally landed a lucky ball in the far corner of the court.

"Forty-love," Flynn said and then finished the game with another ace.

As they shook hands and walked off the court, Steven looked at him. "Want to go somewhere for lunch?"

Flynn shook his head. "Sorry, mate. I'd love to, but I'm going to have to take a raincheck. I'm covering for my cousin and his new wife at the soup kitchen while they're on their honeymoon. They're always short staffed."

"I could come and help."

Flynn smiled in surprise. "Really? That would be great."

Steven shrugged. "No worries. What are friends for?"

Flynn gave him the address and then picked up his gym bag and headed for the showers. "I'll see you there."

Traffic was reasonably light in the tunnel as Flynn crossed the harbor. He drove through the city and was pleased when he found a parking spot not far from Jennifer's Kitchen. He locked his car with the remote and prayed it would still be there when he finished. The bright red Ferrari looked out of place in the dirty inner city backstreets, but he had no other option. Steven pulled up behind him in a more subdued, navy-blue Audi. Together, they entered through the open back door of the soup kitchen.

Sister Mary Catherine greeted Flynn with a welcoming smile. Surprise lit up her face, but she was polite enough not to question his presence. He understood her reaction. He didn't often stop by.

"Hi, Sister Mary Catherine. It's good to see you. I thought with Callum and Grace both away, you could use some extra help."

She beamed. "Absolutely! It's good of you to come."

He introduced Steven and after thanking them for giving up their time, she quickly put them to work. It was almost time to open the doors to the people who relied on Jennifer's Kitchen for a hot meal.

"Flynn, if you and Steven don't mind, I'll put you both on serving. Jayde's got everything sorted for you. She'll help you with anything you need to know."

Flynn's heart skipped a beat. It was ridiculous to think it might be the same Jayde. He made a deliberate effort to keep his tone casual. "Jayde?"

Chapter Seven

Sister Mary Catherine nodded. "Yes, Jayde Hassad. She volunteers here once or twice a week. Come on. I'll introduce you both."

With that, the old nun wiped her hands on a cloth and moved out of the kitchen to where three large bain-maries had been set up, all filled with steaming food. Flynn's gaze zeroed in on the black-haired woman who stood stirring a dish of mashed potato.

It's her.

She wore a simple skirt and blouse beneath a large floral apron. She turned upon their approach. When she noticed Flynn, her smile faltered.

Sister Mary Catherine stepped forward. "Jayde, we're extremely fortunate to have a couple of extra volunteers with us today. I'd like you to meet Flynn Craigdon and Steven Walker. Flynn's a cousin to Callum. Steven works with Flynn. They've dropped by to help while the honeymooners are away."

Flynn stuck out his hand. "It's nice to see you again, Jayde."

"And you."

She shook his hand. He tried not to think about how good her hand felt in his. Sister Mary Catherine's eyes widened in surprise. "Oh, you two know each other already?"

"Yes," Flynn replied. "We met through my brother, Noah."

Jayde switched her attention to Steven and greeted him with another handshake. While the two of them exchanged pleasantries, Flynn came to terms with the fact there was obviously more to the hot little barmaid than he'd first thought. She regularly volunteered at a soup kitchen. That told him a lot about her character. It made him like her even more.

No! I can't let myself think like that! She belongs to Noah!

The main doors to the soup kitchen opened and people began pouring in. Flynn was too busy serving to pay much attention to Jayde. Still, he was acutely aware of her standing a few yards away from him, interacting with and serving the patrons. It was obvious from her manner she was at ease among these people. She had a kind word and a warm smile for even the most reticent among them and she knew many of them by name.

During a break in the traffic, she turned to him and smiled. "I must admit, I'm surprised to find a man like you getting his hands dirty in a soup kitchen."

"What do you mean, a man like me?" he asked, slightly affronted.

She stared pointedly at his crisp white business shirt, designer tie and navy-blue suit pants he'd changed into after his tennis game. "Oh, I don't know. You just don't seem the type."

He narrowed his eyes at her. "And what type is that?"

"You know. A rich, privileged white male who's never done a hard day's work in his life."

He sputtered in outrage. "Never done a hard day's work? I'm a lawyer in a busy city office! What do you think that entails?"

She shrugged nonchalantly. "I don't know. Sitting behind

a desk all day. Writing letters and emails. I can't imagine it's too taxing."

Flynn could hardly believe her audacity. He opened his mouth to give her a piece of his mind, but just in time caught the teasing glint in her eyes.

The little minx… She's winding me up…

Stifling his protest, he deliberately returned his attention to the steamed green beans and peas in the bain-marie in front of him. From the corner of his eye, he saw Jayde grin triumphantly before focusing her attention on the elderly woman in front of her.

"And how are you today, Dorothy? You're looking well."

"Thank you, Miss Jayde. I'm feeling great. The summer air's been good for my lungs. It took me so long to get rid of that cold I picked up last winter."

"Well, I'm glad to hear you're all better."

"Wish I could say the same for my eyes. They've been giving me hell these past few months. Cataracts, the doctor says."

"Maybe you need to have them looked at by a specialist," Jayde suggested.

The old woman merely shrugged. Jayde spooned a serving of beef and gravy onto Dorothy's plate. The woman then moved on to Flynn. With his gaze still on Jayde, he distractedly spooned a serving of peas and beans onto Dorothy's plate. Half of it fell on the floor.

Flynn flushed with embarrassment. "Oh, I'm so sorry!"

"Geez, I thought I was the one who was blind," the woman muttered and shuffled off to Steven's stand.

Flynn was mortified. He glanced at Jayde and found her trying to stifle her laughter. Seeing the humor in the situation, he reluctantly smiled and then returned his attention to the next patron in line, this time taking particular care to ensure the vegetables landed wholly on the plate.

Afterwards, Flynn volunteered to stack the dishwashers. Steven agreed to help him. They were only halfway through the task when Steven gave him a nudge.

"Now I know why you're so out of sorts."

Flynn pretended confusion. "What are you talking about?"

"Earlier. At the tennis court. It's that girl. Jayde."

"Don't be ridiculous," Flynn said dismissively, keeping his attention on the dirty plates.

"You're not going to get away with it that easily, Craigdon. I saw the way you looked at her. You couldn't take your eyes off her. Not that I blame you. She's hot. How long have you known her?"

"You saw nothing, Steven."

Steven shot him a knowing look and grinned. "Ah huh."

With an effort, Flynn stemmed his irritation. "You don't know what you're talking about."

"At least now I know why you volunteered to help out here while your cousin's away."

Flynn slammed a plate into the dishwasher and turned to his friend. "Shut your mouth, Walker. She's just a girl I know. In fact, she's dating my younger brother."

Once again, Steven shot him a knowing look, but this time wisely remained silent. They finished stacking the dishwashers in silence and then joined the others where they sat together at a table at the far end of the kitchen. With an effort, Flynn kept his gaze away from Jayde.

Sister Mary Catherine smiled at him. "Thank you so much for stopping by, Flynn. You too, Steven. You were a great help."

Flynn inclined his head. "It was no trouble at all, Sister Mary Catherine. I promised Callum I'd help out whenever I could. Who's doing all the cooking with Grace away?"

Sister Mary Catherine looked at Jayde. "We were fortunate Jayde was here today. She took over the cooking duties.

I'm afraid I've never been too good in that department." She looked at Jayde again. "Are you sure you can't come in again tomorrow? I'm sure the patrons would appreciate it. They can tell when it's me doing the cooking!"

She laughed self-deprecatingly and the others joined in.

"I wish I could, Sister Mary Catherine," Jayde said, "but I'm afraid I only have two days free this week."

The nun smiled good-naturedly. "Well, two days are better than none. I guess I'll have to hone my skills and hope for the best on the other days."

"You never know, Flynn here might be a genius in the kitchen," Jayde said. "Perhaps you could ask him to do some cooking?"

Flynn tensed in surprise. Jayde shot him a cheeky look. He relaxed and grinned. "I'm afraid not, Sister Mary Catherine. I can hardly boil water, let alone cater a two-course meal."

"So your wife does all the cooking, does she?" Jayde asked, her eyes wide.

"No. I'm not married. I usually eat out, or I order in. Surely you've heard of Uber eats?"

"Sounds like someone with far too much money," Jayde murmured under her breath.

Flynn let the comment slide. He glanced at his watch. It was after three. As much as he wanted to prolong the time in Jayde's company, he needed to get back to the office and attend to a few things before the day ended. He pushed away from the table and stood.

"I must get going."

Sister Mary Catherine nodded. "Of course. Thank you again for coming, Flynn. You too, Steven. We hope to see you here again soon."

Steven acknowledged her comments with a nod and followed Flynn out. On the way back to his office, Flynn reached for his phone. Though he hadn't asked how long

Jayde had been volunteering at the kitchen, it was more than feasible Callum knew her. Flynn wanted to probe him for information. If his cousin asked why Flynn was phoning him on his honeymoon, Flynn would pretend he needed to give his cousin an update on the soup kitchen. Decision made, he dialed the number.

"Flynn! How's it going?"

"Fine, Callum. And you?"

"Kicking back with a platter of fresh seafood and a beer with my beautiful wife by my side. Fiji is great this time of year."

"So I've heard. Listen, I just wanted to let you know everything's under control at Jennifer's Kitchen. You don't have to worry about a thing."

"Gee, Flynn. That's mighty kind of you. I didn't expect you to give up your entire week."

Flynn blushed. "Yes, well… I only stopped by today to help during the lunch service. Sister Mary Catherine seems to be coping well. And she has Jayde, of course. You didn't tell me you knew her." He tried to keep the accusation out of his voice.

"I didn't get a chance. I was kind of busy getting around to all the guests at the wedding. I noticed you were rather interested in her, though. What's with that?"

Flynn pretended innocence. "What are you talking about?"

"I might have been busy with my new wife, Flynn, but I'm not blind. I saw the way you looked at her. I thought you were going to combust."

Heat crept up Flynn's neck. "She belongs to Noah."

"Is that right?"

"Yes."

"Is that what Noah told you?"

"Yes. Kind of. He told me he's in love with her."

"Oh, hell." Callum sighed. "Poor Noah." He paused. "It looks to me like Jayde's the kind of girl who makes up her own mind."

Flynn had no answer for that, but there was no hiding from how Noah felt. Still, it wouldn't hurt to find out more about her, make sure she was worthy of his brother's heart.

"What do you know about her?" he asked.

"She's a nice girl. She started coming in a few months ago. Helps out at the kitchen once or twice a week. She's kind to the people who come there and she's always happy to do whatever needs to be done. She even helps Grace with the cooking."

"Volunteering in a soup kitchen isn't on everyone's list. What's her story?"

"I don't know. It's none of my business. Maybe she's just a good person trying to do her bit for the less fortunate? There are some of us still around."

Flynn grimaced, a little embarrassed. "Of course there are. Maybe I should help out a bit more often."

"You do your bit," Callum reassured him. "We could never have achieved what we did if you weren't prepared to work pro bono on the legal stuff. And then there's the donation you made to the building fund. That was far from insignificant. Everyone does what they can, Flynn. Helping comes in many forms, not all as hands-on in the soup kitchen."

Flynn swallowed past the sudden lump of emotion that had lodged itself in his throat. "You're a good man, Callum Craigdon. I'm glad you decided against devoting yourself to God. We need people like you on our side."

"Hey, I'm still devoting myself to God, just in a different way. Marriage is a vocation, too."

"Yes, of course. Grace is a lucky woman. I wish I were half the man you are."

"I see you, Flynn Craigdon," Callum replied quietly. "I see behind the brashness, the flash cars, the fast women. You're a good guy. You're doing your bit to help make the world a better place, no matter what you say. You don't fool me."

Once again, Flynn was overcome with emotion. Callum and his other cousins were just as close to Flynn as his biological brothers. They meant the world to him and he'd never do anything to hurt them, starting with Noah.

It was less than a week until Christmas and Noah had never felt less cheery in his life. Just when he thought he'd finally found a woman who liked him, he was forced to question himself yet again. Time after time, during his teenage years and beyond, he'd been paralyzed with shyness when it came to women.

It wasn't that he didn't like them. He loved everything about women. The way they looked, the way they laughed, the way they smelled. Sweet, sexy, delicious. It was just that whenever he found the courage to engage a woman in conversation, he inevitably messed everything up.

He guessed it had something to do with his looks. He'd worn glasses from a young age and had always been self-conscious about his appearance. His mom had tried to get him to wear contacts, but he'd struggled with putting them in and out. Most of the time, his efforts failed and inevitably ended in tears. Eventually, his mother had agreed that contacts weren't for him.

Even with the glasses, his eyesight hadn't been the best. He wasn't good at sports, inevitably dropped the ball, or tripped over it, or had any number of other misadventures that meant he was never picked for a team. After a while, he stopped trying out and buried himself in books. During break times, when most other kids were playing games outside, Noah could be found in the school library.

Most of his family thought it a minor miracle he'd managed to graduate from the police service. Though his brothers hadn't laughed when he'd told them he wanted to be a cop, he could tell they thought he didn't have it in him. After all, a cop had to be confident, a good communicator, tough, brave, have a healthy—some would say inflated—self-esteem, and an undoubtable air of authority. Noah was none of those things.

It had been his dream from a young boy to join the police service and he was determined to make it come true. Granted, the first few years as a junior constable had been difficult, but then he'd set his eye on becoming an internal affairs investigator. Now, with the newly created Law Enforcement Conduct Commission, he'd landed his dream job.

It wasn't the job for everyone, but it suited Noah perfectly. He still got to investigate allegations of crime, but he could do most of the work from his desk. He wasn't in any danger of being shot at, or otherwise losing his life. He didn't have to fear being accosted by a criminal high on drugs. No one would be pulling a knife on him; no house calls to domestic disputes that were unpredictable and could easily get out of hand. It was a good solution and it brought him a great deal of satisfaction. At last he'd found his place in the world.

If only he had a woman with whom he could share it… At twenty-eight, he was certainly of an age to settle down.

"How are you, old boy?"

Noah looked up from his position at the Beaches bar in time to see Christopher take the stool beside him. He was immediately reminded of watching his half-cousin move in on Jayde at the wedding. Noah pushed his glasses back up his nose and merely grunted an acknowledgement.

Seeming unperturbed, Christopher signaled the barman and asked him for a beer. Noah ordered a refill.

"What are you doing here?" Christopher asked when the barman walked away.

"Having a drink. This *is* a bar."

Christopher grinned. "It is indeed. Beaches bar. Owned by Jayde Hassad's father. But I'm sure you knew that already, right? Your presence here wouldn't have anything to do with her, would it?" He winked.

Noah scowled. The last thing he wanted was Christopher sticking his nose into his business. It was bad enough he'd caught the man flirting with Noah's date.

The drinks arrived and Noah busied himself filling his mouth with the cold, yeasty brew. Christopher did likewise and then set his glass back down.

"So, what's with you and the delectable Ms Hassad? You couldn't take your eyes off her at the wedding."

Noah swallowed a sigh. It was clear there would be no rest from Christopher until Noah gave him what he wanted.

"Not that it's any of your business, but you're right," he said. "I like her. I like her a lot."

Christopher merely smiled. "So, why do you look so glum?"

Noah sighed. It would be good to talk to someone about the way he felt and though Christopher wouldn't have been his first choice for a confidante, his half-cousin was there and obviously interested. What harm could it do?

"The thing is, I don't know how she feels."

Christopher grinned. "Oh, the age-old question. She came as your date to Callum's wedding. That should tell you something."

Noah shrugged. "Yeah. But I haven't been able to read her signals. I don't know if I'm in the friend zone or if she feels something more."

Christopher reached over and squeezed his arm. "You need to go for it, old boy. Just put yourself out there. Take her out for a drink, or maybe even dinner, and afterwards, just do it. Kiss her. You'll soon know if you're in the friend zone."

Noah looked at him. "Really? You think I should just go for it?"

"Why not? That's what I'd do. But you'd better act fast. I noticed your brother sniffing around her, too. We both know Flynn's never backward in coming forward with the ladies. If you want her, you'd best do something about making her yours before your brother makes a move."

Noah compressed his lips and nodded. Flynn's reputation around women was notorious. It seemed every other month he had a new woman on his arm. The family had lost count of the number of ladies who'd passed through Flynn's life. It seemed he'd hardly started with one and there was another one being introduced. It hadn't been that long ago he'd dated an attractive woman by the name of Casey. Now it seemed he had Jayde in his sights. Noah tensed.

No! Jayde is mine!

All of a sudden, he was determined to make it so.

Gulping down the last of his beer, he turned back to Christopher. "Thanks. I really appreciate the advice. Sorry to rush off, but there are things I need to do."

With that, he left.

Chapter Eight

Christopher stared after Noah's departing back. His poor half-cousin had it bad. He wondered just who Jayde Hassad was, to inspire such passion in not just one Craigdon male, but two. There was no way Christopher had imagined Flynn's heated gaze whenever he'd looked at the woman.

Pulling out his phone, Christopher opened a search engine and plugged in Jayde's name. Nothing. Christopher frowned. Strange. She was a twenty-something young woman. At the very least, she should be on Instagram. Or Facebook. Or Twitter. And yet, according to the results of his online search, Jayde Hassad didn't exist.

Christopher's instincts started humming. Something was awry. Jayde had told him she led a boring life. A barmaid, working for her father. As if that was all there was to it. Christopher had pretended to laugh about it at the time, but now more than ever he didn't believe her. Even if she was as plain and boring as she pretended, he should have found a trace of her online.

This required further investigation. It always paid to stay ahead of the crowd. Who knew? The information he gathered on her might one day come in handy. It was always good to have people in his debt, especially when some of those very people had been given his entire inheritance, lock, stock and barrel.

Scrolling through his contacts, he found the name he was looking for. He dialed the number and waited for the man to pick up.

"Detective Marchant."

"Aaron! It's good to hear your voice. It's been way too long."

The response from the man on the other end of the phone was much more restrained.

"Christopher. What can I do for you?"

"I'm so glad you asked, Aaron. I need a favor."

In short order, Christopher relayed his request.

"Jayde Hassad. The name doesn't ring any bells. I'll see what I can do. But this is the last time, Christopher. After this, we're even."

"Oh, dear boy. You're so funny." Christopher was still laughing when he ended the call.

Sophia Craigdon pulled her car into the Sydney Harbour Hospital parking lot and found a vacant space. Switching off the ignition, she swallowed a weary sigh. She ached all over. It wasn't just the physical pain from the beating she'd suffered at the hands of a madman. She also hurt emotionally. Though she was incredibly glad Archie had stepped up and saved her life by giving her his blood, the shock of discovering he was her biological father still hadn't gone away.

For most of her twenty-two years, Sophia had known her father didn't love her. Though she tried so hard to please Henry Craigdon, to get his attention, to win his praise, nothing she did ever mattered or penetrated his cold exterior. Now she knew why.

Henry Craigdon wasn't her father. And he'd known it. Had known it right from the very start. No wonder he'd treated her with such contempt. Even as a small child, she'd felt it.

Knowing her mother had kept the truth from her all these years made her blood boil.

Elizabeth had watched her husband treat Sophia with disdain and had said nothing. At least not to Sophia. Perhaps her mother had tried to reason with Henry, plead with him not to take out his anger on her daughter, but whatever had been said and done, it hadn't been enough. Sophia had grown up without her father's love and up until now, she'd been confused and bewildered as to why.

And it wasn't only Sophia her mother had deceived. Uncle Archie had also been kept in the dark. Uncle Archie…her biological father. It still seemed so surreal.

Flynn, Noah, Logan… They weren't her cousins as she'd always believed. They were her half-brothers. Along with those siblings she'd always thought were her blood. Jett, Callum, Joel, Nicholas and Isabella… Not her full brothers and sister, but halves. It was a lot to get her head around. The confusion and turmoil of her thoughts was made even worse by the persistent headache that had plagued her ever since the attack.

The doctors had assured her everything appeared normal on her CT scan, but that didn't make the pain go away. They'd urged her to take pain killers as required and give herself time to heal. It was important she rest and relax, de-stress from her everyday life.

Ha! As if I can do that! My whole world has just fallen apart!

Well, not her *whole* world. She still had Jarrod. Her husband. And thank goodness for that! He'd been so wonderfully kind and considerate and loving. He'd been just as horrified by her attack as she was. On top of that was his guilt. She'd been half beaten to death by one of his friends, Tony Mattheson, a former cop. Though she didn't blame Jarrod for an instant, he wasn't quite as quick to forgive himself. After all, Sophia had voiced concerns about Tony in the past. It didn't matter that those concerns had been in relation to Tony's son, Travis.

Travis…

Sophia's heart tripped over in a fresh wave of pain. The six-year-old was fighting for his life after being beaten by his father… The same man who'd attacked Sophia. While Sophia's injuries were slowly healing, Travis was still in the ICU. According to Isabella, he still hadn't regained consciousness.

Sophia bit her lip against a surge of emotion and made her way across the parking lot. She walked into the main building of the hospital and pressed the button for the lift. She was there to visit with Travis. Or at least get an update on his condition. She sent a silent prayer heavenwards as the lift made its way up to the ICU.

The nurse who met her outside the ward recognized her. This wasn't the first time Sophia had stopped by to check on her former student.

"Sophia. How are you feeling?" the nurse asked in a subdued tone.

"Getting there. How's Travis?"

The nurse smiled. "He's awake!"

Sophia's heart skipped a beat. She pressed her hand against her chest and almost sobbed out her relief.

"Thank goodness! Is he okay? Can I talk with him?"

"He seems to be doing all right, but it's still early days. The best news is that he's regained consciousness. We're quietly confident it will only get better from here. His mother is in there with him. I can ask her if she minds if you pop in. We usually allow only one visitor at a time."

"Of course. I'll wait here."

The nurse disappeared and Sophia found a vacant chair not far away. With shaking hands she pulled out her phone and sent a message to her husband.

Travis is awake! He's going 2 b ok!

Jarrod sent a reply right away.

Fantastic news! Have u spoken 2 him?

Sophia quickly texted back.

Not yet. Hopefully soon. I'm @ the hospital now.

Say hi 2 him 4 me. Love u xxx

Will do. Love u 2 xxx

Sophia dropped the phone back into her handbag. At that moment the nurse reappeared, followed by Travis' mother. She looked tired and drawn and pale, but there was the tiniest spark of hope in her eyes.

"Melinda!" Sophia exclaimed.

The two women hugged each other a little awkwardly. When they pulled apart, both of them had tears in their eyes.

"I just heard the good news," Sophia exclaimed. "Is it true? Is Travis awake?"

Melinda nodded and swiped at the tears on her cheeks. "Yes. Isn't it wonderful?"

Sophia smiled and nodded and swallowed past the lump in her throat. "It is. It absolutely is."

And then Melinda frowned. "How are you feeling?" Her gaze roved over Sophia's face, which still bore faint evidence of her beating.

"I'm fine," Sophia said quietly.

Fresh tears formed in Melinda's eyes. "I'm so sorry for what he did to you, Sophia—"

Sophia held up her hand, cutting Melinda off. "Hey. We've already been over this. It wasn't your fault."

"But still…"

"No buts," Sophia said firmly. "Now, do you think I could duck in and see Travis? I promise I won't be long."

Melinda gave her a wobbly smile. "Of course. He'll be thrilled to see you."

With that, the nurse took Sophia into the ICU and left her with Travis. The little boy looked battered and bruised and pale, but his eyes lit up at the sight of Sophia.

"Mrs Craigdon! What are *you* doing here?"

Sophia brushed away her tears and smiled. "Travis! It's so good to see you!"

She walked slowly forward and gently squeezed his hand. "How are you feeling?"

He grimaced. "Pretty sore. And thirsty. Do you think I could have a drink?"

Sophia looked around for the nurse and put in Travis' request. A few moments later, the nurse returned with a plastic cup filled with ice chips.

"We need to take it easy for the first little while Travis," she said and offered him the cup. "It's been awhile since you had anything to drink. Suck on some ice chips for now. If you tolerate that, we can give you some water, okay?"

"Okay." Travis took the cup and tapped a small piece of ice into his mouth.

"How's that?" Sophia asked.

Travis smile. "The best thing I've ever tasted."

She smiled back. Her heart was filled with gladness that it appeared he'd survived the brutal attack without permanent damage. Mindful of how much he needed his rest, she left him a few moments later, promising to return the next day.

As she left the hospital, her earlier thoughts about her mother filtered back into her consciousness. Some of the anger had now left her. There was nothing like spending time with a critically ill child to put things into perspective. Though Sophia had lacked Henry's love, he'd made sure her needs were met. She hadn't been ill-treated, certainly not in the way Travis had. For that, she was grateful. Besides, her father—Henry—was dead.

What good would it do to carry grudges? He was never going to be able to put things right. It was a timely reminder of how fragile life could be. One never knew when it would be taken from them. Life was too short to remain angry at the people she loved, and that included her mother.

With a weary sigh, Sophia popped a couple of painkillers and washed them down with some water she found in her car. Her last thoughts as she departed the hospital were of Travis. He was going to be okay. She broke into a slow, sad smile.

For the second time that week, Flynn found himself outside Jennifer's Kitchen. He'd phoned ahead and Sister Mary Catherine had confirmed Jayde was volunteering there that day. As soon as he heard that, he couldn't get out of the office fast enough.

"I have an outside appointment. I'll be back in a couple of hours," he'd told his junior secretary, Emily.

No matter how many times he told himself to stay the hell away from Jayde, he couldn't do it. The truth was, his inability to eradicate her from his thoughts was irritating. Women came in and out of his life with astounding frequency. He'd never felt the slightest inclination to commit for more than a month or two to any of them. Inevitably he got bored with them, or they became too clingy, and he moved on to someone else. It had been that way forever.

But now things were different. It felt like the ground had shifted beneath him. What had once provided sure and solid footing now felt fluid and unpredictable. And it had everything to do with *her*. That was infuriating.

Flynn entered the soup kitchen through the back door, pushing it open with his shoulder. Jayde stood at the stove with her back to him, stirring something on the burner. The smell of cooking meat, garlic and onion filled the air.

"Something smells good," he said.

She spun around and acknowledged him briefly with a surprised nod before returning her attention to the stove. Sister Mary Catherine came forward to greet him.

"Flynn! So great to see you again. I hope this means you're here to help." She smiled.

"Of course. I thought you might like another pair of hands."

The old nun patted his arm. "Extra help is always appreciated. We'll never turn you away."

He grinned at her. "I'm all yours, Sister Mary Catherine. Put me to work."

"You might regret that," Jayde quipped.

She winked at him and Flynn's gut clenched with need. He deliberately turned away.

Jayde concentrated furiously on the huge pot of stir fry cooking in front of her. It was almost done, but she wasn't yet ready to relinquish her position at the stove. Sister Mary Catherine had put Flynn in charge of emptying the cooked rice into the bain-marie and right next to that was where she had to put the stir fry. With her heart still beating fast, she needed a moment to get her pulse rate back under control.

It wasn't fair. No man had a right to look so good. A charcoal-gray designer suit. Pristine white shirt. Dark red tie. Shiny black boots. And what was she thinking, encouraging him like that? She'd *winked* at him, for Pete's sake! Until she knew what part he played in her investigation, she had no right to flirt with him. She needed to keep her distance, keep a cool head, remain objective.

Then there was Noah. It seemed he spent all his spare time at her father's bar, especially when she was working there. And though he was cute and sweet and funny, she wasn't attracted to him at all. He was a means to an end. A way to infiltrate the Craigdon clan and though that made her feel guilty, it was the truth. Nothing personal. She was only doing her job.

But right now she had to get through another lunch service with Flynn standing only a few yards away. She was sure her handler had no idea the difficulties she sometimes encountered during the course of her work. She'd willingly taken on the assignment to investigate the persistent rumors that had surrounded Henry Craigdon and she'd darn well see it through to the end, but she was sure there were far easier ways to make a living.

With her heart rate now back firmly under control, she switched off the heat under the pot and picked it up and carried it across the kitchen. She set it down on the counter near the bain-marie right next to Flynn's and began transferring the food into the warming pans. He watched her work in silence, but she was acutely aware of him the whole time.

"Looks as good as anything I've had delivered to my apartment in an Uber," he said. He followed the comment with a grin.

This time she refused to let his charm affect her. "I'm surprised a lawyer who works in such a busy city practice has time to spend in a place like this."

He gave her a look of mock outrage. "I'm more than happy to give back to the less fortunate. It's not all about making money."

"Oh, so you work for Legal Aid?" she asked, knowing full well he didn't.

A flush of embarrassment stained his cheeks. "No. I…ah… I'm employed at Sydney Legal."

She forced herself to react with surprise at the mention of the highly reputable law firm. It was one of Sydney's oldest legal establishments. Its lawyers commanded a premium for their services.

"I see," she replied. "So sometimes it *is* all about making money."

Flynn looked uncomfortable. "There's nothing wrong with that," he said in a defensive tone.

"Of course not. It just doesn't gel with the fact you're here volunteering your time at a soup kitchen. You're missing out on hundreds of dollars in billable hours."

His answering smile relaxed and did funny things to her insides. "As I said, it's not all about making money."

She finished what she was doing in silence. Flynn stood by and watched. As if unable to bear the silence another minute, he spoke again.

"Did you know Sydney Legal has a direct connection to my family?"

"Really?" she replied, interested despite herself. This was something her research hadn't unearthed.

"Yes, my aunt's father and her uncle were the founding partners. Of course, it wasn't called Sydney Legal back then."

"What was it called?"

"Doherty & Associates. My aunt's maiden name was Doherty. It was a small, but lucrative law firm in the city. Apparently they were the go-to firm to the rich and famous. More than that, they had a stellar reputation for being honest, hardworking and fair. Twenty years after they first opened their doors, they were approached by Frederick Wentworth who was in partnership with Wilfred Harton at the time. The Doherty brothers were offered an astronomical amount of money and they sold the firm and became senior partners of Harton & Wentworth. Of course, Aunt Elizabeth's father and her uncle have been dead almost a decade now. A few years ago, Harton & Wentworth—"

"Re-branded themselves as Sydney Legal. I remember." She smiled. "Are there any other lawyers in your family?"

"Nope. Just me."

"What about celebrities? Famous actresses? Rock stars?" She grinned, enjoying their banter.

"No. My brother Logan was a famous sailor for a time. He was part of the Australian Olympic team once. Does that count?"

"The Olympics? That's pretty impressive. Does he still sail?" she asked, knowing full well the answer.

Flynn compressed his lips and shook his head. "No. He had a bad accident. Lots of broken bones. They didn't heal so well. He's fine, but he's not up to professional sailing anymore."

"Too bad," Jayde murmured.

When she'd read all about the accident during the course of her research, Logan Craigdon had been a nameless, faceless person who meant nothing to her. Now she recalled the glum surfer dude she'd met at the wedding and couldn't help but feel a twinge of sympathy.

Flynn's expression had sobered. "Yeah. He's been down on his luck, lately. That's for sure."

She thought fast. Having Logan Craigdon close at hand could work to her advantage. It would give her the opportunity to get up close and personal with another significant member of the Craigdon family.

"You could always encourage him to come and help out here," she suggested in a casual tone. "We have fun, don't we? And Sister Mary Catherine could always do with the help. It might be just what he needs."

Flynn merely shrugged. The main doors to the soup kitchen opened and patrons began streaming through. As they lined up with plates and were served, Jayde couldn't help but notice how friendly and open Flynn was with them. Not everyone felt comfortable around the less fortunate, but Flynn seemed to take them in his stride. He greeted every single one of them, and though he didn't know their names, he made them feel welcome.

It left her with a warm feeling inside.

Chapter Nine

From the corner of her eye, Jayde saw the dark-blue, unmarked BMW slide into the Beaches parking lot. It was her handler, Brian Heller. A veteran cop who'd also spent years undercover. He was there for their regular briefing.

She casually finished wiping glasses, then set the cloth on the bar. She looked across at the young barman who was working the morning shift with her.

"Hey, Toby. I'm gonna take my break now. Are you all right with that?"

"Sure, Jayde. We're hardly overrun with customers. Take as long as you want."

She murmured her thanks and untied the apron at her waist then tossed it on the counter. Then she strode across the room and pushed open the door that led outside. There was an external staircase behind the building that provided alternative access to her rooms on the first floor. It wasn't visible from the street. She'd used it many times since taking the job at Beaches. Brian was equally familiar with it.

"How are things?" she asked him as he followed her into her apartment.

"Can't complain," Brian replied and then lowered his bulk to the couch.

"Can I get you a coffee?"

"Sure. Black with one."

"I've only got instant."

Brian grinned. "Makes no difference to me."

She filled the kettle and set it to boil and then rejoined him in the living room. She took the seat opposite.

"How are you progressing with the Craigdon investigation?" he asked. "Find anything useful?"

"Well, I compiled a thorough dossier on every member of the family, right down to Henry's illegitimate son. I've been working hard getting to know some of them. I've managed to gain an introduction to three of Henry's sons."

Brian nodded with approval. "Good girl. Anything else?"

"Yes, I've also managed to befriend two nephews and I've been introduced to a third. I'm hoping to gain their trust enough that they might shed some light on their uncle's activities."

The kettle boiled and Jayde excused herself to make the coffee. A short time later, she returned with two cups of steaming hot brew. She set one down in front of her handler and kept the other one for herself. She returned to her seat on the couch.

"It sounds like you've been busy," Brian said around a mouthful of coffee.

"Yes. I was helped along when I managed to get invited to a Craigdon wedding."

Brian smiled in surprise. "How did you manage that?"

Jayde merely grinned. "I did nothing untoward, I assure you."

"I don't care what you did. The fact is, the DEA had been watching Henry for years before he died. We never got enough on him to make an arrest. He was always one step ahead of us. Now he's out of reach."

"Maybe, maybe not. Henry's company, Craigdon Enterprises, is now owned by one of his nephews."

"Really? That's a little odd. From what I recall, Craigdon had a number of sons and a couple of daughters. Why would he leave his precious company to a nephew?"

"I'm not sure anyone knows the reason behind it. Even the family seems baffled. The nephew in question isn't a property developer. Anything but. Logan Craigdon is a ship builder. Well he designs super yachts to be exact. Before that, he used to sail competitively. Even made the Olympic team when he was younger."

Brian frowned. "Very strange. Seems there might be something fishy about this. Perhaps this Logan fellow was already involved in Henry's drug business? Maybe putting him in charge of the legitimate business was a brilliant smokescreen, gifted to the nephew on Henry's deathbed? Why else reward the man so handsomely?"

"Yes. I'm not sure of that, yet."

"How did Henry's children do?"

"Some did well and some less so. There doesn't seem to be any rhyme or reason that I can ascertain. Of course, no one was treated better in the will than Logan Craigdon."

Brian looked thoughtful. "You need to dig deeper into this Logan character, find out the extent of his involvement in his uncle's affairs."

Jayde nodded. "I'm happy to do that of course, but the thing is, Logan Craigdon isn't running Craigdon Enterprises."

Brian frowned again. "No? Who is?"

"One of Henry's sons," Jayde explained. "Nicholas Craigdon. He's been employed by Craigdon Enterprises since before he left school, but he's never held any position of power. Since the change in ownership, Nicholas has been appointed Managing Director by Logan. It's Nicholas who has the day-to-day responsibilities of running the company."

"Interesting. Maybe this Nicholas is an innocent pawn and has been put in charge of the legitimate business affairs to enable

Logan to carry on with the less scrupulous money-making activities behind the scenes. Do you think that's a possibility?"

"I guess it's possible. I don't know him well enough to say."

"Of course, another possibility is that they're both in it together."

Jayde merely shrugged.

"You said Logan designs and builds yachts?"

"Yes."

"Another interesting tidbit," Brian mused. "Tons of illegal drugs are brought in across the water every year. Our border forces are stretched to the limits intercepting boats. As a waterman, this Logan character would have plenty of connections with other boatmen. Interesting indeed."

Jayde frowned. She'd met both Logan and Nicholas at Callum's wedding. Both of them had been regulation Craigdon male perfection, but they'd also been polite and courteous. Logan had been a bit distant, but Noah had explained his brother's dour mood. Neither of the men had triggered her radar that something was awry.

Still, if the DEA had been watching Henry for years before his death, it was obvious he'd been a big fish.

"What kind of money are we talking?" she asked.

Brian compressed his lips. "At the time of Craigdon's death, the narcotics guys estimated his annual turnover to be in excess of half a billion dollars from the sale of illegal drugs alone."

Jayde gasped. She'd had no idea they were talking that kind of money. She told her handler as much.

"Yes. It's big business. That's why it's so important for you to discover if any of the remaining Craigdon family members were involved in it then, or have since stepped up and taken over where Henry left off." He paused. "I'm sure I don't need to tell you that you'd be looked upon most favorably if you could get enough evidence on even one of them that would allow charges to be laid. The big boss would be more than pleased."

Brian's meaning was clear. The promotion Jayde had been angling for might be within her reach if she managed to pull this off. She felt a little uncomfortable at the thought of continuing to spy on Noah and Flynn, but those were her orders and she was first and foremost a cop. Noah of all people should understand.

"What about Christopher Barrington?" she asked.

Her handler frowned. "Barrington? Where does he fit into the picture?"

"He's Henry Craigdon's first-born, illegitimate son. His mother's Evelyn Baker. She had an affair with Henry before she married Frank Barrington."

"The mining magnate?"

"Yes. Frank legally adopted Christopher when he was twelve."

"Does this Christopher work for Frank?"

"No, not as far as I can tell. He was employed by McClintock Properties in their contracts department until recently."

"Did he inherit anything under the will?"

"No."

Brian thought for a moment. "So he's probably not the one who'd be in line to take over Craigdon's drug business."

Jayde nodded. "Probably not, but he's a bit of a sleaze. There's something about him that makes me uneasy."

"Keep an eye on him."

"No problem. Is there anything else?"

"How are you doing with the intel against your father?"

The change of subject brought with it a rush of icy anger, followed swiftly by a renewed sense of cold hard determination. Brian knew all about her tumultuous past, including the recent tragic loss of her brother. He also knew how important it was for her to see her father in jail.

"I'm proceeding slowly. It's imperative I gain Dad's trust. So far, so good. He has no reason to suspect his daughter. He trusts me with Beaches. Next, I'm angling to be included in his discussions with his suppliers."

Brian nodded, pleased. "Good. Don't forget, we need hard evidence. Recorded conversations, video footage. Whatever you can get."

She looked at him. "You can count on me, Brian."

He held her gaze. "I know I can." He paused and then added, "By the way, Henry Craigdon was a regular here at Beaches. He and your dad were tight. We could never prove they were doing business together, but that didn't mean we didn't all think that. See if you can prise some information out of your dad about Henry. John might inadvertently give us the breakthrough we need. Especially when he has no idea you have an ulterior motive." Brian chuckled. "Imagine the irony if one of Henry's drug cronies was the one who ended up breaking open this case, and all without a clue. It would be priceless."

Jayde smiled and nodded slowly, her thoughts now centered on the knowledge the Craigdon family were far more entwined with her family than she'd ever guessed. She wondered if any of the current Craigdon stock were aware of it and if so, what they intended to do with that information. Time would tell.

Elizabeth's stomach quivered with nerves. Pacing the thick carpet of the music room, she clenched and unclenched her hands. In between, she kept checking the time. She'd asked Sophia and Archie to meet her at Craigdon Manor. They were both running late. Though she'd already spoken to Archie about the secret, he was far from reconciling himself to it—or to her. In particular, he was hostile about her continued refusal to come clean about their ongoing affair. They hadn't shared a bed since he'd discovered her treachery.

As for Sophia, until now, she'd refused to come anywhere near her mother. She hadn't returned any of her calls. Elizabeth couldn't live with the guilt, the anxiety, the pain of it any longer. Being at odds with two people she loved more than anything was destroying her. The heart attack might not have killed her, but being hated by her family could very well finish her off.

And then she heard the front door open and a fresh wave of nerves rushed through her.

"Is that you, Archie?" she called. "I'm in the music room."

"No, Mom. It's Sophia."

Elizabeth's youngest daughter appeared in the open doorway. At the sight of her grim expression, Elizabeth was filled with dread. It was Christmas Eve. A time for family, for love and celebration. A time she'd always held dear. But from the stiff and unyielding way Sophia held herself, it was obvious she hadn't softened toward her mother. She looked like she was about to endure the worst moments of her life.

"It's good to see you, darling. Thank you for coming." Elizabeth pecked her on the cheek and was grateful when Sophia didn't pull away.

"I'm only here because Jarrod convinced me it was the right thing to do, being Christmas and all."

Her words pierced Elizabeth's heart, but she refrained from commenting. A moment later, there was a knock on the front door and then Archie appeared. He looked almost as grim as Sophia. He acknowledged Elizabeth with a brief nod, but gave Sophia a hug.

"How are you feeling, honey? You had us all so worried. When we were told how that madman attacked you and how badly you'd been injured..." He shuddered. "I'm so glad you're okay."

Sophia gave him a shaky smile. "Thanks, Uncle—I mean—" She looked stricken.

"It's all right Sophia," Archie replied. "Call me whatever you're comfortable with. It's going to take both of us time to adjust to this new reality."

He turned and shot Elizabeth an accusing look. She flushed, but held his stare. Yes, she'd made a mistake keeping the truth from them, but her reasons for doing so were sound and she refused to be made to feel like this forever. That was the reason she'd asked them both to meet with her.

Drawing in a deep breath, she eased it out and let go some of the tension inside her. It would do none of them any good if she went into this conversation feeling defensive. With that thought in mind, she spoke.

"Thank you so much for coming. I really appreciate it. We haven't actually had a chance to talk about what happened and I don't want to go into Christmas without clearing the air."

Sophia looked bored, but Elizabeth could tell she was listening. Archie merely stared hard at the floor.

Elizabeth sighed softly. "There's nothing I can do to change things. I made the decision many years ago to keep the truth of Sophia's parentage a secret. I still believe the decision I made back then was done for the right reasons. And I honestly, if not perhaps naïvely, thought I could take that secret with me to my grave. I wanted to spare both of you the distress."

She glanced at Archie. "As you said, the two of us were still married to other people. That wasn't going to change. How could knowing Sophia was your daughter have made any difference to how things were?"

"At least it would have provided me with an explanation for why Daddy treated me so abominably all those years!" Sophia cried. "Do you know how many times I beat myself up, thinking it was *my* fault he didn't love me? All the times I tried to please him, over and over again. Desperate for his approval. Desperate for his love. And all the time you knew why he treated me the way he did. Why he'd never love me, no matter what I did. And you said nothing!" Sophia's voice broke on a harsh sob.

Elizabeth was filled with anguish. This was exactly what she'd hoped to avoid during all those years she'd kept the secret and now she saw she'd failed dismally. Her heart clenched with pain.

"Oh, honey! I'm so sorry! I'm so sorry! I thought I was sparing you the heartache of knowing the truth, but all I've done is cause you more grief! It's all my fault. I only wanted to protect you—and because I loved you so very much. I didn't want you to think you were an outsider, someone who didn't belong. I wanted you to grow up thinking you had a legitimate call to the Craigdon name, the same as your brothers and sister.

"I was still pregnant with you when Henry and I made the decision to keep my affair a secret. At the time, I had no idea he'd hold your parentage against you. None of this is your fault! You were completely innocent of wrongdoing. I lost count of the number of times I railed against him, shouted at him for treating you differently than the others. But he'd just look at me coldly and tell me I was the one responsible for your pain."

As the awful memories bombarded her, Elizabeth gasped on a sob of anguish, but she forced herself to continue. She might never get the chance to explain again. She looked at Sophia.

"There were so many times I wanted to tell you the truth, but by then it was too late. Now that you know what it's like to love someone so deeply, maybe you can understand where I'm coming from."

She paused and encompassed both of them with her gaze. "I didn't want to hurt either of you. I was all too aware it wouldn't change the way Henry regarded you, Sophia, but I was horribly afraid it would change the way you felt about yourself. You were a Craigdon, being raised as such alongside your brothers and sister. I didn't want to tamper with that or damage your relationship with them.

"I accept that telling you the truth might have helped you to understand your father's unforgivable behavior, but I… I couldn't do it. I was afraid of how you'd react. Terrified of losing you, losing your love, your respect."

She looked at Archie. Through her entire monologue, he'd remained stony-faced. Now he turned to her with pain-filled eyes.

"I wish you'd told me. It might not have changed anything on the surface, but you robbed me of years knowing Sophia was my daughter… *My daughter*… Watching her grow up, her first day of school, her high school graduation. It would have meant so much more to me if I'd known."

His gaze shifted to Sophia. "I've always loved you, Sophia. You've always had a special place in my heart. But the love an uncle has for his niece… It isn't the same. One day, if you're ever blessed with children, you might understand." He paused. When he spoke again, his voice was low and husky with emotion.

"It's only right you know I bear some guilt. There was a time I suspected you might be my daughter, but I never found the courage to ask."

Elizabeth started in surprise. She'd had no idea the thought had even occurred to Archie. His admission eased some of her guilt.

His gaze zeroed in on her. "I'm ashamed to make that admission, Elizabeth, but that's the truth. The timing was right for her conception, but… I didn't want to know. I was scared to know. I was still married, had young children of my own. Knowing for sure I had a daughter, that there was proof of my affair… It would have forced my hand. There was no way I wouldn't have claimed you as my own and…that would have had consequences…for everyone."

His gaze took in both of them. His expression turned beseeching. "You have to understand, I had responsibilities I couldn't discard. So did you, Elizabeth. Though I was shocked and angry that you kept this from me, the more I've had time to think about it, the more I've come to understand. You did what you thought was best for everyone and you did it out of love. In many ways, I'm grateful you kept the secret."

His unexpected admission made Elizabeth gasp. She stared at him in disbelief. Tears burned in her eyes.

Archie turned to Sophia. "This is hardest for you. Your mother's right. What happened had nothing to do with you—not the affair, not your conception, not keeping back the truth. But I hope one day you might find it in your heart to forgive me and your mother and love me as your father. You're the daughter I always wanted and never knew I had."

His voice cracked with emotion. Tears streamed down his cheeks. Elizabeth and Sophia were also crying. Almost at the same time, they turned to each other and embraced.

"Oh, Mom!"

"Sophia! My darling! I'm so sorry. I never wanted to hurt you. I love you so much!"

"I love you, too!"

Archie threw his arms around both of them and they made room for him, laughing and crying at the same time. Elizabeth felt like a mountain had been lifted off her shoulders. She tilted her head heavenward and whispered a heartfelt prayer of gratitude.

Chapter Ten

It was Christmas Eve. Christopher sipped at the single malt Scotch he'd treated himself to in deference to the occasion and surveyed the dimly lit bar. The place was nearly empty. Bing Crosby's "White Christmas" played on the juke box. An attempt at a decorated Christmas tree stood in the far corner, near the old brick fireplace. It was safe to say its patrons weren't drawn there for the décor.

Harry's Bar was the perfect place for hiding out. Hidden down a narrow alleyway in the city, most people didn't even know it existed. Those that did, preferred to keep its location a secret. No one wanted it to be overtaken by the "in crowd"—the bloggers, the Instagrammers—with their phone cameras at the ready for any shot worthy of uploading to social media. Unlike the Beaches bar in Balmoral, Harry's Bar prided itself on the fact it wasn't frequented by actors, celebrities, politicians. Just ordinary people hoping to escape the pressures of the world and hide out for a few hours.

Taking another sip of his drink, Christopher was interrupted by the sound of his phone buzzing in his pocket. Pulling it out, he checked the screen.

No caller ID.

No matter. A lot of people Christopher knew weren't crazy on advertising their number. He answered the call and smiled when he recognized the voice on the other end of the phone.

"Christopher. It's Aaron Marchant."

"Detective. How nice of you to get back to me so quickly. I hope you're about to give me an early Christmas present?"

"I'm not sure about that. There isn't much. Jayde Hassad doesn't show up in any of the police databases. The best I could do was dig out some family history. Her mother died last year. Cancer. Her brother OD'd in June. The most interesting thing I found was that she's the daughter of John Hassad."

"You say that as if it should mean something to me."

"John Hassad is a notorious drug dealer. A big time player. Has networks all over Sydney, but particularly on the northern beaches. The police have been trying to get him for years, with no luck. He's a clever bastard, that's for sure."

Christopher frowned. For years, he'd watched Henry come and go from Beaches. That was the reason Christopher started frequenting the bar in the first place. He'd been curious about what drew his father there, over and over again. And though it was clean and modern and the views of the harbor were spectacular, the bar tended to cater to a much younger crowd. He'd never been able to work out Henry's attraction to the place. Now he couldn't help but wonder if something else had drawn his late father to the establishment, time and time again…

"And Jayde? Is she involved in the family business?" he asked.

"I can't tell. She's never been charged. Not even an arrest. The brother showed up on the search, though. John Hassad Junior. Numerous charges for drug possession. A couple for dealing, but only small amounts. He'd done time. At least six months. Both times for drug offenses. No surprise he died from an overdose."

"*Mm.* I see. Well, thanks for that. You've been most helpful."

"Don't forget what I said. This was the last time."

Christopher's fingers tightened around his phone. He lowered his voice to a menacing growl. "Listen here, Aaron. Have you forgotten about that nasty piece of footage I have on my phone? No? I didn't think so. Listen close, Aaron. I'll tell you when we're done. Are we clear?"

The silence drew out… "Yes. We're clear."

"Good."

With that, Christopher ended the call.

The sound of Mariah Carey's dulcet tones singing a Christmas tune floated in the air of Beaches. Despite the fact it was Christmas Eve—or perhaps because of it—the place was rocking. Jayde had been flat out serving drinks for the past several hours and her feet were killing her. In deference to the occasion, she'd put on extra staff, and all of them were busy.

"Good crowd tonight," her father said, raising his voice over the music and the noise of conversation.

Tonight was one of the rare nights he'd shown up during business hours. Busy serving a customer, Jayde merely acknowledged his comment with a nod and continued to fill the beer glass. When she was done, she handed it to the patron and then took his money. He shot her a cheeky grin. She winked back at him. He laughed and with his beer in hand, turned away.

Her father's assessing gaze followed the man for a moment and then turned back to Jayde. "Too bad you didn't show up here sooner. You're good for business. Half the men in this room are hankering after you."

Jayde remained silent. She took the open appreciation she received from many of the patrons in the spirit it was offered.

A bit of harmless flirtation that left both parties feeling good. She didn't do this to increase business. She did it solely to ingratiate herself with her father as a valuable member of his team. The more he trusted her, the more likely he was to let her into his inner circle, including sharing details of his drug trade.

After the death of her mother right before Christmas the year before, Jayde had used her police contacts to track down her brother. She'd found him working at Beaches. It was obvious he was a front man for their father's more nefarious activities. Jayde had tried to appeal to his sense of decency and when that didn't work, to the fear of getting caught.

"Do you know how much jail time you're facing if they catch you?" she'd asked, horrified that he'd been caught up in their father's business.

Junior had merely laughed. "They won't catch me. Have you forgotten? Dad's been doing this all our lives. He's still the king."

Jayde had been appalled. It killed her to know her brother had gone down the same path as their father. It made her choice of career even more ironic. Of course, she kept her occupation a secret from Junior, too. In fact, she hadn't offered her father any explanation at all when, a week after her brother's overdose, she'd returned to Beaches and asked for a job.

At some point, his curiosity had gotten the better of him. After all, she'd appeared from nowhere. He hadn't seen her for twenty years. She'd never before expressed a desire to spend time with him. When he asked what she'd been doing since she left school, she'd kept her answers deliberately vague. A secretarial course. Business management. Working as a temp in an office.

"So why do you want to work here?" he'd asked.

She had an answer at the ready. "It pays better than secretarial work. Plus, my lease is up. I noticed you have an empty apartment upstairs. I thought I might be able to make use of it." Maintaining her subterfuge, she gave him a cheeky grin.

Her father had given her a searching look, but eventually shrugged and turned away. "You can start waiting tables. If that works out and you decide to stick around, I'll give you a job behind the bar. That's my best offer."

"I'll take it," she said and then spontaneously gave him a hug. Though she found everything about him distasteful and blamed him for her brother's death, he was still her father. And though he'd been mostly absent from her life, he was the only one she had.

But instead of returning her embrace, he'd looked startled and ended the contact with unseemly haste. Jayde had tried to conceal her hurt behind a shaky grin.

"When do you want me to start?"

That had been six months ago and she was now firmly entrenched in the place. Her father had recently given her the responsibility of counting the till at the end of the evening and for locking the money away in the safe. He'd shown her where it was, behind the desk in his office, and had given her the combination.

The first time she'd opened the secure door, her heart had beaten almost out of her chest. She wasn't sure what else he stowed there. Drugs? Bundles of cash? Burner phones? To her disappointment, there was nothing more than a small stack of legal documents providing evidence of his ownership of the bar. Still, his increasing trust in her was a step in the right direction. She was determined to gather enough evidence to bring her father down.

To that end, when the last of the patrons left and she'd locked up for the night, she found her father in his office and sat down opposite him with a sigh.

She scrubbed a hand over her face and yawned. "Boy, am I glad to see the end of today. It was madness out there. Don't those people have a home to go to? It's Christmas Eve, after all."

Her father smiled. "I can remember when you believed in Santa Claus. You begged me to let you stay up late so you could watch him coming down the chimney. You wouldn't believe he could fit down there."

Jayde forced a grin. "You'd told me a long time before the chimney didn't work. It was all blocked up, you said. That's why we couldn't light a fire. I was concerned Santa might not make it down."

Her father chuckled. "You always were too smart for your own good."

She looked at him. For some reason, he appeared to be in a good mood. Maybe it was the Christmas spirit making him sentimental. She didn't know, but while he was in the mood to reminisce, she wanted to take advantage. In particular, she wanted to quiz him on his relationship with Henry Craigdon.

"Do you remember a guy by the name of Henry Craigdon?" she asked as casually as she could.

"Henry? Of course I do. Why do you ask?"

She shrugged. "His nephew hangs out here sometimes. He mentioned him once or twice," she lied.

Seeming to accept her partly fabricated explanation, her father continued. "Poor bastard dropped dead from a heart attack earlier in the year. Back in February, I think it was."

"How did you know him? Was he a friend of yours?"

Her father chuckled. "I wouldn't call him a friend. More like a business associate."

She widened her eyes in mock innocence. "Oh. I didn't

realize you were into property development. Isn't that what Henry Craigdon was? A property developer?"

Her father nodded. "You're right. He was. Among other things." He shot her an assessing look and then continued. "I think it's time you learned how your old man makes a living."

Once again, she feigned confusion. "You mean, Beaches? We made a killing tonight. I can see how you can afford to drive that Lexus." She chuckled.

He laughed along with her. "You don't know the half of it." He paused. "Now that Junior's gone, I need another right-hand man. Or maybe I should say, right-hand woman."

She frowned. "What are you talking about? I thought I was already managing the bar. I've taken over all of Junior's duties, and a few others as well. I've been liaising with our suppliers. I've negotiated a better rate on those mixer drinks. I've also introduced a couple new lines. I've been meaning to talk to you about that, but I haven't had the chance. But the new lines are selling well. I think they're going to be good for us."

Her father shook his head slowly from side to side, grinning. "Look at you go, girl! A real little entrepreneur! Too bad you didn't come on board years ago. I could have had a garage of Lexus cars by now."

She laughed, basking in his praise, not at all phased by the fact she'd just lied straight to his face. She hadn't negotiated better rates on the mixer drinks. Neither had she spoken to any suppliers. But she was betting on the fact her father wouldn't know that. In the six months since she'd been there, he'd barely expressed an interest in the bar beyond collecting the takings from the safe.

"You're right," her father said. "Junior managed the bar. But he also did other things."

"Like what?"

"Do you remember why I walked out on your mother?"

She nodded. "I was seven. Mom told you to stop selling drugs or get out. You left."

Despite the years that had passed since that fateful day, Jayde felt a surge of familiar pain. Her father had taken his son with him, leaving his daughter behind.

He looked at her with grudging admiration. "Right. You have a good memory."

"Dad, just because it's Christmas Eve, doesn't mean we have to take a walk down memory lane. Where are you going with this?" Jayde asked, forcing irritation into her tone.

The ruse worked. Her father sat forward and cleared his throat.

"The thing is, Jayde. I'm still selling gear. That's how I make the big money."

She did her best impression of appearing shocked. "Dad! All these years? You're still selling drugs?"

He merely shrugged and offered her an unrepentant smile. "A man's gotta make a living."

"But the bar's doing great! Besides, it's illegal!" Jayde said, aghast as she continued with the ruse. "What if you get arrested? You'll go to jail for life!"

Her father chuckled. "I've been doing this a long time, sweetheart. They haven't caught me yet!"

She shook her head and looked unconvinced. "Is that what you meant by doing business with Henry Craigdon? He was selling drugs for you?"

"Not for me. He was selling them for himself. He had an extensive network of dealers in the eastern suburbs. I've always controlled the north. We never infringed on each other's turf. We respected each other that way.

"Henry had been involved in the business almost as long as me. I was his main supplier. I tell you, I nearly cried when I heard he'd dropped dead. He was one of my best customers."

"He left behind a heap of kids. Were any of them part of it?" She held her breath waiting for his answer.

Her father shook his head. "Not that I know of. I only ever dealt with Henry. He used to pick up the gear himself. Never missed a shipment. Business just hasn't been the same since he kicked the bucket. There's a big hole in the market right now." He paused and shot her a sly look. "There's an opening if you're interested."

She looked at him disapprovingly and reacted in the way he'd expect. "Really, Dad? You know exactly how I feel about drugs. Especially after Junior's overdose."

Her father waved her comment away and scoffed. "Junior. He should have known better. He was weak. Got himself hooked on the gear. Made the fatal mistake. If you want to be part of this business, you can't touch the stuff."

"Is that what happened to Henry? Was he taking drugs? Is that what caused the heart attack?"

"No. Henry was smarter than that. The word on the street is that he had a heart attack while having sex with his lover. I don't know how true that is, but he's always been a player. That was common knowledge.

"Like the night he killed Janelle Craigdon. Apparently they were on their way back from a dirty weekend. Henry was driving them back to the city. He was drunk. Swerved to miss a kangaroo. Ran off the road and hit a tree. He managed to survive, but his woman didn't."

Jayde's mind worked furiously. She'd met Henry's wife at the Craigdon wedding, but for the life of her, she couldn't recall the woman's name. "Who's Janelle Craigdon? His wife?"

"Ha!" Her father scoffed. "Not likely. Try his *brother's* wife."

Jayde gasped in shock. "Oh, my goodness! When did this happen?"

"Oh, it must be ten years ago now."

She thought of Flynn and Noah and Logan, all sons of Henry's brother. She wondered if they had any idea their mother had been having an affair with their uncle.

"Did he go to jail?" she asked.

"No, of course not. Henry had friends in high places. As far as I know, he wasn't breath tested at the scene. Nor was there any blood taken at the hospital. No proof that he'd been drinking."

"Then how do you know about it?"

Her father's grin widened. "Where do you think he was in the hours before he climbed behind the wheel?"

"Here?"

"No. Not here. We'd met out in the country. The Hunter Valley. I wanted to inspect the quality of a product before I paid for a shipment. I invited Henry along. We met up at a bar. That's when I met Janelle."

Jayde sat back in her chair, feeling genuinely shocked. She didn't know any of the Craigdon brothers well enough to come out and ask them about their mother.

What if they don't know?

The circumstances surrounding Janelle's death weren't important to her investigation. After all, if what her father said was true, the perpetrator was now dead. There wasn't anything anyone could do. It was probably best for all concerned if she didn't say anything.

A distant knock on the front door caught their attention. She looked at her father, but he appeared unsurprised by the late arrival. He pushed back his chair and strode out of the office. She followed him. Her father crossed the dimly lit bar and unlocked the front door.

"Dimitri! It's good to see you. You're right on time."

"Merry Christmas!" the man replied in heavily accented English. He walked through the open doorway carrying a large Styrofoam box.

Jayde stood back in the shadows, hoping her father might forget she was there. He let Dimitri carry the box all the way to the bar. Pulling out a knife, her father cut through the seal and pulled out bottles of gin. Underneath were clear plastic bags filled with white powder.

As if suddenly remembering her presence, her father swung around to face her. "We're going to be busy here for a while, Jayde. Best get yourself to bed. You've had a big day. You've earned your rest."

"But—"

"Merry Christmas, sweetheart. I'll see you in the morning." His tone brooked no further argument.

"Merry Christmas, Dad." She went through the motions of pecking him on the cheek and turned away.

Making her way back across the floor of the bar, she started up the internal staircase that led to her apartment above. She trod heavily on the stairs, making sure her footsteps sounded all the way to the top. She unlocked her door, opened it and closed it. Then, on silent feet, she tiptoed back down the stairs, coming to a halt a few steps from the bottom. She was still invisible to the men below her, but could hear every word they said.

"It's good quality shit. Better than the last lot," Dimitri was saying.

"Just as well," her father said. "I made sure Petrov knew I wouldn't be paying for second-class gear. That shit he tried to pass off as coke last time… What a joke. He thought I wouldn't be able to tell the difference. As if I haven't been involved in this business for more than half my life. It's bullshit. That's what it is."

There was a pause and then her father said, "Well, let's get the shit packed away. No sense taking the risk someone could see us."

"It's Christmas Eve, John. Who's going to see us?"

"No matter. It doesn't pay to take unnecessary risks. Come on. Give me a hand, will you?"

Jayde heard them moving across the wooden floor. It sounded like they were over near the restrooms. She remembered Brian telling her they needed hard evidence. She reached into the pocket of her jeans and pulled out her phone. Moving down a couple more stairs, she pressed the record button and directed it toward the noise.

The creak of old floorboards caught her attention. She couldn't remember any part of the bar sounding like that and yet her father and the other man were still there. She could hear them talking. She crept down further until she stood on the very last step. She peered carefully around the corner in the direction of the restrooms. She made sure the phone was still recording.

Her father stood above an opening in the floor. *A trapdoor!* A moment later, he disappeared from view. There was obviously a basement she'd been unaware of. Given the age of the building, the discovery of an underground room shouldn't have been surprising. A dim light came on, illuminating the stairway that went below the floor. A few minutes later, her father reappeared.

"Give me the box," he said.

Dimitri handed him the large box and her father once again disappeared down the stairs. Jayde kept recording, hoping they'd say something incriminating. So far, all she'd managed to capture was her father and his associate storing a box in the basement. Big deal.

The good news was, as soon as her father left, she'd open the trapdoor herself and locate the box downstairs. She'd be sure to take photos of what lay inside. She was one step closer to seeing her father put away for good. That thought made her smile.

Chapter Eleven

Flynn squinted against the bright morning sunshine that poured through his open window. He'd forgotten to draw the curtains.

"Shit," he muttered and then winced as a headache pounded behind his eyes.

He'd gotten in late the night before after celebrating with some single work friends over Christmas drinks. Now he was paying the price.

"Merry fucking Christmas," he mumbled and gingerly sat up in bed.

He needed to use the bathroom and he also needed some painkillers. Not necessarily in that order. Thankfully both were located in the same room. With a sigh, he pushed off the covers and set his feet on the floor. Next, he stood up. He swayed for a moment, but then righted himself and managed to make it to the bathroom without incident.

It wasn't often he overindulged. The problem was Jayde Hassad. He couldn't stop thinking about her and it was driving him insane. This time last year, he'd woken with a cute blond by his side. They'd enjoyed early-morning sex, followed by breakfast in bed and a stroll along the beach before he'd sent her home. This Christmas, he'd woken alone. And it was all Jayde's fault.

It seemed she'd ruined him for any other woman. Before Jayde, he'd been a serial womanizer. All of his friends and family knew it. They accepted it as completely as he'd accepted it for all of his thirty years.

But ever since he'd met the black-haired minx, his life had changed. *He'd* changed. And as far as he was concerned, it wasn't for the better. Before, when he spotted an attractive woman, he'd zero in on her, ascertain her availability and if she were agreeable, he'd ask her out. Now he found himself hesitating.

Worse still, he'd begun comparing every woman he came across to *her*…and inevitably they failed to measure up. That was the reason he found himself alone on Christmas morning for the first time in his adult life. It was downright embarrassing.

Of course, he could always call her and ask her out, but it wasn't that easy. Noah fancied himself in love with her and though Flynn was almost certain she didn't share his feelings, the thought of going after his brother's woman filled him with distaste. Not to mention how Noah would feel if he found out. It was a dilemma for which he had no answer and it didn't help alleviate his desire to see her one bit. It had gotten to the point where it was almost a physical ache. Even worse than his headache.

He swallowed a couple of painkillers and suffered under a hot, stinging shower. Flynn felt almost normal as he pulled on a T-shirt and board shorts. Feeling restless, he considered going for a walk along the Manly Corso, but he wasn't in the mood for window shopping, and crowd watching didn't hold any appeal. What he really wanted was to see Jayde, talk to her, hear her laugh.

And then he thought of the soup kitchen. Jennifer's Kitchen prided itself on offering a hot meal every day of the year, including Christmas Day. It was a Tuesday. The same day of the week Jayde had volunteered there once before. It was a long shot, but it was possible she might be working there today.

A surge of nervous excitement went through him at the thought. He wouldn't be doing anything wrong as far as Noah was concerned. Flynn was merely volunteering at the soup kitchen. If Jayde happened to be there, well... He could hardly help that.

Decision made, he hurried downstairs and opened the door that led into his garage. He climbed into the Ferrari and gunned the engine. The loud roar echoed off the walls. The sound of the powerful engine never ceased to thrill him. Along with the possibility of seeing Jayde, driving the sports car also lifted his mood. He left his building with a smile on his face, his heart beating with anticipation.

It was Christmas Day. Jayde ought to be at church or treating herself to a big cooked breakfast. Maybe even spending time with her father, further gaining his trust. Instead she was poring over bank records belonging to the Craigdon men.

Brian had dropped them off the day before, but with the crowd they'd had late into the night at the bar, she hadn't gotten a chance to take a look at them. Beaches was closed for Christmas Day and wouldn't open until tomorrow. That gave her the time she needed to examine the records and see what they revealed about the Craigdon family.

So far, she hadn't found any red flags. She'd started with Flynn's accounts. There were no large deposits, apart from his one-million-dollar inheritance. Curiously, that money had also been withdrawn a few weeks later. She wondered what he'd bought with it.

Other deposits included a regular generous salary, share

dividends and receipts from property investments. He'd made six-figure profits from the sale of a couple of townhouses in the city. No wonder he could afford to live the high life.

She'd also analyzed the bank accounts of Noah, Nicholas, Logan and Callum. Once again, she'd found nothing out of the ordinary, apart from their inheritances and trust accounts. One thing was for certain, none of their accounts looked like those of drug dealers.

She hoped she was being objective and not downplaying anything because she liked them all. Way too much. Flynn, in particular. There was always a chance the men had other accounts in someone else's name, but that would be risky. It would also involve an extra degree of trust that, in her experience, most drug lords didn't have. Despite her being at Beaches for more than six months and being his blood relation, it was obvious her father still didn't trust her completely.

Jayde glanced at her watch. It was going on for eight. If she were going to help Sister Mary Catherine with the cooking, she'd best get a move on. Today they were making a special meal, in honor of Christmas Day. She and Sister Mary Catherine had planned the menu a couple of weeks ago: Baked ham with a honey and mustard glaze, mashed potato, steamed beans and roasted corn. For dessert, there was plum pudding with vanilla bean custard. Jayde was keen to get started.

Noah opened his eyes and stared up at the ceiling. It was Christmas Day and just like all the other Christmas Days he'd celebrated, he woke in his bed alone. He resisted the urge to feel sorry for himself. He was a good and decent guy, with a secure job and a comfortable apartment overlooking Manly beach. In fact, he was only a few blocks from Flynn.

Noah was sure there was a woman out there who'd take one look at him and be wild with desire—for him. He wanted so much for that woman to be Jayde, but he had a sneaking suspicion she didn't feel as strongly about him as he did about her. He sighed quietly. At some point, he'd get together with his brothers and his father and celebrate Christmas dinner, but for now he had the luxury of sleeping in.

After a while, he reached for his glasses and pulled them on. He threw off the sheets and padded barefoot across the room to his balcony, dressed only in the boxers he'd slept in. Pushing his glasses higher on the bridge of his nose, he surveyed the beautiful day Sydney had served up for Christmas.

The sky was a clear blue, with hardly a cloud in sight. The sun was warm on his skin. People lined the promenade below him, walking or jogging with dogs and strollers, in groups and on their own. There were also plenty of people dotting the sand and enjoying the water.

The day was so perfect, he was tempted to join them. He'd been knee-deep in an investigation for more than three weeks. He'd barely had time to go to the gym and couldn't remember the last time he'd jogged along the beach or gone for a swim.

Feeling inspired, he strode back inside. After a quick shower, he dressed in jogging gear and then headed toward the kitchen. He switched on the coffee maker.

A shot or two of caffeine and he'd be on his way.

Flynn stepped into Jennifer's Kitchen through the rear entrance. The kitchen smelled of sugar and spices and honey. The first person he saw was Jayde. She stood at the stove lifting lids on saucepans and checking the contents. As if sensing his presence, she looked up. A becoming blush stained her cheeks. She offered him a quick smile and then looked away.

"Merry Christmas!" he greeted her.

"Merry Christmas!" she replied, keeping her gaze fixed on the saucepans.

He moved closer, unable to stay away. "Smells good. What are you cooking?"

"Plum puddings. They're almost done. "I'm about to start making the custard."

"Do you need a hand?" Flynn could hardly believe it when the words fell out of his mouth. He didn't cook. Ever.

It seemed Jayde was recalling that. She looked at him with a dubious expression.

"Really? I thought you told us last time you couldn't boil water? Are you sure you're up for the task?" She smiled to take the sting out of her words. A teasing light shone in her blue eyes.

He grinned. "If you give me clear and concise instructions and stand very close and watch every single move I make, I'm pretty sure I can pull it off."

She laughed. Sister Mary Catherine walked into the kitchen, smiling. "That's a joyous sound on this lovely Christmas morning," the old nun said. "Merry Christmas, Flynn. It's wonderful to see you again. Are we lucky enough to have your help today?"

He spread his arms wide. "I'm at your service, Sister. Let me know what you need done."

"As long as it doesn't involve cooking," Jayde teased.

He poked his tongue out at her and she laughed again. Mary Catherine was right. It was a joyous sound. Husky, full-throated laughter that filled him with a rush of desire. With a deliberate effort, he directed his attention elsewhere.

"Then you can help me set the tables, Flynn." Sister Mary Catherine moved to where a large cardboard box stood on the counter. "I bought a few decorations to make the place feel a bit more like Christmas. Red tablecloths, white napkins, bonbons, miniature Christmas trees. What do you think?"

"I think it sounds great. Very festive," he agreed and collected the box from her. "Lead the way, Sister."

Out of the corner of his eye, he saw Jayde smile. He felt her gaze on him all the way out into the dining room. Flynn couldn't remember a time in his recent past when he'd enjoyed Christmas morning more.

Jayde was stacking the last of the dirty plates in the dishwasher when Flynn came up to her. He'd been washing pots and pans in the sink and now wiped his hands on a tea towel and set it to one side.

"We had a great turnout today," he said. "I think the pudding went down really well. It was a treat."

"Yes. It's nice to do something a little special to recognize the significance of the occasion. I think they enjoyed the Christmas touches."

She smiled and tried not to notice how the cuffs of his red polo shirt cupped his bulging biceps. For a guy who made his living behind a desk, he sure was in good condition.

"I think so too," Flynn replied. "And I heard plenty of compliments for the chef. They were raving about the ham." He winked.

She laughed. "I can only take credit for the dessert. Sister Mary Catherine glazed the hams."

"I'm sure it was a joint effort, and one these people appreciated. Not everyone's willing to give up their Christmas Day to help the less fortunate." Flynn's tone was full of sincerity. His gaze was filled with admiration.

Jayde inclined her head. A rush of warmth went through her at his words. "Thank you. That's very nice of you to say. And I could say the same thing about you. I'm sure you have a dozen different places you could be, including being with your family. Yet, here you are."

An intriguing blush stained his high cheekbones. He merely shrugged and then changed the subject.

"What are you doing after this? Do you fancy a walk along the beach?"

Jayde's heart skipped a beat at the look in Flynn's eyes. The barely banked hunger in them took her by surprise. She felt an answering need deep inside her. Her pulse took off at a gallop.

There were so many reasons why spending time alone with Flynn Craigdon was a bad idea. First and foremost, he was part of her investigation. But the more she probed, the more it appeared unlikely the surviving Craigdon men were involved in anything illegal. Even her father had more or less vouched for them.

Still, it probably wasn't the wisest thing to be fraternizing with Flynn while members of his family were still part of an active investigation. She opened her mouth to decline his invitation, and found herself nodding instead.

"That sounds lovely. Where would you like to go?"

"How about Manly?"

Her eyebrows rose in surprise. The closest beaches to Jennifer's Kitchen were in the eastern suburbs—Bronte, Clovelly, Bondi, Coogee, to name a few.

"What's so special about Manly?"

He grinned. "Spoken by someone who obviously wasn't raised on the lower north shore."

"You're right. I was born in Nepean Hospital."

Flynn's eyebrows rose. His eyes sparkled. "Oh, so you're a westie."

She rolled her eyes. "Spoken by someone who obviously *was* raised on the lower north shore."

"Are you calling me a snob?" he asked in mock outrage.

She shrugged nonchalantly. "If the shoe fits…"

She joined in his laughter. After finishing with the tidying up, they bid Sister Mary Catherine and the other volunteers farewell and walked outside. Flynn headed toward a shiny red Ferrari.

"Your car?" she asked.

"Yes. Where's yours?"

"I caught a bus."

He flashed her his charming smile. "Then it's your lucky day. Jump in."

Feeling more excited than she had a right to, Jayde waited for Flynn to open her door and then slid onto the smooth leather seat. It was the first time she'd ridden in such an expensive car. She felt like a movie star.

Get a grip, Jayde. It's just a car. And Flynn is just a man. You're acting like a besotted school girl! You're twenty-seven, for heaven's sake!

To her chagrin, the pep talk didn't make any difference. As Flynn slid behind the wheel and shot her a sexy grin, it was all she could do not to drag him into her arms. His full, sensuous lips looked so kissable. She itched to run her palm across his freshly shaven cheeks. The scent of his expensive cologne tickled her nostrils.

Dragging her gaze away from him, she stared through the window at the beautiful day. Flynn put the car into gear and pressed on the accelerator. The powerful car surged forward. With confidence and precision, he blended into the traffic heading north over the Harbour Bridge.

The traffic was lighter than usual. Probably because most people were at home with their families, resting after indulging in Christmas lunch. It wouldn't be until much later, after the heat had gone out of the day, that people would emerge and swarm the cafes, the ice cream parlors, the beach. She was sure that was why Flynn had suggested they head to Manly now. There would be far fewer crowds so early in the afternoon.

Though she'd been born and bred in the western suburbs of Sydney, Jayde was more than familiar with the northern beaches. Her father's bar was located on the lower north shore. She'd also spent many hours at Manly beach, along with several million visitors to Sydney every year.

Manly was an iconic tourist destination. The Corso was the focal point of Manly's central business district. It was originally built in *circa* 1854 as a boardwalk for tourists across Manly's harbor pier and the beach. Most of the street had no vehicular traffic, making it a broad pedestrian precinct for shoppers and visitors. The Corso was lined with popular surf shops, boutiques, pubs, cafes and galleries and there was almost always live street entertainment on offer. It was a happening place with a happy, energetic vibe. Jayde understood why Flynn might enjoy it.

As if privy to her thoughts, Flynn shot her a grin. "You do realize we're heading to the best beach in Sydney?"

She chuckled. "You sound a little biased."

He shrugged. "Probably. I live not far from the Corso."

"View of the beach?"

"Oh, yeah."

"What else?"

"Well, let me tell you, we have the best ice cream in the world."

Her eyes opened wide. She shot him a teasing grin. "In the world? That's a lofty claim."

"It is. But wait until you try it. You'll agree with me."

"What if I don't like ice cream?"

He stared at her in horror. "You don't like ice cream?"

She laughed. "Would it be a deal breaker?"

He appeared to give her question serious consideration and then he glanced at her and smiled.

"Nah. It just means more for me."

She laughed again. "How do you figure that? Surely you'll just buy a cone for yourself."

Once again, he pretended to look horrified. "A cone? No way! A cone's never enough. It's the tub, or nothing!"

She giggled, loving the way he made everything so fun. She couldn't remember the last time she'd felt so lighthearted. It seemed most of her life she'd been worried. Worried that her parents were fighting. Worried when they finally split up. Worried there wouldn't be enough money when it was just her and her mom. Worried about Junior and how he was faring with their dad.

Later, when her mom got sick, Jayde had spent nights worrying about what would happen if the cancer spread and her mom lost the fight. And then her worries were justified when the doctor told them she had only months to live. Jayde had taken leave from her job and had nursed her mother to the very end.

Though she wouldn't have given up that time with her mother for anything, it had been the most difficult time of her life. Sarah Hassad had died ten days before Christmas. Jayde had passed the first anniversary of her death as a guest at Callum Craigdon's wedding. At least the wedding had helped keep the sad memories at bay.

If any good had come of her mother's death, it was the impetus to search out her brother. It had been years since she'd seen him. Tragically, they'd barely had six months to reconnect before Junior died of an overdose.

"Hey! Are you all right?"

Flynn's voice was filled with concern. She looked at him and managed a tight smile.

"Of course."

"I was only joking about the ice cream. We can always go and get coffee."

She shook her head. "No, ice cream sounds great."

He looked at her. "You sure?"

"I was only kidding you. I love ice cream."

He grinned. "Atta girl!"

Though on an ordinary day, finding a parking spot anywhere near the beach was almost impossible, with the crowds smaller than usual, Flynn pulled the car into a shady spot not far from the Corso. He came around to her side and opened her door. She murmured her thanks and climbed out.

The light breeze lifted the hem of her floral print mini sundress and sent it fluttering high around her thighs. A fair amount of tanned skin was exposed to Flynn's interested gaze. Flushing with embarrassment, she grabbed the hem with both hands and held it down in place.

"Darn breeze," Flynn said with a grin.

He followed it with a look that sent warmth rushing through her. She silently castigated herself for the instinctive rush of attraction, but she couldn't deny she enjoyed his attention.

They crossed over a parking lot filled with cars. A homeless man sat on the pavement, his back against an ancient fig tree. He called out to them as they passed. Flynn paused and fished in his back pocket for his wallet. With a murmured greeting, he dropped a one-hundred dollar note into the man's tattered and dirty hat.

"God bless you," the man said, giving Flynn a toothless grin.

"No worries, mate. Merry Christmas! You take care."

They continued to walk toward the Corso. Jayde looked at Flynn. "That was very generous of you."

He shrugged. "It's only money."

"Spoken by a man who's never had to wonder where his next meal's coming from." She shot him a sideways glance. "How much did your uncle leave you in his will?"

"A million."

"Nice, but I would have expected someone with the wealth of Henry Craigdon to have left you more."

Flynn shrugged again. "It's none of my business how he chose to leave his money. I was only a nephew, after all. It was a nice gesture, but I honestly didn't expect him to leave me anything. Besides, I'm a man of simple pleasures and I do well enough with my career."

She lifted her eyebrows. "Simple pleasures? A Ferrari? An apartment on the beach?"

"Hey! I bought those with my own money."

She stared at him, filling with curiosity. "Wow, you must be a darned good saver. Either that or you're one of the highest paid lawyers I know. Business is obviously booming."

He shrugged dismissively. "Like I said, I do all right."

Her curiosity only deepened. "So what did you do with your inheritance?"

He bit his lip and a flush stained his cheeks. She didn't think he'd respond. When he finally did, his embarrassment was obvious. "I donated my inheritance to the soup kitchen."

"You mean Jennifer's Kitchen?"

"Yep."

"Wow! I'm impressed," she said and meant it.

He winked, his good humor restored. "You should be."

They smiled at each other and somehow their gazes caught and held. Jayde's heart turned over. Her chest tightened on a wave of nerves. For a moment, she struggled to breathe.

"Tell me about your family," Flynn asked, breaking the moment.

"What do you want to know?"

Chapter Twelve

"I want to know everything."

The look Flynn gave her sent another rush of nervous excitement flooding through Jayde's veins. With an effort, she got control over her jittery pulse. They kept walking and she began to talk about her past.

"Well, you already know I was born in the western suburbs. My mother was a hairdresser. My father was…a businessman. They divorced when I was seven."

"Has your father always been into bars?"

Jayde thought of the illegal drugs her father had dealt in all his life. Her earliest childhood memories included shadowy strangers meeting with her father in the backyard and the arguments between her parents that inevitably followed. Back then, she'd been unaware that they were arguing over her father's illegal drug business.

She looked at Flynn and realized he was waiting for an answer. "Um, no. Not always."

"So, do you have any siblings?"

"A brother. John. He was named after my father. We always called him Junior."

"Does he live in Sydney?"

She shook her head and bit her lip against a stab of pain.

Though she'd been separated from her brother for most of her life, reconnecting with him after so many years apart had felt amazing. Now he was gone forever.

"No," she managed. "He… He died in June this year."

Flynn came to a halt. He turned to her, his face filled with concern. "Oh. I'm sorry."

The tenderness in his eyes almost did her in. She blinked away a rush of tears. "It's fine."

"How long have you been working at Beaches?" Flynn asked, tactfully changing the subject.

Jayde felt a wave of relief. The less she spoke about her brother, the better. "Six months," she said.

Flynn frowned and she was reminded how quick-minded he was. His next words confirmed it.

"So did you start working there before or after your brother died?"

Jayde closed her eyes against a blast of raw emotion. Her brother's death from an overdose was the reason she'd decided to turn traitor and betray her father. She despised everything to do with illegal drugs. Now they had cost her the life of her brother. It was time to bring her father's operation to an end, even if that meant putting him in jail for the rest of his life. He'd made his choices long ago. Now he'd pay for them.

Once again, Flynn's face creased with concern. "Are you all right?"

She managed a tight smile. "Of course. I was… I was thinking about my brother."

Flynn moved closer. He reached out and cupped her cheek. "It's Christmas Day. Let's talk about something more cheerful. I know, ice cream!"

She offered him a grudging smile.

"There it is! That's better. You have such a beautiful smile."

They stared at each other. The rising sexual tension between them had been growing from the beginning. Flynn's head descended. Jayde's eyes fluttered closed. The next thing she felt was his warm, sensuous lips moving over hers.

The kiss was sure and confident. His lips increased their pressure, demanding a response. She was helpless to resist its fiery call. Giving into the temptation, her arms crept around his neck. Right there, in the middle of the Corso, with people looking on, she kissed him back.

It felt like it went on forever and then it was over far too quickly. When they pulled apart, they were both breathing hard. With her heart thumping, Jayde fought to catch her breath. All the time, she told herself she'd only let the kiss go on for so long because she wanted to put him at ease, to keep him from thinking for even a minute that she might have an ulterior motive for spending time with him.

Flynn dropped his arms from around her waist and stepped away. "I'm sorry. I shouldn't have done that."

She looked at him, confused. He had no idea who she was. She couldn't fathom why he'd regret kissing her. "Why not?"

"Because you belong to my brother."

Understanding flashed through her, along with irritation. "I belong to no man."

Flynn looked uncomfortable. "That's not what I meant. It's Noah… He likes you. *Really* likes you. He's always been shy. He never had the courage to ask a girl out, not even in high school. And then he brought you to Callum's wedding. We were all surprised. But in a good way. It might not seem like a big deal to you, but if you knew his history, you'd see what I mean. Like I said. He really likes you. He's my brother. I love him. I'm not going to hurt him like this would."

Jayde stared up at Flynn. She'd never met a nicer guy. There was no way this guy was a drug dealer. He was just too nice. If that made her naïve, then so be it.

"You're such a great guy," she said softly. "I admire your loyalty. The only thing you're forgetting is that I don't like Noah in that way."

"But—"

"Don't get me wrong, he's a terrific guy, so smart and sweet and sensitive. But he's not for me. I think of him as a friend. Maybe even a brother."

"But maybe, given time, you could come to feel differently?" Flynn persisted.

Jayde shook her head. "Do you have any female friends, Flynn? I mean women you like, and enjoy their company but you've never slept with them?"

"Yes, of course… One or two. My junior secretary, Emily."

"How old is she?"

"Twenty-three."

"Is she attractive?"

"Yes."

"And yet you've never slept with her?"

His face twisted in a look of horror. "Of course not! She's my secretary. She's…Emily!! The thought of doing anything like that with her is… Hell, I don't even want to imagine it."

"But maybe if you spent more time with her you'd feel differently?"

"I already spend eight hours a day with her."

"I mean outside of work. In a social setting."

He shook his head. "No. It wouldn't matter where we were, she'd still feel like a friend. Maybe even like a little sister. You can't force physical attraction. You're either turned on by someone or you're not."

He shot her a look so filled with heat it made her stomach clench with need. They stared at one another. She broke the tension by clearing her throat.

"I agree. That's exactly how I feel about your brother."

Flynn fell silent, his brow furrowed in thought. Then he looked up at her. "You sure?"

"I'm sure."

Once again, Flynn fell silent. He reached for her hand and laced his fingers with hers and began walking toward the beach. Then she heard him sigh.

"Have you told Noah?" he asked.

"Not in so many words, but I'm sure he knows we're just friends."

Flynn looked grim. "And I'm just as sure he doesn't know that. Trust me. If you're really never going to feel that way about him, he needs to know. You need to be blunt with him. Tell him straight out. It's the only thing guys understand."

"Okay. I can do blunt."

"Good."

They were on the edge of the pavement that led down to the beach. It was more crowded down there. The footpath was filled with people walking and jogging. Some were pushing prams. Flynn drew her over to an ice cream shop. They joined the short queue.

"What's your favorite flavor?" he asked.

She grinned. "That's easy. Salted caramel."

"Yum. Good choice. I'm kind of partial to salted caramel myself."

"So that's your favorite, too?"

"No. It's strawberry all the way for me. Even better when it's filled with chunks of real strawberries." He kissed his fingers in the way of the French. "*Mm.* Delicious."

She grinned. Flynn put in their order for ice cream. Though he wanted to get her a tub, she laughingly insisted they settle for cones. A short time later, he handed her a waffle cone piled high with two scoops. She licked at the icy treat.

"*Mm.* Delicious."

Flynn's gaze was arrested on her mouth. She licked her lips self-consciously. He groaned.

"What is it? Do I have ice cream on my face?" she asked. She reached up and touched her cheek.

Flynn chuckled and drew her in for a casual hug. "No. You're fine. I was just enjoying watching you eat your ice cream. You do it oh so delicately!"

"I like to take my time. I want it to last."

"I can always buy you another."

"No. I don't need another. But I do want to savor every bit of this one."

They wandered away from the crowds and found a spot on the big rock wall that formed the boundary before the beach. With legs dangling over the side, they ate their ice cream and shared a bit more about themselves.

"Tell me about your work as a lawyer," she said.

"What do you want to know?"

She already knew from her research that he specialized in family law, but he didn't know she knew that. Instead, she pretended ignorance.

"What kind of lawyer are you?"

"I work in family law. Divorces, property settlements, child custody disputes."

She pulled a face. "Sounds awful."

He laughed. "Sometimes it is. No, scratch that. Yes, it is. Quite awful."

"Then why do you do it?"

He looked out over the beach and sighed. The sand was dotted with people and families enjoying the summer day. Children running and laughing and making sandcastles. Couples kissing, applying sunscreen to each other's backs. It was a happy scene and a stark contrast to the grim expression on Flynn's face.

She touched his arm. "Flynn? Are you all right?"

He smiled, but it didn't reach his eyes. "Of course. I was just thinking about work. It's sometimes kind of depressing." He turned to her, his expression now earnest.

"The problem is, a lot of the time I'm surrounded by liars."

Her heart skipped a beat, but she forced herself to appear unaffected by his words. She kept her tone casual. "What do you mean?"

Flynn grimaced and scrubbed at his hair. "My clients, the opposing lawyers, sometimes even the kids. Everyone in a family law matter has their own agenda and they'll lie, cheat and deceive to achieve their goal."

She shook her head, a little shocked. "Is it really as bad as that?"

"Of course. People will do and say anything if it means getting one up on the spouse they despise at that point. The kids are often dragged into it. They're coached by one parent to say one thing and the other parent urges them to say the opposite. Then there are the kids themselves. Some of them are totally switched on. They know how to play the game. They give the court false evidence because they know it will mean any decision that's made will be one to their liking. The evidence given by the adults against each other is even worse. They'll say anything to get custody or a bigger piece of the pie."

She looked at him, appalled. "But what about the evidence? Surely they have to back their claims up with proof?"

"You'd think so, but there are far too many judges who are swayed by mere rhetoric. It shouldn't be like that, but it is."

When he turned to her again, his eyes were bleak. "That's why honesty is so important to me in my personal life." He picked up her hand and squeezed it. "That's why it's nice to know I can trust you to tell me the truth. You're a good and decent person, Jayde Hassad. Believe me, until I met you, I was beginning to believe people like you no longer existed."

She laughed to hide her discomfort. Guilt poured through her veins and settled in her stomach in a heavy ball of dread.

If only you knew…

She suppressed a shiver of apprehension. She hoped Flynn never found out the truth. Though she couldn't help but deceive him, she realized it would destroy him if he discovered she was every bit the liar he'd accused others of being. Not only that, she was also pursuing a personal agenda. She was sure that would be the final straw for him.

And then his face cleared. He smiled gently.

"Hey, I'm sorry. I shouldn't have let the conversation get so heavy. "It's Christmas Day. Let's just rejoice and be happy."

She managed a laugh, relieved that he'd dropped the subject. She finished off her ice cream. Once again, his gaze zeroed in on her mouth. And then he reached for her hand and tugged her to her feet.

She stared at him. Her heart beat fast. Almost in slow motion, she saw him rest his hands on either side of her hips and draw her close. Like a moth to a flame, she went to him without resistance. Once again, his mouth came down on hers and she was lost.

Pressed tightly against him, she felt the evidence of his desire. Her heart raced, her nipples tightened, heat flooded to her core. Unable to stop herself, her arms went to his shoulders. She clung to him. Another kiss, and another—each one more passionate than the last. It was as if the world had fallen away and there was nothing and no one but the two of them.

And then reality set in. Jayde dropped her arms and stepped away. She looked around, feeling embarrassed. Joggers parted around them. And then her gaze landed on Noah. He was dressed in sweats and had obviously been jogging, along with everyone else. The look of shock and devastation on his face told her all she needed to know.

"Noah," she said weakly.

Flynn tensed in shock. Noah stared at them a moment longer and then turned and kept running.

"Oh, God…" she said.

Flynn looked grim. "I'll talk to him."

Jayde looked up at him. "Let me talk to him first. I owe him that much."

Flynn looked far from convinced, but finally nodded. "Okay."

It had been three days since Christmas. Three days since Jayde had spent a blissful few hours with Flynn and she was still annoyed at herself for kissing him. She was supposed to be investigating him and his family and their potential links to the drug trade. What the hell was she doing kissing him?

But it had been so good… And she was more and more convinced Flynn and the rest of his family had nothing to do with Henry's drug business.

Now she found herself outside the building that housed Noah's office. She'd gotten his number from Flynn and had called him several times, leaving messages every time. He hadn't once phoned her back. He'd also stayed away from Beaches. It was the longest she'd gone without seeing him. It was time to take a more direct approach.

She could only imagine what had gone through his head when he spied her and Flynn in a passionate embrace. Though she hadn't given Noah any indication she returned his interest, she *had* gone with him to his cousin's wedding as his date. She could understand why he might have thought there was something more between them.

Taking the lift up to the fifth floor, she stepped out into a tastefully furnished reception area and walked up to the front desk.

"Can I help you?" the attractive young woman behind the desk asked.

"I'm here to see Noah Craigdon."

"Do you have an appointment?"

Jayde wished she could simply flash her badge. It would make this so much easier. Unfortunately, she didn't have the freedom to do that. Instead, she gave the girl her name.

"Please let him know I'm here. I'm sure he'll be willing to see me."

The girl merely nodded, but she picked up the phone and spoke quietly into it. Jayde turned away and took a seat in the row of fabric-covered chairs that stood against the wall. A moment later, the girl hung up the phone.

"He's on his way. He won't be long."

Jayde had only turned the first page of the glossy magazine she'd opened when Noah appeared through a side door. He regarded her somberly through his glasses. She tried out a smile.

"Hi, Noah. It's good to see you."

He merely inclined his head and then stepped backwards, indicating for her to follow him. Collecting her handbag from the seat beside her, she followed him through a rabbit warren of partitioned desks until he finally came to a halt inside an office. He took a seat and she did the same.

"Nice digs," she said by way of breaking the ice. It was true. The offices were fitted out better than the average government building.

He merely shrugged. "It's okay."

She fiddled with the strap of her handbag. Now the moment was upon her, she was beset with nerves.

"Look, Noah. I'm sorry for not making it clearer that the two of us are…friends. Only friends."

"But what about the wedding? Why did you agree to attend with me?"

A guilty blush heated her cheeks. "I… I thought I was coming as your friend."

"Bullshit! I've been coming to Beaches for months, hanging out. You're not stupid. You knew what kept drawing me there. You knew I liked you. That's why I invited you to Callum's wedding. You weren't coming as my friend! You were coming as my date!"

She winced at the hurt in his eyes. She deserved every last bit of his angst. Of course she'd been aware of his interest. She'd used it to her advantage to get closer to his family. Though she'd done it for noble reasons, the deception behind her actions now filled her with guilt.

"Flynn knew how I felt about you! I blame him as much as I blame you!"

Jayde sat forward in her seat, intent on clearing Flynn's name. This was nothing to do with him.

"No, Noah. You're wrong. This isn't Flynn's fault. He told me how you felt. He warned me off. Told me he wouldn't take his brother's girl. The thing is, I'm not your girl, Noah. I never have been. It's not Flynn's fault I've fallen for him. He did everything he could to dissuade me."

Noah's lip curled up in disgust. "It didn't look that way to me. He was hardly fighting you off."

"Please, Noah. I know you're hurting and I'm so sorry you found out that way. Flynn and I… We're taking things slow. Neither of us know where this might lead. Right now, your brother's feeling terrible about all of this. He wanted to go to you right away. I asked him to let me talk to you first. He agreed."

"Good old Flynn," Noah said bitterly. "Always the one to get the girl. It's never been any different."

Jayde bit the inside of her lip. She hated that she was the

cause of Noah's pain, but neither would she apologize for her feelings for his brother.

"Maybe it's a numbers game," she suggested in an effort to focus Noah's attentions elsewhere.

Noah looked only mildly interested. "What do you mean?"

"Well, Flynn strikes me as someone who's always had plenty of women in his life, right?"

"Yes. For as long as I can remember. Even back in primary school the girls would flock to him."

Jayde could well imagine. With his combination of good looks and confidence, she'd bet Flynn had been able to have any girl he chose.

"And what about you, Noah? Were there always plenty of girls in your life?"

Noah looked away, uncomfortable. "No. I wasn't like Flynn."

"But there were some? One or two?"

"Yeah. I guess."

"Do you see where I'm going with this?" she asked.

"Not really."

"Flynn had a swarm of women. You had one or two. Who do you think had the best odds of finding someone to fall in love with?"

"Flynn, of course. Because he's better looking, more charismatic, not so introverted," Noah replied morosely.

Once again, Jayde sat forward in her seat. She needed to make him see. "No, Noah. That's where you're wrong. Yes, Flynn had the best odds, but not because of that. Like I said, it's a numbers game. You have to get more points on the board. Go out more, meet girls, date, have fun."

"I'm not into casual relationships. I've never had a one night stand," he admitted. He stared down at his desk in embarrassment.

"There's no shame in that, Noah. In fact, many women would find your attitude refreshing. I do."

He looked up, surprised. "You do?"

"Yes. I'm not keen on one-night stands, either. I don't think it's good for either party. I'd much rather be in a long-term, committed relationship with someone who loves me and wants to be with me for longer than it takes to sober up after a big night."

Noah sighed and then nodded. A tiny smile turned up his lips. "Too bad I don't do it for you, Jayde. We could be so good together."

She smiled back. She stood and walked around to his side of the desk. To his surprise, she pressed a soft kiss upon his cheek. "Can we still be friends?"

His smile widened. "Yeah. Of course. I'd like that."

Chapter Thirteen

Flynn tried to concentrate on the statements in front of him, but he kept reading the same paragraph over and over and still couldn't have said what it meant. Ever since Christmas Day he hadn't been able to get Jayde off his mind. The kisses they'd shared had blown his mind. He couldn't get enough. It was so unlike him and it scared him a bit.

For all of his life he'd loved being around women. He'd had more high school girlfriends than he could count. In the past he tended to lean toward leggy blonds, he'd also dated redheads, brunettes and black-haired women. He'd never met a woman who held his heart longer than a month or two. And that's how he'd liked it.

Though his parents had remained married until the tragic death of his mother a decade earlier, Flynn had never been inspired to take a stab at the institution himself. Now he'd found out his parents' seemingly happy marriage hadn't been so happy at all. His father had cheated on his mother and the product of that affair was Sophia. He had yet to find out if his mother had known about the affair and accepted it, or if she'd been completely oblivious the whole time.

Then there was the fact he specialized in family law. He made his money off divorces. He'd worked out a long time ago that marriage wasn't necessarily forever. Most people fell out of love and as soon as that happened, it seemed like they then fell into hate. It never failed to amaze him how two people who'd once declared their undying love, could want to tear each other apart down the road.

Of course, it was the kids he felt sorry for. They were the truly innocent victims in the whole sorry story. It wasn't their fault their parents had gone from loving each other to not being able to stand the sight of each other, sometimes in a fairly short period of time. And the anger…the vitriol…the hate… The very thought of arriving at that point with someone he'd once loved made him shudder.

So, he'd opted out of marriage and long-term relationships. Sometimes he even called it quits before their first argument. He'd decided it was far better to end things while the going was still good—while they were still being civil to one another, at least—than to see the relationship spiral out of control and become something filled with spite and maliciousness.

But with Jayde, things felt different. He wanted to see her, to be with her, all the time. He hadn't seen her since Christmas Day and that was driving him insane. He couldn't sleep; he couldn't concentrate. He couldn't even beat Steven at tennis. It was embarrassing and he didn't know what to do about it. He'd certainly never felt this way before. It alarmed him that he felt it now.

He barely knew her. What was it about her that was so special? There was no doubt she was beautiful, but he'd dated plenty of beautiful women before. She was also smart and funny. Ditto. The truth was, he couldn't put his finger on what made Jayde Hassad so unique, so important to his peace of mind.

All he knew was that he felt good when he was around her and he wanted her to feel good, too. He wanted to protect her from life's difficult moments, from hardship, loss and pain. He wanted to cocoon her in a world where there was nothing but sweetness and kindness. Where nobody got hurt.

It was ridiculous the way he felt. He'd totally lost his mind. He'd never been one to engage in silly feelings. He never got emotional. Well, maybe when his mother died. But she'd died in a car accident, well before her time. And he missed her.

Still, there was no denying Jayde had cast a spell over him and there was nothing he could do about that. The best thing to do was to go with it and see where it might lead. No doubt it would burn itself out in time, like all of his other relationships had. In the meantime, he must see her again. There was nothing else for it.

With that thought in mind, he pushed away from his desk and headed out of his office. Being the Christmas season, the reception area was dark and empty. It was only idiots like him, or workaholics, who turned up in the office over the Christmas break.

He went down to the staff carpark and climbed into his sports car. Gunning the engine, he swung out of the lot and blended into the traffic. All the way across the bridge, he tapped impatiently on the steering wheel.

This is madness! What am I doing? I don't even know if she's working today!

Though she'd asked him for Noah's number, Flynn hadn't thought to ask for hers. He'd been distracted by the sight of Noah and the awful way he'd looked. Now Flynn was on his way to Balmoral on nothing more than a hope and a prayer that the woman he craved to see would be there.

He pulled into the parking lot outside the Beaches bar. There were a number of cars already there. It was three in the afternoon, but it seemed that was early enough for some patrons. He'd been hoping the lunch crowd might have dispersed already and it was too early for dinner. But it seemed he was destined to talk to her among a crowd of people.

Pushing open the front door with his shoulder, he stepped inside. His gaze zeroed in on the bar.

She's here!

Behind the counter, serving drinks, smiling at the customers. It took her a moment to notice him. When she did, her eyes widened in surprise. A becoming blush stained her cheeks. He was flooded with warmth and satisfaction, glad she was as affected by him as he was by her.

He found an empty space along the bar and took a seat on a vacant stool. It took her a few moments to finish serving another customer, but finally she was there, in front of him. Smiling a little cautiously, like she wasn't quite sure what to say.

He knew how she felt. He felt the same way. Nervous. Tongue-tied. Churned up inside. It was weird. He never felt this way. Not around women, not around clients, not even when he was facing down the stern visage of a judge he instinctively knew was offside.

And yet, here he was, almost sweating, wondering what to say. The last time they'd been together they'd shared the most amazing kisses. Each one burned him all the way through. Hours later, it was all he could think about. No, scrap that. It was all he'd been able to think about for *days*. Ever since it happened.

I'm still thinking about it. About doing it again…

"Hi," she said.

"H-hi," he stammered and then blushed.

"How are things?" she asked.

"Fine." It came out on a squeak. He cleared his throat and tried again. "I'm fine. Busy."

Her gaze moved over him, taking in his suit and tie. "You're back at work already?"

"Yes. I had a few things to do. I see you're back at it, too."

She grinned and he felt it all the way to his gut.

"Oh, yeah. My father's the boss. There's no rest for me. The only day we were closed was Christmas. As for New Year's, that's our biggest night of the year."

Flynn digested her words. He was disappointed he wouldn't get to watch the fireworks with her, or share a drink and celebrate the incoming year, but maybe they could celebrate earlier? Like tonight.

"What time do you get off?" he asked.

"Six."

"I'd like to spend some more time with you. Our date got kind of interrupted the last time."

She raised her eyebrows in silent query. "Date? Is that what it was?"

He held her gaze. "Yes."

Emotion flared in her eyes. She swallowed. "I spoke to Noah. We sorted things out."

"Is he okay?"

"Yes. I think so."

Flynn compressed his lips. "I should call him."

"Yes. That might be a good idea."

Flynn would talk to his brother and smooth things over. It wasn't Flynn's fault Jayde didn't feel the same way about Noah. His brother would understand. He knew better than most that no one had control over who they fell in love with.

He glanced at Jayde. She stared down at the counter. He cleared his throat on a sudden rush of nerves.

"So, what do you say? Want to go for a drive?" he asked. His heart beat double time while he waited for her answer.

"Okay."

Excitement leaped in his veins. "Okay." He grinned. "I'll pick you up at six."

Then Jayde shook her head and his spirits plummeted. "No."

He tried to contain his disappointment and kept his tone light. "No?"

"No. I'll pick *you* up. We can go for a ride on my motorbike. Is that okay with you?"

He smiled slowly. "You have a motorbike?"

"Yes. A real beauty. A Harley-Davidson Street Glide. She goes like the wind."

He felt her excitement. His gut clenched. He wanted to leap over the bar and take her in his arms. He wanted to strip her naked, kiss her senseless, until they were both breathless with desire. His body hardened at the thought.

"I have a spare helmet, if that's what you're worried about."

Her comment interrupted his feverish fantasies. He managed a smile. "I guess I'll see you at six, then."

She winked and blood rushed to his cock. "Six it is."

The rest of Jayde's shift passed in a blur of excitement, nervousness, and demanding customers as the bar filled with its usual busy late-afternoon crowd. She lost count of the number of times she looked at the big old wooden clock that was perched up on one of the oak beams that ran the length of the ceiling.

From the moment she'd accepted Flynn's invitation, she'd been second-guessing herself. Her father was certain Flynn hadn't been involved in Henry's drug business. The Craigdon bank accounts supported that fact. She'd found no evidence of Flynn's involvement, but that didn't mean she was completely comfortable going out on another date.

He was part of her investigation. What if he found out? What if he thought the only reason she wanted to spend time with him was because she was trying to gather dirt? That might have been her motivation in the beginning, especially with Noah, but somewhere along the way, things had changed. Not only was she almost certain Flynn and his family were in the clear, she'd developed feelings for Flynn that just wouldn't go away. Strong feelings. Feelings she'd never had before. For anyone.

She barely knew him and yet she yearned to be with him. She missed him when they were apart. She thought about him all the time, what he was doing, who he was with. She also thought about their kisses. She wanted to kiss him again. And more. So much more. She liked him. She liked him a lot. And that scared her to death.

After her tumultuous childhood, she'd been wary of entering into any serious relationships. She'd dated casually from time to time, but she'd never given anyone her heart. She'd fiercely protected herself from getting too involved. She didn't want to go through what her mother went through. She didn't want to watch her family get torn apart.

And though the circumstances weren't the same, they weren't all that different, either. Her father hadn't told her mother about his involvement in illegal drugs until well after they were married. As far as her mother knew, he owned a bar, was a businessman. When she discovered the truth, their relationship was never the same. Though Jayde had been oblivious to the cause of the tension at the time, that had been the beginning of the end. Her mother had finally given her father an ultimatum: Either give up the drug dealing or get out. He left, taking her brother with him.

Her shoulders slumped on a sigh. A relationship built on lies and deceit had no chance of survival. Her parents had shown her that. Flynn had no idea she was a cop. Nor did he know she was investigating his family. She didn't have to imagine how he'd feel if he found out. Any chance they might have as a couple would go up in flames, disintegrate without a trace, leaving nothing but regret—and possibly a broken heart.

Broken heart? Am I in love with him? How can that be?

She didn't know how it had happened, but it was true. Somewhere along the way, she'd fallen in love with Flynn Craigdon. Despite the investigation, the complications with Noah and all the other reasons she shouldn't have, it had happened just the same.

She wished she could say she was happy about it, but the knowledge scared her half to death. What was worse, she didn't have a clue how he felt. It was obvious he was interested in her, but what did that mean? Right from the outset she'd pegged him as a love 'em and leave 'em kind of guy. Her research had uncovered his penchant for beautiful women and his habit of moving on after only a few months. Either he was terrible at choosing potential life partners or he was a commitment phobe. She guessed it was the latter.

Do I really want to become just another one of Flynn Craigdon's exes? A woman he wines and dines and charms for a month or two, only to be discarded when he tires of me?

No, she didn't. She'd never been that kind of woman and at twenty-seven, she wasn't about to start. The only problem was, how could she resist him? She'd already proven herself weak when it came to Flynn Craigdon. If he wanted to kiss her again, what would she do? Particularly when every fiber of her being craved more of him.

When six o'clock came round, Jayde was no closer to making a decision. Flynn arrived back at the bar looking gorgeous in black leather pants and an expensive leather jacket. Her heart skipped a beat and then galloped away. The tight pants cupped his ass and emphasized the strength and length of his legs. The jacket hugged his broad shoulders. He looked like a bikie. Like a real bad boy. The only things missing were a bandanna and a tattoo or two.

And then he smiled a slow, sexy smile and the fantasy was complete. Her stomach quivered with nerves. She turned away from him, hiding her reaction while she pretended to be busy with last-minute drink orders. When she felt more in control, she bid farewell to the other staff members and wished them a good night. Steeling herself against the impact, she joined Flynn on the other side of the bar.

"You certainly look the part. Do I take it you know how to ride?" she asked.

"Of course."

She shot him a doubtful look. His eyes widened in mock outrage. "What? You don't think I'm telling the truth?"

She laughed. "Not at all. You're full of surprises, that's all. You're a divorce lawyer. You live by the beach in an apartment. You drive a Ferrari. If I had to guess, I'd say you were more into cars than motorbikes."

"I'm into lots of things," he murmured.

He gave her a slow once-over. Heat trailed in the wake of his gaze. She shivered with desire. Her nipples tightened into nubs. When his gaze met hers again she nearly gasped aloud at the desire that burned inside them.

Flustered, she broke eye contact and tugged down the ends of her T-shirt. That reminded her she needed to change into something more suitable for riding.

"I need to go upstairs for a minute," she said. She turned and headed toward the internal staircase.

"I'll come with you," Flynn said.

She opened her mouth to protest, but then closed it again. What did it matter if he knew she lived in the apartment above the bar? It wasn't exactly a secret. As she made her way upstairs, she was conscious of Flynn following a few steps behind her. She didn't dare turn around and see if his gaze was on her ass, but she had a sneaking suspicion it was. She had a sudden urge to twerk, but then decided against it—just in time. She was still confused about whether she was ready to throw caution to the wind. Better not to inflame him unnecessarily.

Leaving him standing in her living room, she hurried into her bedroom to change. She pulled on a clean T-shirt and switched her jeans for leather pants. Flynn wasn't the only one with biking gear. As she pulled on the tight pants and zipped up her jacket, she wondered what he'd think. She didn't have to wait long.

The expression on his face told her all she needed to know. He might not be in love with her, but there was no doubt he was in lust.

"Oh, God," he breathed. "You look so hot."

Desire curled a heated trail across her stomach and centred in her core. The nerves she'd held at bay rose once again to the fore. She felt edgy, nervous, excited and turned-on, all at the same time. Concealing the topsy-turvy emotions behind a cheeky grin, she winked.

"I hope it was worth the wait."

He groaned. "You have no idea."

The fire in his eyes burned brighter. He stepped forward with intent. On a sudden burst of panic, Jayde turned away. Collecting two helmets from a cupboard in the kitchen, she headed straight for the door.

"Pull it shut behind you," she threw over her shoulder and hurried back down the stairs.

Chapter Fourteen

Flynn was on fire. Pressed up against Jayde's back, his chest was tight and his cock was rock-hard and throbbing. The feel of the powerful engine beneath him only added to his torment. He'd been stunned when she'd appeared in skintight leathers, grinning from ear to ear. The only thought that had run through his mind was that he had to have her. He had to take her in his arms and love her senselessly. He wouldn't be able to think straight until he knew what it was like to bury himself in her warmth.

Then she'd made her escape and he'd been forced to put his amorous intentions on hold. Now he clung to her slim waist as they raced along the Pacific Motorway toward the Central coast and he was loving every minute of it.

She rode with grace and confidence, taking tight corners with ease. It was obvious this wasn't the first time she'd had the Harley at full throttle. The heady feeling of having his arms around her while they flew down the freeway on a powerful motorbike filled him with euphoria. He couldn't remember the last time he'd felt so good.

More than an hour later, she slowed the bike and eased off the highway. They turned down a narrow road. Weaving in and out among the trees, they at last came into an open clearing.

Jayde parked the bike near a walkway where a sign indicated the path led to the beach.

Flynn swung his leg over the bike and fiddled with the strap of his helmet. He pulled it off and waited for Jayde to do the same. In silence, they stood and grinned at each other as the adrenaline of their ride began to wear off.

"You like?" she asked.

"Oh, I like. I like a lot." His voice was rough with emotion and once again blood rushed to his groin. Her eyes flared wide, but she didn't respond. Instead, she turned and headed in the direction of the beach.

Fortunately, it was still light enough for them to see the path in front of them. Flynn followed Jayde slowly along the paved walkway. It was overgrown with lantana and other shrubby bushes. At one stage he ducked under an overhanging banksia tree to avoid getting scraped across the face with it.

"Are you okay?" Jayde asked over her shoulder.

"Yep, all good."

Around the next corner, the view to the beach opened up in front of them. Jayde stopped. She bent over and undid the strap of her boots and then tugged them off, along with her socks.

"Bare feet?" he teased.

"It's the beach. Of course bare feet!"

He followed suit and then offered to carry her boots, along with his. She happily handed them over and then started jogging across the sand. With her arms spread wide, she danced around in a circle.

"Oh, it feels so good! I love the beach!"

He smiled at her antics and followed behind her more slowly. Finding a high spot, he deposited their boots on the ground and then shrugged out of his jacket. The summer evening was warm and now they'd stopped, the humid air felt stifling. His hands went to the clasp on his pants and he paused momentarily.

"What the hell," he mumbled and then shucked off his pants.

"Flynn! What are you doing?" Jayde squealed.

He looked at her and shrugged. "I'm hot."

She grinned. "I won't deny you're good looking, but hot? That might be taking it a little too far."

He grinned back at her and then pulled off his T-shirt. He stood before her in only his boxers. She squealed again, but at the same time, her gaze was fixed on his six pack. Though he spent most of his time seated behind a desk or at a bar table, he made it a priority to stay fit and healthy and along with his regular tennis game, he put in frequent sessions at the gym. In the fading light, he saw Jayde's eyes widen with appreciation. Her mouth gaped. Her tongue stole out. She stopped just short of licking her lips.

He smiled inwardly. It pleased him to know she found him attractive. Though he'd always found it easy to impress women, this was the only woman who counted. Her response to his kisses had been telling, but it didn't hurt to have a little extra affirmation.

"You like?" he teased.

She laughed. "Oh, I like. I like a lot."

Just like that, the air between them was charged, like an arc of electricity had passed between them. Flynn's heart hammered against his ribs. His cock throbbed. Need filled every pore.

"Jayde…"

She took a step toward him and then another. When she got close enough, she reached out and touched him. Her palm lay flat against his chest and then her fingers walked across his pectorals. She raked her fingernails over his nipples. His breath hissed.

He stood stock still and endured her sensual torment. When he couldn't stand it another moment, he stilled her hand.

"Jayde…?"

She gave him a nervous smile and then turned and ran toward the water. She paused only long enough to tear off her jacket and pants. After a moment's hesitation, her T-shirt quickly followed. With a shout, she ran into the ocean in just her underwear. Flynn watched, grinning.

Jayde cried out with laughter as the waves enveloped her, covering her in frothy foam.

"Are you coming in?" she shouted above the noise of the waves.

Flynn didn't need any further encouragement. He walked into the water and then dived under a wave. Coming up for air, he shook the water out of his hair. Jayde stood a few feet away from him, staring at him. Once again, desire thundered through his veins.

Jayde's heart thumped. Flynn was gilded in the last rays of the sun. It glinted off his wet hair, his face, his chest. Her gaze kept returning to his well-defined muscles. He looked like a male model, all golden perfection. A fine sprinkling of darker hair lined his pectorals. Her fingers itched to touch him.

This is madness! I've gone mad! That's what this is! Utter madness!

No matter what it was, it didn't make a difference. She wanted him. She burned for him. She had to have him. Mind made up, she walked toward him, jumping over the waves. She reached up and framed his face between her hands and pulled his head down to hers.

The moment their lips touched, every other thought and concern disappeared. All that mattered was the feel of his lips on hers. Warm and supple, firm and confident, he kissed her like a man who knew what he was doing. It was just as good as the first time and yet again, she couldn't get enough.

With a low growl, Flynn swung her up into his arms and

carried her from the water. He set her far enough up the wet sand that the waves wouldn't reach them. He followed her down and covered her body with his. She reached up and threaded her arms around his neck and kissed him again.

The heat of his body was in stark contrast to the coolness of his skin. He tasted salty. That, mixed with the smell of his spicy cologne and she was dizzy with desire. He reached around and unclasped her bra. Her wet panties quickly followed. Then he pulled away just long enough to tug off his boxers and kick them out of the way.

The sand was damp and firm beneath her. She frowned slightly at the thought of it getting into all of her cracks and crevices and then Flynn pressed full-length against her and she forgot everything but the man she wanted more than anything.

His erection pressed impatiently against her belly as he kissed her over and over again. Tongues entwined, passions rose, Jayde's heart was thumping. He moved against her and her legs fell open and then his cock pressed against her entrance.

"Flynn!" she gasped.

He lifted his head. "Do you want me to stop?" he rasped.

She shook her head. "What about a condom?"

"Do you have one?"

"No."

"Neither do I."

Flynn pressed his forehead against hers, breathing hard. Coming to a decision, Jayde lifted his head and stared him in the face.

"I want you."

"But—"

"I don't care. I'm on the pill. Free of disease. You?"

"I'm not on the pill, but I'm disease free. Is that enough?"

She laughed and he captured it in his mouth. Once again,

their kisses quickly caught fire and burned out of control. Flynn moved until he was again positioned between her thighs. In one hard thrust, he entered her.

Jayde gasped from the impact. Her inner muscles stretched to accommodate him. At the same time, he began to move, slowly at first and then with increasing intensity. Jayde's climax began to build, filling her with urgency. She clung to his shoulders, urging him on. Burying her face in the crook of his neck, she nipped at his salty skin. His buttocks flexed, his hips thrust and all of a sudden she was there—at the precipice.

Crying out, she toppled over the edge and was freefalling into pleasure. A moment later, Flynn joined her. He shouted out his release and then collapsed against her, breathing hard. And then he rolled off her and drew her against his side.

"I'm sorry, Jayde. I've never done that before." He looked abashed and a little bewildered.

She gave him a wry smile. "I'm not sure I believe you were a virgin."

He shook his head and grinned. "No, not that. I mean, I've never lost control like that. I should have waited until we had protection, no matter what you said."

Jayde frowned. "Don't tell me you're regretting what we just did?"

"No, of course not," he hurried to reassure her. "It's just that... You drove me past the point of common sense. I've never felt like that before. Like I had to have you. Like I couldn't wait. It's...disconcerting."

Though Jayde knew exactly what he meant, it didn't do her ego any good to hear him describe their lovemaking as disconcerting. Rolling away from him, she stood and brushed off the sand. She looked around for her bra and panties and hopping, first on one foot and then the other, managed to put them back on. Then she headed to where she'd left the rest of her clothing.

"Jayde! I didn't mean it like that. Come on, Jayde! Let me explain."

He'd followed behind her, with his boxers in his hand. She forced a smile. "There's nothing to explain. I understand. I really do. Now, you might want to put on those boxers before you pull on your leather pants. We don't want anything getting caught in the zipper."

With that, she turned her back on him and began to get dressed.

Flynn cursed under his breath and hurriedly pulled on his clothes. Still wet and covered in sand, it was no easy task. He moved higher up the beach to a dry spot covered with spindly grass and sat down and pulled on his socks and boots. When they were both finished dressing, they headed back up the hill the way they'd come. The sun had finally set which made it more difficult to see. Once again, Jayde led the way forward. He suspected this wasn't her first visit to the area. In an effort to break the silence that had fallen between them, he put the question to her.

"You're right," she replied. "I come here as often as I can. It's only an hour from Sydney. Far enough to allow me to open up the throttle and give my bike a good run. The beach is off the main drag, so most of the time there aren't many people here. Only a few locals. This time of night, I usually have it all to myself."

Flynn frowned. Though he hadn't noticed anyone around, it concerned him that she came here at night on her own. He told her as much.

She turned briefly to face him. He saw a flash of irritation before she turned away and continued the ascent.

"I'm a big girl, Flynn. I know how to take care of myself."

He opened his mouth to argue further and then shut it again.

He wasn't her father, her brother, or her boyfriend. He had no right to offer an opinion on her activities, no matter how much he wanted to. They might have just had sex but that didn't give him the right to tell her what to do. The weird thing was, he'd slept with countless women. None of them had filled him with such a proprietary feeling, or the desire to keep her so safe.

He'd always been a supporter of feminism and firmly believed women were just as capable as men. He'd never had reason to question that. But now, when he thought of Jayde potentially putting herself in harm's way by being alone on the beach without a man's protection, it unsettled him.

Why do I care so much what she does? It's like she said: She's a big girl. Capable of looking out for herself.

The best thing to do would be to forget about the whole thing. Yes, that was the problem. He was overthinking everything. Instead, he should be replaying the incredible feeling of having her beneath him at last. The silky warmth of her moist womanhood, her muscles clenching around him. It had been exquisite, sensational, better than he could ever remember…

And then he'd gone and ruined it by his awkward and bumbling explanation. There was no point in trying to explain any further. He'd messed it up so much already. The best thing he could do was ignore what he'd said and hope she did the same.

Flynn was still thinking of Jayde on his way to work the next day. After parking his car in the staff parking lot, he waited in line at the coffee vendor's outside his building. After bidding her farewell the evening before, he'd spent the rest of the night tossing and turning and reliving their interlude on the beach. No matter how he looked at it, there was no denying it: He'd fallen for her.

It filled him with mixed feelings. All his life, he'd been content to play the field. To love and be loved, but to never lose his heart. He enjoyed the company of women, both in and out of the bedroom, but he'd never wanted to tie himself down to one forever. Until now.

He'd never felt this way toward a woman. He'd spent the night dreaming about long term, maybe even forever. *Fuck! Am I crazy?* But he couldn't help it. He wished he knew how she felt.

Oh, she liked him well enough and she'd definitely enjoyed the sex, but did her feelings run any deeper? What if he was the only one who felt this way? He shook his head at the irony. For so long, it had been him who'd done the loving and the leaving. He was sure he'd left behind a few broken hearts, but that had never given him pause. He'd never promised forever. It wasn't his fault if they misread the signals, or hoped he might change his mind.

But now it was *his* heart that was in danger of getting broken and he was the one who could very well be misreading the signals. It was a situation that was totally foreign to him and he wasn't exactly sure what to do about it.

"Next."

Flynn stepped up to the counter and put in his order for a large long black. As he moved to one side, he caught sight of his friend and colleague, Steven Walker.

"Hey, mate. How's it going?" he asked with a grin.

Steven slapped him on the back by way of greeting. "Flynn! Merry Christmas! What are you doing here?"

"I had to get on top of a few things at work. You know what it's like this time of year. Christmas brings out the best and the worse in us. How about you?"

"Same. Remember the Romano case? Yeah, well, it continues to give me headaches. We still haven't managed to get him bail. He's screaming from the rafters."

Flynn commiserated with his friend. That's why Flynn had gone into family law. Though it could be incredibly gutting to watch two people who'd once declared undying love for each other turn into rabid animals as they tried to tear each other apart, it was a different kind of stress compared to knowing he had someone's liberty resting on his shoulders. There were always stories about defendants who were refused bail, had to sit on remand awaiting their day in court, who were eventually found not guilty.

The system wasn't perfect, but everyone involved in it did their best. Like Steven. He had a reputation for being one of the best defense lawyers in Sydney. Romano was lucky to have him, even if he didn't see it that way at the moment.

"What's the biggest hurdle to his bail?" Flynn asked.

Steven sighed. "He's considered a flight risk. Last time he was given bail, he hopped a plane to far north Queensland. It took them a month to track him down. The prosecutor's made it abundantly clear the court shouldn't be prepared to take that risk again. At least they know he'll show up for trial if he's on remand."

"Sounds like a headache all right," Flynn said.

Steven grimaced. "Yeah. You don't know the half of it. Romano's hinted he's willing to spill secrets on some of the other big players in the drug world if he can get a deal. When I pressed him for details, he gave me the name of John Hassad."

Flynn frowned. The name was familiar, but he couldn't put a face to it.

Hang on a minute… Wasn't that the name of Jayde's father? Still, the name "Hassad" wasn't uncommon…

"Hassad? Who's he?" he asked, keeping his tone casual.

Steven moved closer and lowered his voice to a conspiratorial whisper. "That's the thing. I didn't know who he was, either. You and I, we obviously run in different circles," he joked.

Flynn chuckled. "I guess it can only be a good thing that we aren't familiar with the who's who of the drug world."

"Yes. So, anyway, I decided to do some research. Guess what I found out?"

Flynn shrugged. "What?"

Steven's eyes gleamed with excitement. "He's Jayde Hassad's father. The girl you were keen on from the soup kitchen. Remember?"

Flynn tensed. "Of course I remember," he said, trying hard to hide his shock.

Steven touched his arm. "I just thought you ought to know, before you…you know… Before you go and get your heart broken."

Steven laughed and thumped Flynn on the back. Flynn forced himself to laugh, too. Steven knew better than most about Flynn's reputation as a womanizer. There was no way Steven seriously believed Flynn's heart might be at risk.

"Thanks for letting me know, Steven. And for looking out for me. I can always count on you to have my back."

Steven pointed toward him and grinned. "No worries, mate. Anytime."

Chapter Fifteen

Nicholas Craigdon had a headache. It had been with him most of the morning. Leaning forward, he picked up the phone on his desk and buzzed his executive assistant.

"Hi, Harper. Do you mind bringing me a couple of painkillers?"

His fiancée reacted with surprise. "Are you all right?"

He smiled at the concern in her voice. It made him feel good knowing he finally had someone to care about him.

"I'm fine," he said. "It's just a headache. But I've had it all morning. I don't think it's going away by itself."

"I'll be right in."

True to her word, Harper appeared in his office a few moments later carrying a glass of water and a packet of paracetamol.

"Here," she offered, handing them over.

He took the packet and popped a couple of pills into his hand and then washed them down with the water.

"Thanks."

She moved closer and cupped his cheek, her gaze filled with worry. "Are you sure you're not coming down with something?" Her hand moved to the back of his neck. "You're a little warm."

Nick sighed. "No. It isn't that. I've been going through the list of names I found in Dad's safe. I discovered them not long after I took over as managing director, but there were so many entries and they didn't make sense. I set them aside until I had more time to study them. A few weeks ago, I pulled them out again."

He glanced up at her, feeling grim. She looked alarmed at his expression.

"Nick? What is it? What have you found?"

"There are pages and pages of entries. Names, dates and monetary amounts. It seemed there was no rhyme or reason to the entries. The only consistent thing was they were in chronological order. The type of paper changed from time to time, along with the type of pen used to make the notations. It was as if it was a running record Dad kept, adding to it as necessary. At least, that's what it looked like."

Harper perched on the edge of his desk. "Did you work out what it all meant?"

He bit his lip and nodded. "Yes."

She looked at him and waited for him to speak again. His shoulders slumped on another sigh.

"Each person on the list was employed by Craigdon Enterprises while Dad was alive. All but one of them left our employment after his death. That seemed a little unusual, but then again, many of them had worked for Dad for a number of years. I figured they'd remained loyal to him, but when I came on, there was a new kid in town and their loyalty to my father died with him."

"Okay," Harper murmured. She gave Nick a look of encouragement to continue.

"Over the past weeks, I've managed to speak to more than half of these former employees. I was shocked when every single one of them came flat out and told me they weren't employed as laborers."

Harper frowned. "Then what were they doing for your father?"

Dread and disappointment formed a hard ball in his gut. It was difficult enough to tell Harper the truth. How much harder would it be to tell his brothers and sisters? His mother? Still, he'd been determined to solve the mystery and now he had to live with the truth of it.

"The thing is, it was all a ruse," he continued. "A clever cover. Each of them were listed as Craigdon employees on the books and at first glance you could be forgiven for assuming they were laborers on the building sites, but what they really did was sell drugs for my father."

Harper gasped. Her eyes were wide with shock. "Are you sure?"

Nick nodded, feeling grim. "Unfortunately, yes. The men confirmed it. Of course, none of them would go on the record, which means there's no proof and with Dad now gone, it's hardly a matter the police will concern themselves with. The men will deny telling me anything and the police will have no evidence to the contrary. The only people who'll be hurt if this becomes public knowledge are the people I love and they were completely innocent of any of this."

"How do you know?"

Harper voiced the question so softly, for a moment Nick thought he'd been mistaken. He stared at her in disbelief. "How can you even ask that? You've met my family. Which one of them do you think could have been involved in something like this?"

"You're right," she said quickly. "I'm sorry. Of course none of them could have been part of such a heinous scheme." She shook her head. "I just don't understand your father's motivation. I took the liberty of looking over the accounts when I first started here. Even before Henry's death, the accounts were looking good. He had several building ventures on the go and all of them were set to make him a lot of money. Why would he dabble in illegal drugs?"

Nick compressed his lips. "Who knows? Dad was always driven by money. He was convinced it was the only thing that mattered. The earliest entries on his list were from fifteen years earlier, but he could have been doing it way before then. This might only be the newest list he created. Who's to say?"

Harper moved to stand beside him. She cradled his head against her stomach and ran her fingers through his hair, massaging his temples. "Oh, Nick. No wonder you have a headache. What are you going to do?"

Nick took refuge in her soft caress. He blew out his breath on a heavy sigh. "There's one employee on Dad's list who's still employed by the company. Igor Petrov. He's one of our head foremen. He's been with Dad more than fifteen years. I need to confront him with my suspicions. Tell him what I found out. See if he's willing to shed any more light on what went on…and why."

Harper framed his face between her palms and pressed a kiss against his forehead. "Oh, Nick. I'm so sorry. This must come as such a shock. I'm here for you. Now and always. If there's anything I can do…?"

He managed to smile and putting his arms around her waist, pulled her in close against him. Tilting his face upwards, he waited expectantly for a proper kiss. She willingly complied. With Harper's soft lips pressed against his, he felt his strength return. She gave him the confidence to do what needed to be done. She loved him and he loved her. Each day he thanked God he'd found her.

Flynn returned to his office, his head buzzing with questions. He'd had no idea John Hassad was a bigwig drug dealer. Then again, it was only on the say so of a criminal.

Romano was hardly a credible informant. Flynn should go directly to the source and ask Jayde. Surely she'd tell him the truth.

Just as he threw himself in the chair behind his desk, his phone rang. Checking the screen, Flynn frowned.

Christopher. What did his half-cousin want? In Flynn's experience, Christopher was never the bearer of good news. No doubt he wanted to talk to Flynn about the lawsuit Christopher had filed against Henry's estate. Well, Flynn was staying the hell out of that one. Christopher had his own lawyer. He could go to him with his questions.

Flynn let the call go through to voicemail. Less than thirty seconds later, Christopher rang again. The third time, Flynn cursed and answered the call.

"Christopher. What the hell do you want?"

"*Tut, tut,* Flynn. That's no way to greet your cousin. It being Christmas, and all."

Flynn gritted his teeth against the condescension in Christopher's tone. "I don't have time for a social call."

"Oh, but I have some very important information. Something I'm sure will be of interest to you."

"If this has anything to do with your lawsuit—"

Christopher laughed. "Of course not. I have that well in hand. No, this has to do with a little someone by the name of Jayde Hassad."

Flynn blinked in shock, momentarily silenced. "What about Jayde?"

Christopher's chuckle grated in Flynn's ear. "Oh, yes. I thought that might get your attention. See, I've recently discovered her father's a kingpin in the illegal drug industry."

Flynn's mouth gaped. First Steven, now Christopher. *What's going on?*

"How do you know this?" he demanded.

"I'm not at liberty to reveal my sources, but believe me

when I tell you, the information is reliable. *Very* reliable. I suggest you take a step back and have a good hard look at little Miss Hassad. As difficult as that is, you need to look past those big tits and baby blues and see the real woman underneath. Her father's a big-time drug dealer, Flynn. Surely that tells you all you need to know about her."

With that, Christopher ended the call. Flynn stared down at his phone. Doubts swirled in his gut.

Is it true?

Though Christopher hadn't exactly proven himself trustworthy over the years, he'd sounded so certain about the accuracy of his information. Then there was Romano. What good was it fishing for a deal with false information? It would be a simple matter for the prosecutor to investigate the legitimacy of Romano's claims. Surely he wouldn't be stupid enough to piss them off with claims that weren't true.

Flynn stared down at his desk, his mind a whirl of confusion. What if Jayde knew all about her father's business? What if the bar was all a front? Worse still, what if she was part of it? She worked at Beaches as a barmaid. But what if she did other stuff for her father, too? Errands that were conducted under the cover of darkness.

What better way to do it than to live on the premises? No one would suspect her. He'd noticed there was both an internal and an external staircase to the upstairs apartment. She could come and go from the place as she pleased without raising the slightest suspicion.

But did he really believe she was the type of person who could be involved in such heinous acts?

No!

The Jayde he knew couldn't be a drug dealer. It just didn't fit. Then again, how well did he really know her? He'd been overwhelmed by her beauty, her sense of humor, her spirit of adventure and generosity. She volunteered at a soup kitchen, no less. But did that mean she couldn't be involved in something far seedier?

He had to talk to Noah. Though he worked in internal affairs, he still had connections. He could ask a few questions, find out the truth.

The thought sent Flynn into a tailspin of denial.

What if I don't want to know the truth?

The only thing he knew for sure was that he'd fallen hard for Jayde Hassad. What if it turned out she was a drug dealer? Could he live with that? No, of course he couldn't. Then maybe he was better off not knowing. Maybe that was the better path to take.

Flynn groaned aloud with anguish and shook his head from side to side. He was torn between doing the right thing—telling Noah and discovering the truth and putting into action a series of events that could see Jayde go to jail—or he could cover for her and say nothing and hope everything worked out for the best.

What to do?

Jayde wiped over the counter of the bar and tried to stop thinking about Flynn. Ever since their bike trip, he'd been on her mind constantly. No, scratch that. He'd been on her mind from the day she'd met him. Inexplicably, even knowing the kind of guy he so obviously was, she'd been drawn to him. Now that she'd kissed him, held him in her arms, felt him move so powerfully inside her, she wanted him even more. It was madness, but there was nothing she could do about it.

The phone rang in her pocket. She fished in her jeans and pulled it out. She checked the screen.

Brian.

She was filled with a surge of anticipation. She'd called her handler earlier that day and arranged a meeting so that she could bring him up to speed on her father's activities. She also wanted the opportunity to ask him if he'd discovered a connection between the remaining Craigdons and Henry's drug dealing. She was hoping with all her heart her instincts would prove true and that Flynn in particular had nothing to do with any of this.

"Brian. How are you?"

"Great. I'm right outside."

"I'll meet you upstairs."

With that, she ended the call. She looked across at her colleague who was with her on the morning shift.

"Toby, I'm going to take my break. Are you all right here for a bit?"

"All good, Jayde. Take as long as you like. I've got it covered."

She nodded. Thankfully the bar wasn't usually busy in the morning. Most of the time, it was just her and one other staff member rostered on. From lunchtime onward, the traffic picked up as people came in to dine. It was no surprise the evenings were the busiest of all.

Jayde headed outside and took the external stairs that led up to her apartment. She could have brought Brian in through the bar, but she preferred to keep him out of sight. As a former undercover officer, he preferred it that way, too. Though he was only a few short years from retirement, there were plenty of people still roaming the streets who Brian didn't want to recognize him. She understood his need to remain as invisible as possible.

"How are things?" he asked as she opened the door. He followed her inside.

"Not too bad." She went to her bedroom and came back with the dossier of information she'd collected on the Craigdons. She'd been looking over the documents every night before she went to bed, hoping to find something she'd missed.

"I've been analyzing those bank records," she said. "I've looked at all the main players. I couldn't find anything suspicious. Nothing appears to stand out. If they're siphoning huge sums of money out of a drug enterprise, they're doing a good job of hiding it."

"Have you looked over all seven years' worth?"

"Yes. I've found nothing. Flynn seems to be exactly what he purports to be—a busy, successful lawyer. Noah turns up for his shift every day, as does Logan. Their pay packets confirm it. Callum was a priest. He's now the proprietor of a not-for-profit soup kitchen. He's put every penny of his inheritance into building accommodation for the poor. I just can't see him running drugs. Christopher is also not displaying any suspicious behavior. He's currently suing his late father's estate. He's asking for one hundred million dollars. He'd be unlikely to do that if he's on the take from Henry's drug enterprise."

She paused and looked at Brian. "As far as I can tell, the Craigdon men aren't involved in the drug trade. What's more, I spoke to my father about Henry. Apparently he was one of my father's best customers. As far as Dad knows, Henry operated the business alone, or at least without the assistance of his sons and nephews. Dad says he never dealt with anyone other than Henry."

Brian nodded. "Interesting. Too bad we didn't learn about that earlier, before Henry Craigdon bit the dust. It would have been nice to see him behind bars."

Jayde nodded in agreement and then forced herself to ask, "How about you? Did you find anything?"

Her chest went tight as she waited for him to answer. She couldn't deny how important his response was to her. If there were even the slightest chance Flynn was involved in his late uncle's illegal enterprise, then that would be the end of them.

There was no way she'd be in a relationship with a criminal. She'd spent all of her adult life fighting crime. In particular, she'd been running her own personal war against drugs. In her opinion, drug crime was the worst crime there was. It destroyed people's lives; turned addicts into criminals. Most break and enters, robberies and assaults were committed by drug users, to say nothing of murders.

If Flynn was part of that scene, even on the fringes, all bets were off. She'd pursue him just as doggedly as she'd pursued her father and she wouldn't stop until they were both in jail.

"We've been doing some surveillance on the Craigdon men," Brian said, giving her a searching look.

Her cheeks heated with embarrassment. She avoided his gaze.

Oh, God. Does he know about the bike ride? The interlude on the beach?

She was grateful when he continued to speak.

"So far, we've seen nothing untoward in their behavior. No secret meetings with known dealers. No suspicious drop-offs. We've also tapped their phones. Again, nothing. It seems they lead perfectly boring lives. It appears it was only Henry who was involved." Brian grimaced. "The lucky bastard got away with it. His crimes died with him."

"At least we still have my father in our sights." Jayde showed him the photos and videos she'd taken on her phone. "Apparently, he's expecting another shipment tonight," she added.

Brian watched the footage with interest. When he was finished, he gave her a nod of approval. "You've done good. Well done. Get us more like this and we'll soon have enough to arrest him."

Jayde eyed him solemnly. "Consider it done."

As Brian departed, she walked back into her bedroom and set the dossier of information on the desk beside her bed. She was relieved to discover Brian and the other investigators had found nothing against the Craigdon men. She was quietly hopeful that meant they were in the clear. That her gut instincts hadn't been wrong. With a bit of luck, she was done with looking closely at the Cragidons, once and for all.

Chapter Sixteen

Flynn had stopped pretending he could focus on the application for an injunction that sat in front of him and instead found himself driving toward Balmoral. He needed to see Jayde. He had to know the truth. He wouldn't involve Noah. He'd go to her and put it to her straight out. He hoped to God she was honest and that any explanation she offered was believable.

With many businesses still closed for the holiday period, the traffic on the bridge wasn't as heavy as usual. He pulled into the Beaches parking lot in less than half an hour after leaving the city. He'd taken a gamble she'd be in.

He pushed open the door and gazed over the heads of several patrons, seeking her out. A nineties pop song was playing on the jukebox. Several people were seated at the booths that lined one wall. His gaze scanned the bar. He didn't see her.

"Shit," he cursed. He still didn't have her number. He had no way to contact her.

And then she appeared from beneath the bar, holding a bag of ice. She'd been bent over and out of sight when he'd looked the first time. He breathed a sigh of relief. He'd come this far and he was fired up. He was determined not to leave without answers to his questions.

"Flynn," she said, greeting him with a smile.

He hadn't spoken to her since they'd had sex, but his only response was to glare at her. He wanted to make it clear this wasn't a social call.

Her eyes widened in surprise. She looked uncertain and confused. Her eyes asked him a question. He indicated with his head that he needed to speak with her in private. Wisely, she didn't argue. Instead, she returned the bag of ice to the freezer, spoke to her colleague and came around to Flynn's side of the bar.

"Let's go upstairs," she murmured and started across the room.

Flynn followed behind her. She opened the same door they'd entered before and started up the stairs. When they reached the top, she unlocked another door and stepped inside her apartment. He followed her.

She turned to him with her hands on her hips, her expression somber. "What's the matter?" she asked in a no-nonsense tone.

He'd come there for answers, but he wasn't sure where to start. As upset as he was about the possibility she was involved in the drug trade, he believed in the tenet of their legal system that someone was innocent until proven guilty. He'd give her a chance to explain.

"Your father is John Hassad."

She looked bemused. "Yes. I don't think that's a secret. I already told you my brother was named after him. That's why we called him Junior."

He continued to stare at her, feeling grim. "I've been told your father's a kingpin drug dealer. Is that right?"

Some of the color left her cheeks. She blinked a couple of times. No doubt she was surprised he'd discovered that information.

"Is that right?" he repeated, intent on getting an answer.

Slowly, she nodded. "Yes, that's right."

He looked at her in horror. "What the *hell?* You *know* he's a drug dealer! What are you doing here, working for him?"

"Flynn, it's not what you think." Her posture was stiff, uncompromising.

His anger got the better of him. "You know he's a drug dealer, and yet you work for him. How do I know you're not involved in selling for him? It would be so easy, using the bar as a ruse. It's the perfect cover."

She stood there calmly. It only infuriated him further. He dragged a hand through his hair. "I can't believe it! I didn't even see it! Didn't suspect you for an instant!"

"Flynn! Please! You're wrong! I'm aware of my father's reputation and how he makes his money, but I've had nothing to do with that. My brother died from a drug overdose! I can't abide anything to do with drugs! How can you think I'd not only condone the sale of them, but actively take part in it?"

Flynn stared at her. "I don't believe you. No barmaid that I've ever known could afford a bike like that!"

Jayde's breath came fast. She held on to her temper by her fingernails. She understood how Flynn might jump to conclusions after discovering her father's true line of work, but she'd done nothing to deserve his accusations.

She glared at him. "How *dare* you! I saved for *years* for that bike! Every single penny came from my honest, hard work."

At the ferocity of her response, he backed off a little. His breath sounded harsh in the silence. He stalked forward a few paces and then spun around and stalked back. It was as if he wasn't sure what to say or what to think. She could feel his frustration and confusion. A part of her couldn't believe the irony that he'd once been firmly in her sights for the very same reason. Now he thought *she* was the one involved in drugs.

"Flynn," she said in a calmer voice. "It's true I've always been aware of my father's involvement with illegal drugs. Some of my earliest memories are of him sitting at our kitchen table, weighing powder and counting pills. I remember asking him about them once. He told me they were happy pills. I asked him if I could have one. He said I was happy enough."

Flynn's expression turned bleak. "How old were you?"

"Three or four."

"Hell."

"My mother eventually gave him an ultimatum: Either he give up what he was doing or they were done."

"I remember you told me your parents divorced," Flynn murmured.

"Yes. My father took my brother with him when he left."

"That must have been tough. I can't imagine growing up without my brothers…being separated from them."

"Yes. I mourned Junior like he was dead. I'd also effectively lost my father. It was twenty years before I saw either of them again. Six months after I reconnected with them, Junior was dead from an overdose."

Her voice hitched as the sad memories bombarded her. Flynn was immediately by her side. His earlier anger forgotten, he pulled her into his arms and held her close. She took comfort from his warmth and his strength. Tears she'd long since held at bay burned behind her eyes and then spilled over. She blinked furiously in an effort to stem the flow.

The tears fell softly, sliding down her cheeks. She cried quietly, soaking his shirt. When she was done, he handed her a clean handkerchief.

"Thank you," she murmured and turned away so she could wipe her face and blow her nose.

When she was done, she turned back to him and sighed. "Where was I?"

"You were explaining about your father. What I don't

understand is, if you always knew what he was, why did you come and work for him?"

She looked at him a long time and debated about what to tell him. There was no way she could tell him the truth. She was an undercover officer in the midst of an active operation. She'd blow the whole thing wide open if she said anything. So she told him what she could and hoped it would be enough.

"My mother died last year, right before Christmas. After her death, I vowed to seek out my brother. I found him living and working with my father at Beaches. I naïvely thought we could make up for lost time."

She offered a sad smile. "What I didn't realize was he was already an addict. And why wouldn't he be? He had a ready supply of drugs right under his nose. I don't even know if my father made him pay for them. Not that it would have stopped him. By the time I came back into his life, he was already too far gone. He would have found the money for the drugs, or stolen it."

"And your father didn't care?"

"No, I don't think he did. He came to Junior's funeral, but I didn't see him shed a tear. Not even one. It was like he'd completely disconnected. He came straight back here after the service. The wake was held here. Only a handful of people turned up. I didn't know any of them. Dad went right back to work, as if nothing had happened. I heard him later on the phone telling someone he needed another runner. I left soon after."

She looked him straight in the eye. "I can't force you to believe me, but I give you my word, Flynn. I've *never* had a part in my father's business. I detest everything about illegal drugs and I'll do whatever I can to see him behind bars. I don't care that he's my father. He lost the right to call himself that when he walked out on me and my mother. The only thing driving me now is to avenge the death of my brother."

Flynn listened to Jayde's words and his heart went out to her. He didn't know how he'd ever imagined she could be part of the illegal drug trade. It was obvious how distraught she still was about her brother and even more obvious how determined she was to see her father go down.

He thought about his uncle. Many years earlier, when Flynn was still a teenager, Henry had approached him about selling E's at school. Flynn had been shocked. Not only about the discovery his uncle was a dealer, but that he wanted Flynn to sell them to his friends. Flynn had quickly turned him down and hurried from the room.

To his relief, his uncle never approached him again. Flynn hadn't told anyone about it, neither his father, his mother, nor his brothers. Still, he'd never forgotten it. All these years later, the memory still had the power to upset him.

Jayde must have noticed something in his expression. She frowned. "Flynn? What is it?"

He looked at her for a long moment, debating about whether to tell her. And then he decided he would. He liked her. Really liked her. Probably more than that. If they were ever to have a chance together, she needed to know everything. He didn't want there to be secrets between them.

"My uncle was a drug dealer. I don't know the extent of it, but he was definitely involved in the scene."

To his surprise, Jayde barely reacted to his announcement. She continued to regard him somberly. Then she asked, "How do you know?"

He told her about Henry approaching him in high school and how he'd turned his uncle down.

"And that was it? He didn't approach you again?"

"No."

"Did you say anything? Tell anyone?"

"No."

"Why not?'

Flynn shrugged and looked away. "I don't know. I guess I was shocked, scared, confused. I didn't know what to think. I just wanted to forget about it; pretend it never happened."

She nodded slowly and his shoulders slumped in relief. He'd told her his deepest secret and she hadn't run screaming from the room.

"I already knew about your uncle."

Her words fell into the silence and startled a gasp from him. "You knew? How?"

"From my father. He told me Henry was his best customer. He'd sell drugs to your uncle at wholesale and Henry would up-sell them through his own network of dealers. My father had his business on the north side of the city. Your father was established in the east. They agreed not to infringe on each other's turf. It seemed to work."

Flynn stared at her in disbelief. Though he'd known firsthand his uncle was involved in drugs, he'd had no idea it had been as advanced and structured as that. A part of him had hoped his uncle's involvement hadn't extended beyond a few pills. It was clear that wasn't the case. It was also clear Henry's drug dealings had gone on for a long time. It had been fifteen years or so since Henry had approached him.

"Did your father talk about my uncle's death?" he asked.

"Of course. He was disappointed he'd lost his most valuable customer."

"So my uncle was dealing, right up until his death?"

"That's what I understood from my father."

Flynn shook his head slowly from side to side, still trying to come to terms with the afternoon's revelations. He caught Jayde looking at him with an uncertain look on her face.

"What is it?" he asked.

She bit her lip and appeared to be weighing up whether to respond.

He took her hand and squeezed it. "Please, Jayde. Whatever it is, I can take it. I don't want any secrets between us."

A look of panic flashed across her face, but slowly she began to speak.

"I'm not sure if you know about this already, but just in case you don't… I think you have a right to know."

"Know what?"

"It's about your mother."

He frowned. "My mother? What's my mother got to do with anything? She's been dead ten years."

Jayde nodded, her expression grim. "Yes."

"Go on," Flynn urged.

Jayde relayed the story her father had told her about the car accident that had taken Flynn's mother's life.

Flynn made an impatient sound in the back of his throat. "I know about this. Uncle Henry was behind the wheel."

"Yes. But what you might not know is that he was drunk when the accident happened."

Flynn gasped in shock. "No! That's not possible! He would have been breath-tested at the scene. And if not then, later. At the station. Your information's wrong."

Jayde merely shrugged. "You might be right. I have nothing to back it up. Only what my father told me. But he knew your uncle well. My father had been out drinking with your uncle the same night your mother died."

Flynn shook his head. "No," he said firmly. "I don't believe it. It was an accident. A terrible accident. Just like Uncle Henry said."

Jayde held up her hands in a sign of surrender. "Like I said. I only know what my father told me. I can't vouch for the accuracy, or otherwise. I just thought you should know."

Flynn refused to believe his uncle had been drunk behind the wheel. There was no way he would have gotten away with it.

Besides, if he'd been drinking surely he would have owned up to that. It had cost Flynn's mother her life.

Then an insidious thought intruded and he couldn't set it aside.

Was that the reason Uncle Henry left me and Noah a million dollars? Was it guilt money? But what about Logan? He'd been gifted a billion-dollar company. How did that fit in?

It's ironic," Jayde continued with a tiny smile.

"What is?"

"That you suspected me of being part of the illegal drug trade. I wondered the same thing about you and your cousins."

Once again, Flynn was shocked. "How could you think that?"

"Like I said, your uncle was my father's best customer. It's a natural conclusion to draw."

Flynn silently agreed.

"So, here we are," Jayde said softly. "You know about my father and I know about your uncle. Both of us deny being involved. The way I see it, we have two choices. We can choose to believe each other, or not. It's that simple."

Flynn stared at her. All of a sudden, the air between them felt charged. He moved closer and reached out to cup her cheek.

"Nothing about you is simple," he whispered. Before he could stop himself, he leaned in and kissed her.

Chapter Seventeen

Flynn felt her initial surprise, but seconds later she came alive in his arms. Like a switch being flicked, she kissed him back with a passion that matched his own. Her arms crept up around his neck and she held him as close as he held her. They devoured each other with their lips, their hands, their tongues. He pressed his erection against the softness of her belly. She cradled his cock with her pelvis.

With frantic haste, they peeled off their clothes and tossed them to the floor. When they were both naked, Flynn lifted her in his arms. Her legs came around his hips. She clung to him, kissing him, loving him.

He stumbled into her bedroom and lowered her down to the bed. He followed her down and covered her body with his. She brought his head back down to hers and kissed him like she couldn't get enough. His lips, his cheeks, his eyelids. Her mouth was everywhere. Her fingers tangled in his hair. She moved beneath him, moaning with need. Her uninhibited lovemaking drove him wild.

He was so hard he thought he might explode, but he wasn't ready for this to be over. Their coupling on the beach had been over way too soon. This time, with the comfort of a mattress beneath them, he wanted to take things slowly. With that thought in mind, he kissed his way down her sternum and then paused at each of her breasts. He kneaded the soft flesh with his fingers and then bent to take her nipple in his mouth. It pebbled under his tongue and he sucked and licked and tasted. She made little mewling sounds of need.

"You like that?" he rasped.

She nodded and let out a breathy sigh. He turned his attention to her other breast and loved it in the same way. She moved restlessly beneath him. Her hand stole between their bodies and closed around his cock. The warmth and strength in her fingers was indescribable.

Her fingers opened and closed around his erection, stroking him in rhythm with his tongue. He licked and sucked her nipples. Her hand clenched and unclenched his cock. Burning with need, it was all he could do not to plunge inside and seek relief in her moist warmth. But he wasn't finished yet.

Pulling gently out of her hold, he slid further down her body. Kissing his way across her stomach, he arrived at the juncture of her thighs. He buried his head against her womanhood, soft, silky and smooth. Dipping his tongue into her sweetness, he traced the line of her slit.

"Flynn!" she gasped, coming half off the bed.

He paused and looked up at her. She was flushed. Her chest rose and fell with her rapid breaths.

"Is it okay?" he asked.

"Yes," she breathed. "It feels amazing. I… No one's ever done that to me."

He was filled with a surge of triumph, coupled with a tenderness he'd never felt before. Of all the women he'd had pass through his life, none had made him feel like she did. He wanted to protect her, keep her safe, love her for all time.

Love? Surely not.

Still, he wouldn't deny what he felt for Jayde was stronger than anything he'd ever felt before. He didn't know if it was love, but it was strange and unfamiliar and exciting—and that scared him half to death.

With his lips and tongue, he explored her innermost places, sweet and silky, like warm honey. She was a drug. He craved her taste. He couldn't get enough. When he couldn't stand it a moment longer, he lifted his head and moved back up to cover her body with his.

"Please, Flynn. I want you."

Her eyes were wide and pleading. Her words were husky with need. A surge of blood rushed to his cock and nearly brought him undone.

"Condom?" he rasped.

"In the top drawer."

He reached across to the bedside table and pulled out a foil packet. Ripping it open with his teeth, he sheathed himself and then positioned himself between her thighs. He entered her slowly, inch by incredible inch. Then she reached for him and pulled him down on top of her and his control snapped.

He plunged into her the rest of the way and the force of it snatched their breaths. She felt wonderful. Hot and tight and wet. And then he started moving, thrusting in and out. She met each thrust eagerly, clinging to him, urging him on.

And then he was there, at the cliff-face, hanging for a split second in time. He heard her cry out and felt her muscles contract around his cock and he could hold back no longer. With a shout of triumph, he surged forward and emptied himself inside her. He collapsed on top of her, breathing hard. She soothed him with soft strokes of her fingers through his hair and murmured sounds of comfort.

Afterward, he rolled off her and drew her against his side. He pressed a kiss against her temple and had almost drifted off to sleep when she shook him by the shoulder.

"Flynn. I have to get back to work."

"*Mm*," he said. He was so comfortable, so relaxed. "Stay."

"I can't stay. I have work to do. It's going to get busy downstairs. I need to be there." Amidst more mumbled protests from Flynn, she climbed out of bed. A moment later, he heard the sound of the shower.

Rolling over, he pulled himself upright and hunted around for his clothes. He pulled on his boxers and suit pants. Looking around for his shirt, he spied a thick file on her desk. The name "Craigdon" was written across the front of it in big bold letters.

His gut clenched with surprise. Dread flooded through his veins. Walking closer, he opened the file and began to flip through the contents. Page after page of handwritten notes, photographs, bank statements and so much more. He stared at them, uncomprehending and then realization set in.

From some distant part of his mind, he heard the shower shut off. A moment later, Jayde appeared, wrapped in a towel. She took one look at the file in his hand and her gaze flew to his face.

"Flynn… Oh, God… Flynn… Let me explain."

He rounded on her, angry and incredulous. "Explain? About what? That you've been spying on me? On all of us?"

He shook his head, trying to clear it of shock and then came at her again. "Who the fuck are you?"

"You know who I am."

"Bullshit. All I know is I've been taken in by a lying, scheming woman who's used her face and body to get me exactly where she wants me. Unsuspecting. Off-balance. Thinking with nothing but my cock. It's just like Christopher said."

She frowned. "Christopher? What does he have to do with this?"

Flynn glared at her. "Forget that. All I want to know is *why?*"

They stared at each other, at a stalemate. His breath came fast, the sound of it harsh in the silence of the room. It was clear there was something going on that he had no idea about. No one compiled a detailed dossier of information on someone's family unless they were up to no good.

With a fresh wave of anger overwhelming him, he narrowed his eyes at her. "Tell me the truth. I deserve that at least. Who are you and what the fuck are you doing messing around with my family?"

Jayde regarded him calmly, but the rapid rising and falling of her chest gave her away. She lifted her head and stared him down.

"I'm sorry, Flynn. You need to leave."

He clenched his jaw. "I'm not going anywhere until you tell me what the hell is going on!"

"I can't do that. I want you to go."

"No."

"*Go!*" she shouted and then pushed him toward the door.

He stumbled, shocked. It was obvious she wasn't going to tell him anything. Short of forcing it out of her, he had no choice but to leave.

Fine.

He'd find out some other way about who the hell she was and why she was spying on his family.

Nick did his best not to appear apprehensive as he looked at the huge Russian who sat across from him. Igor Petrov was massive, from his huge biceps covered in tattoos, to his bald head and equally broad shoulders. His chest was twice the size of Nick's and even under his work clothes, Nick could tell the man was pure muscle. He looked like a bouncer, or a personal security guard for some celebrity. He looked like someone you didn't want to get on the wrong side of.

Still, Nick refused to be intimidated. He'd called Igor there for a reason. The man was the only employee on Henry's list who still worked at Craigdon Enterprises. Nick wanted to know why.

He offered what he hoped was a friendly smile. "Thanks for coming in, Igor. I know you're busy out at that Parramatta job site."

The Russian merely inclined his head and regarded Nick with pale blue eyes. Nick nervously cleared his throat.

"The reason I asked you to come in, is because I have a few questions. I've been talking to a number of my father's former employees. I believe they're all known to you."

He picked up the pages he'd found in his father's safe and began to read off some of the names. He glanced at Igor to ascertain his reaction, but the man's face remained cold and expressionless.

Nick forged on. "I asked around the jobsites about these men. No one had heard of them. I thought that was strange, so I tracked down as many of them as I could find. When I confronted them with the facts, that they'd never worked on a Craigdon jobsite, one by one, they folded. They told me they were drug dealers, moving gear at my father's request. They were quite open about it. I guess they know that with my father's death, they're unlikely to get prosecuted. After all, where's the proof?"

He looked at Igor. "I understand you were part of that operation, too."

If he expected a confession, he was sorely disappointed. Igor barely blinked. Nick tried again.

"These men all nominated you as their leader. Are you telling me they were lying?"

Igor continued to regard him in silence with those unsettling, pale blue eyes. Then he flexed his muscles. Nick tried not to squirm. Holding onto his courage, he took a surreptitious breath and tried again.

"See, here's what I think. My father was using this

company as a cover to launder drug money. He hired men like you and the others on this list to offload his gear and he paid you through the company books. It all looked completely legitimate. In fact, if he hadn't kept this list of names, I would never have suspected anything. It was a brilliant plan, but my father was a stickler for details. He always kept meticulous records. It was his undoing."

Anger flared in Igor's eyes. He spoke with heavily accented English. "You think you're so smart, but you don't know shit. Your father was a brilliant man. You…" His lip curled up in disgust. "You are nothing."

Nick felt a familiar stab of hurt and then quickly pushed it away. He was done with accepting criticism—especially from the likes of Petrov. The man was a drug dealer. The lowest form of scum. Nick was a good and decent man. He was smart, decisive and a hell of a lot more compassionate than his father had ever been.

Petrov was a criminal who profited from the destruction of other people's lives. It angered Nick that Igor would no doubt get away with what he'd done. Unless Nick could find something concrete to pin on him. It was obvious Igor wasn't going to admit to anything. There was no point in wasting any more time. They were done.

"Get your stuff and get out, Igor. Your time at Craigdon Enterprises is over. You'll get two weeks' severance pay in lieu of notice and you want to feel grateful I'm even giving you that."

Igor's cheeks flushed with anger. He pushed back his chair and stood. Nick followed suit. The Russian towered over Nick and outweighed him by more than a hundred pounds. Nick resisted the urge to take a step back.

The man eyeballed him. His breath hissed between his teeth. His eyes glowered with hate. "You're going to regret this, Craigdon. Mark my words." With that, the Russian turned and left.

Shaken, Nick sat back down and took a moment to gather his wits. Firing Petrov had been a stupid move, but Nick had lost his temper. The words had fallen out. The man was trouble. There was no way the Russian wasn't involved. The question was, was it still going on?

It was imperative Nick find out. There was no way he'd stand for Craigdon Enterprises being mixed up in the awful business of drugs. Not only was it illegal, it had the potential to destroy so many lives. To watch someone annihilate themselves over drugs was heartbreaking. Though Nick didn't have any personal experience, he'd seen his fair share of addicts at Jennifer's Kitchen. Callum had once told him how drugs were a scourge on society and it was an ongoing problem that nobody in government seemed willing or able to fix.

But that didn't mean Nick didn't have options when it came to Craigdon Enterprises. He was sure he'd have Logan's full support in weeding out the drug culture Nick's father had apparently encouraged—not only encouraged, but actually participated in and rewarded. It was time for it to stop. Starting with Igor Petrov.

With that thought in mind, Nick reached for his phone and called Joel. His brother was a detective and though he worked in the fraud squad, it was possible he had connections to someone in the DEA. Joel answered on the third ring.

"Hey, Nick. What's happening?"

Nick asked him if he knew of a man by the name of Igor Petrov.

"Sure do. He's on a police watch list. Has been for some time. He's thought to have connections to the Russian mafia. Why do you ask?"

Nick sighed. Using as few words as possible, he filled Joel in.

"What the fuck? Are you sure?"

Nick understood Joel's shock. He'd felt the same way when he realized what had been going on.

"Yeah," he said, his tone grim. "I've spoken to some of Dad's employees. They confirmed my suspicions. They were ostensibly employed as laborers, but all they did was sell drugs. When you look at some of these guys, it's plain to see they're telling the truth. Many of them are addicts. There's no way they were legitimate employees."

"Shit." Joel sounded dazed.

"Igor was Dad's foreman. He was in charge of all of these 'workers.' I just confronted him about it and he denied everything, but if the police think he has connections to the Russian mafia, I'm even more certain I'm on the right track."

"Are these dealers still working for the company?"

"No. They left after Dad died. I'm hoping that means the apparently flourishing drug trade inside Craigdon Enterprises died with their departure. Only Igor remained. I pulled out his personnel file. It appears he actually *is* a qualified concreter. He was legitimately employed as a foreman on Dad's building sites. Somewhere along the way, he and Dad got involved in the selling of drugs."

"Hell. I can't believe it. Dad…dealing drugs! It's inconceivable."

"Yeah. I still can't work out why. I mean, the company was always successful. Dad made a fortune on legitimate enterprises. I don't understand what lured him into the drug trade."

"He always loved the thrill of the chase, and he could never have too much money. He used to tell us that all the time."

"Yeah. I used to think he was just trying to justify his regular absences."

Joel sighed. "So what are you going to do about your discovery?"

"I'm going to tell the police. I want them to investigate. Find out if it's still going on. Maybe you could help me there?"

"Sure. I can contact someone in the DEA. I'll ask them to give you a call. Will that do?"

"Yes. Thanks." Nick paused. "I guess I'll have to tell the rest of the family. No doubt they'll be as shocked as we are. We had no idea about any of this… I can't imagine how Mom's going to take it."

"She's a strong woman. She lived with Dad all those years. She's made from stern stuff. She'll be fine but she's been through some tough times lately."

"I hope this news doesn't set her back…."

"Give me a day or two," Joel said. "I'll make sure the information gets to the right people. It will then be up to them."

"Thanks, Joel. I really appreciate it."

"No worries, mate. That's what brothers are for, right?"

Chapter Eighteen

It was way past late and Jayde was tired. Her back was sore and her feet were aching. On top of that was the knowledge Flynn was somewhere hurting—furious even—and there was nothing she could do about it.

She finished pouring a beer and handed it to the last remaining customer. He gave her a twenty-dollar note.

"Keep the change darlin'," he said and then winked.

"Drink up," she said. "We're closing."

She opened the till and put the money inside. Apart from her solo drinker, Beaches was empty. In a rare moment, her father had arrived just before closing time and had wiped over the tables and lifted the chairs off the floor. All that was left was for her to mop it.

It had been a busy night. Despite the fact she'd been run off her feet, her mind kept straying to Flynn. She hadn't planned to tell him about Henry being drunk behind the wheel. Somehow, it had just come out. His reaction had been so distressing that she'd refrained from adding anything further to his pain. Besides, it was only on her father's say-so that Henry and Janelle had been romantically involved. Best not to inflame matters unnecessarily. Relations between her and Flynn right now were fragile enough.

She cursed herself again for forgetting about the file she'd left on her desk. It had been there for months. When she and Flynn had gone into her bedroom, it had been the furthest thing from her mind. Now she'd pay the price.

As much as she'd wanted to tell him everything, she couldn't. She might have cleared him and his family of suspicion, but there were other things at stake. Namely, the ongoing investigation into her father. Over the months, she'd slowly gained his trust. The taskforce was close to a breakthrough. She was sure of it. But they needed more time. There was no way she was going to jeopardize an investigation that had been years in the making. Flynn would have to wait.

Her phone began to vibrate in the pocket of her jeans. She reached in and pulled it out and checked the screen.

Brian.

She hadn't spoken to him since their last meeting—when they'd all but decided the Craigdon family was in the clear. Now she wondered what he was calling about. Moving out of earshot of her father, she answered the call.

"Brian. How are you?"

"Jayde. I'm glad I caught you. There's been a development."

Jayde's heart skipped a beat. "Does it have anything to do with the Craigdons?"

"Yes."

Icy dread trickled through her veins. She sent a silent prayer heavenward that it didn't involve Flynn. "What is it?"

"One of the guys just had a call from Joel Craigdon. He's a detective with—"

"The fraud squad," she interrupted impatiently. "Yeah, I know. I looked into him. He doesn't have anything to do with the family company. He's just a cop. I dismissed him as a suspect early on."

"Right. This isn't about Joel. The thing is, he called the

DEA with information about his father's company. In particular, about Igor Petrov."

Brian paused and let the name sink in. Jayde's pulse leaped. "Petrov? As in the Russian drug boss?"

"Yes. We haven't been able to pin anything on him yet, but we've been watching him for a while. We knew he was employed at Craigdon Enterprises and suspected his involvement with drugs. Apparently Nicholas Craigdon has discovered evidence to this effect, but so far Petrov is denying everything. Both Craigdons are keen for the police to get involved. They want to make sure no one on the Craigdon payroll's dealing drugs."

"It sounds like we're all on the same side," Jayde said, her tension easing.

"Yes. I think we can probably assume the relatives of Henry Craigdon are not, and have never been, involved."

Jayde eased out a sigh of relief. Though things between her and Flynn were far from settled, at least she no longer had to worry he might be a criminal. And then she remembered something else.

Petrov…

She glanced behind her and saw her father was on the far side of the room. She lowered her voice to a whisper. "Brian, there's a possibility this Petrov might be working with my father. The night I filmed them taking possession of that shipment of cocaine, I overheard Dad speaking. He mentioned something about a Petrov."

"Are you sure?"

"Yes."

"That doesn't necessarily mean it's the same guy, but still… This is good, Jayde. You've done well. Thanks."

"You're welcome."

From the corner of her eye, she saw her father closing the door behind the last patron. Instead of locking it, as she expected, he stepped outside. A few moments later, the door opened again. Curious, Jayde watched as her father and the man she recognized as Dimitri talked in hushed tones.

Quickly, she ended the call and gave the men her full attention. Like the last time he'd appeared, Dimitri carried a large Styrofoam box. Jayde froze momentarily as the implications set in. She thought fast. Tapping on the record button, she tucked her phone back into her jeans. Plastering a bored expression on her face, she sauntered toward them.

She fought to keep her tone casual. "What's going on?"

Her father looked at her. "I'm taking delivery of my latest shipment." He pointed to the box. "Inside there's powder with a street value of more than three million dollars!"

Jayde forced herself to smile. "Wow. That's a lot of drugs."

"Yeah, and an even greater amount of money. Three million bucks is not to be sneezed at."

"Hell, no. I might have to ask for a raise." She grinned.

Her father grinned back. "And I might just give it to you."

To her relief, this time he let her stay while he paid Dimitri in thick wads of cash taken from the safe behind the bar. After Dimitri left, her father turned to her.

"Give me a hand to store these, will you?"

Not waiting for her reply, he picked up the box and took it over near the restrooms, where she'd seen him take the previous box. Closing the distance between them, she held the box while he removed the rug that lay across the floor and revealed the trapdoor beneath.

She forced a chuckle and let her face fill with admiration. "Not a bad hiding spot, Dad."

He winked. "It's where they used to store the kegs in the old days. It does the trick."

Surreptitiously, she slid her phone out of her pocket. Pretending to check her emails, she made sure the phone was still recording and then stowed her phone away. The video footage would be useless, but she hoped to capture some incriminating audio.

She gave her father another disarming smile. "I can't believe you're still doing this. After all these years. Some of my earliest memories are of you counting money and cutting drugs. Aren't you scared you might get caught? You could go to jail!"

Her father scoffed. "Ha! I'm too clever to get caught! I've been doing this for thirty years. Probably more. I haven't been caught yet."

He gave her another wink. "The trick is to set up a legitimate business and run it all above board. That's why I bought Beaches. Everything's done by the letter of the law. Then you can fly under the radar. Employ dealers on the books. Move money in and out. It works a treat. Just ask Henry Craigdon."

She frowned in mock confusion. "I thought Henry Craigdon was dead?"

"Yeah, of course. But before that. I showed him how to do it. It was because of me that he grew so big. The biggest dealer in the eastern suburbs. No one else came close."

"Where do you get your supplies?"

"All over. A lot of it comes in by boat. That was the good thing about Henry. He didn't mind helping me out. We'd help each other. In the early days, he had his own suppliers and I had mine, but every now and then if one of us ran short, we'd borrow gear off the other until we could make good on it again."

"I thought you said Henry was your biggest customer?"

"He was. Over the years, he got lazy. I guess he was getting old. He had quite a few years on me. A lot of the time he preferred to pay me a premium for my gear, rather than seek out his own supply." Her father shrugged as if it were of no consequence. "Hell, I didn't mind. As long as someone paid me for the shit, I didn't care who I sold it to."

He turned back to the trapdoor and bent to lift the door away, revealing an opening beneath. Using his phone to light the way, he reached once again for the box. Jayde handed it to him. As he descended into the darkness, she pulled out her phone and took some footage.

A light flickered on, illuminating the staircase. "Are you all right down there, Dad?" she called.

"All good. I won't be long. Just checking on a few things down here. I stocked up over Christmas. I want to see what's left. No good having the gear sitting here going to waste. It doesn't make me any money sitting on the shelf."

Afterward, back in her apartment, Jayde went through the audio and video she'd captured. Though the video was dark and grainy, the audio was as clear as could be. She smiled.

This is good. This is really good.

Better still, it was obvious there were even more drugs stored underground. If the police acted quickly, they could catch him red-handed. Coupled with the other evidence they had, it would be enough to put him away for many years.

Opening a new email, she addressed it to her handler. She attached the footage and then typed a quick message. The reply came back to her a few moments later.

Good stuff. We're putting together an arrest team as we speak. What time does your father usually arrive there in the morning?

Jayde read the message and her stomach clenched with nerves. She emailed a reply.

Eight.

It was late, but despite the fatigue etching into his bones, Flynn was restless. He'd returned to work after his visit with Jayde, but concentrating on the arguments printed on the pages in front of him was beyond him. His client was seeking an urgent injunction. She was fearful her children were in danger from their father and wanted to ensure they didn't have to spend the scheduled time with him come New Year's Day, pursuant to the existing custody orders.

Flynn's client had made serious allegations against the father of her children. In his affidavit in response, the father vehemently denied them and had tossed out some accusations of his own. Flynn had lost count of the number of times he's seen this kind of tit for tat, especially around the holiday season. It was meant to be a time of goodwill and good cheer. In his experience, it only brought out the worst in warring parents.

Flynn leaned back against his chair and sighed. He ought to be home, having a drink, relaxing on his balcony. At the very least, he ought to be putting his time at the office to good use formulating the arguments he meant to present to the court the next day. But neither of those options held any appeal. He couldn't concentrate and the last thing he wanted to do was go home to his empty apartment.

His mind kept circling back to Jayde. The discovery that his uncle might have been under the influence of alcohol at the time of the deadly crash had stunned him. He still wasn't quite sure what to believe. After all, the information had come from Jayde's father. It was hearsay at its highest. Still, the possibility was troubling and raised questions he'd wondered about over the years along with some new ones he'd never considered. Such as, why his mother had been with Henry in the first place that fateful night.

And then there was the thick file of information Jayde had obviously collected on the Craigdons. He still couldn't work out the motive behind that. She'd told him she'd suspected he might be involved in the drug business, like his uncle.

Is that the reason she'd compiled so much detailed information? Had she thought the Craigdons were competition, a threat to her father's empire?

But that didn't make sense. Jayde had been adamant she

despised everything there was about illegal drugs. She'd appeared so genuine in her distress about the whole thing. Had she been lying about that?

And what's with her refusal to offer him an explanation? What does she have to hide?

The sound of his phone ringing interrupted his frustrated thoughts. He dug it out of his pocket and checked the screen.

Noah.

His heart leaped guiltily. It shamed him to realize he hadn't spoken to his brother since Noah had seen him and Jayde together in Manly on Christmas Day. Flynn had avoided the usual Christmas dinner with his father and brothers. He hadn't been ready to face Noah. Besides, Jayde had asked to speak with Noah first and he'd honored her wishes.

The thing was, though, Jayde had since told him she'd cleared the air with Noah and Flynn still hadn't made contact with him. They lived a few blocks away from each other and yet Flynn hadn't found the time to go and see him. Even now, he debated a few seconds about answering the call and then sighed. He had to front up to Noah sooner or later.

"Noah," he said.

"Flynn."

Noah's tone was low and even. It didn't give Flynn a hint as to how his brother was feeling.

"How are you?" Flynn asked.

"I'm fine."

"Really?"

"Yes, Flynn. I'm fine."

Some of the tension that had gripped Flynn's gut began to ease. He picked up a pen and doodled on the notepad in front of him, wondering which one of them would be first to broach the subject. And then Flynn thought about the other revelations he'd learned. The stuff about Uncle Henry and their mother. The dossier. The drugs.

All of a sudden he wanted to share the information with Noah. He needed his brother's input…and he could do with his support. Flynn was still struggling to come to terms with it all. It would help to talk to someone about it. Someone who'd be equally affected by the news as Flynn was and could understand.

"Hey," he said. "Where are you?"

"At home."

"Do you mind if I come over? I could do with a drink and I don't want to drink alone."

"Since when did a Craigdon have a problem with drinking alone?"

Flynn heard the teasing tone in Noah's voice and smiled. "Okay, smartass. It would be good to see you. Shoot the breeze. Are you up for that?"

There was a moment's hesitation and then Noah said, "Sure."

"See you in half an hour." Flynn ended the call.

Chapter Nineteen

On the way over to Noah's, Flynn took a call from Christopher. He was surprised to hear from his half-cousin, especially so late in the evening. From the pronounced slur in Christopher's voice, it was obvious the man was drunk.

Flynn stemmed his irritation. "Christopher. What's up?"

"I jussh wanted to let you know… The lawshuit… I've changed my mind…"

Flynn sat up straighter in his seat. "You're dropping the suit against the estate? Is that what you're trying to say?"

"No. Not dropping it. But I've lowered my priesh. Eighty-five million. It'sh a fair deal."

"Eighty-five million!" Flynn scoffed. "Why bother? You might as well have left it at one hundred. What difference does fifteen million make?"

"A lot of differench!" Christopher replied, sounding insulted. "Fifteen million dollarsh ish a lot of money! You ought to be pleashed I'm prepared to negotiate."

Flynn shook his head, tiring of the conversation. "Look, Christopher. You were dudded by your father. No one's arguing against that. You deserve to be recognized as his son. You also deserve a portion of his estate. Whether that's one hundred million or eighty-five is irrelevant. I'd hoped we could have worked something out as a family, but I also understand your need to have your day in court. I'll pass on your offer to the rest of the family, but I'm sure they'll think the same way I do. Now that you've instigated legal action, it's best to leave it to the courts to sort out."

"I thought you'd want to avoid any media attenshion? The presh are going to be mighty intereshted in thish."

Flynn gritted his teeth. He knew from past experience that people like Christopher needed their day in court. Anything less and they felt ripped off.

"You do what you have to do, mate. I'm sure you will anyway." With that, Flynn ended the call.

It was closer to fifty minutes later when Flynn pulled his car into the curb outside Noah's apartment block. Like Flynn's, it was a two-bed, two-bath apartment with ocean views. Flynn would have been just as happy to have his brother living in the same building, but there hadn't been an apartment available at the time his brother was looking. Still, it was convenient having Noah so close.

Flynn pressed the buzzer outside the door to Noah's apartment and waited. A rush of nerves flooded through him. He hoped Noah wouldn't be too cut up about what had happened with Jayde. After all that had gone on since, it seemed so long ago now.

A moment later, Noah stood there before him. He wore a T-shirt and shorts. His hair was mussed. There was an air about him that made Flynn think he might have been asleep. Not that he would have blamed him. It was nearly midnight.

To Flynn's relief, Noah's greeting was friendly enough. The two of them hugged briefly and then Flynn followed Noah down the short hallway and into the open plan living room and kitchen. Unlike Flynn, Noah was spotlessly tidy. There wasn't a dirty plate or glass in the sink. Not a half-eaten pizza on the counter. Not a loaf of stale bread in sight and the garbage can that stood near the fridge was far from overflowing.

Flynn flung himself down on Noah's comfortable sofa. The leather was worn, but it was still Flynn's most favorite spot to sit. He could see the beach through the gauzy curtains that framed the view outdoors. This time of night, it was inky black. There wasn't even a hint of moonlight to illuminate the waves.

"What are you drinking?" Noah asked.

"Got any beer?"

"Will a Corona do?"

"Sounds good."

Noah moved into the kitchen and opened up the fridge. He came back to Flynn carrying two bottles and handed one over.

"Thanks," Flynn said and took the proffered drink. He twisted off the cap and gulped down half the contents.

"Looks like you're thirsty," Noah commented dryly.

Flynn sighed and tilted his head back until it was leaning against the back of the sofa. "Yep. If you'd lived through the last few days I have, you'd understand."

"Is it work?'

"Some of it."

"I thought you guys closed down for Christmas."

"We do. But I had an urgent injunction to file with the court." He shrugged. "Christmas and families—you know how it is."

Noah nodded. "I guess we were lucky we didn't have to go through that kind of shit."

"You bet. I wouldn't wish it on anyone. There are no winners and the biggest losers are the kids. It sucks."

Flynn took another chug of his beer. "That's not all." He sighed. "This might come as a shock, but Uncle Henry was a drug dealer."

Instead of the shocked reaction Flynn expected, Noah merely frowned. "How do you know?"

"Someone told me. Someone reputable. I believe them." Once again, he looked at Noah. "I'm afraid there's more."

"More? As if hearing my uncle was a drug dealer isn't enough?"

Flynn grimaced. "This is about Mom."

Noah tensed and his face went blank. "What about Mom?"

"I've been led to believe Uncle Henry was drunk behind the wheel when Mom was killed in that car accident…"

"*What?*" This time the shock on Noah's face was forthcoming.

"I know. I can't believe it, either."

Noah shook his head. "No, I don't believe it. There's no way we wouldn't have heard all this before, or that he would have gotten away with it. I'm a cop! I know how the system works! Henry would have been breath-tested at the scene. And if not then, back at the station. If he'd been over the limit, he would have been charged with driving offenses, in addition to Mom's death."

Flynn compressed his lips. There was nothing he could say. He'd reacted exactly the same way. "So why wasn't he?"

Noah's expression remained stubborn. "Your information can't be true. Whoever it was who told you, wanted to cause trouble. I don't know why. Only you can know that. But I refuse to believe Uncle Henry was drunk behind the wheel."

Flynn remained silent. He tried to think what advantage Jayde hoped to gain or what she hoped to achieve by passing on incorrect information—especially information as sensitive as that—but he could think of nothing. Unwilling to get into an argument about it, he changed the subject.

"I'm sorry about what happened with Jayde."

Once again, Noah looked tense. He lifted the bottle to his lips and took a few swallows of beer. Then he looked back at Flynn.

"How do you feel about her?" Noah asked.

Flynn averted his gaze. "I don't know. I like her. I like her a lot. But there's something off about her."

Noah frowned. "Off? How do you mean?"

Flynn blew his breath out on a heavy sigh. "She's been spying on us."

The shock on Noah's face reflected the way Flynn had felt when he'd found the dossier.

"What the hell? Spying on us?"

"Yes. I found a file of information she'd gathered together. On us. All of us. Cousins, included."

Noah's frown deepened. "What kind of information?"

Detailed stuff. Personal information. Photographs. Bank statements. It was weird."

"Did you confront her about it?"

Flynn grimaced. "Of course I did."

"What did she say?"

"She refused to discuss it with me."

Noah shook his head, looking bewildered. "You're right. That's strange. What's your take on it?"

Flynn sighed again. "I wish I knew. All I can think of is that she was gathering information on the competition. She thought we might have been involved in Uncle Henry's drug business."

Noah shook his head. "Where would she get that idea?"

"I don't know. But I'm sure as hell not done with this. Jayde Hassad's going to do some explaining, whether she likes it or not."

"Does this affect the way you feel about her?" Noah asked quietly.

Flynn paused and then shook his head. "I wish I could say it did. I'm clinging to the hope she has a reasonable explanation for the file. You're going to find this hard to believe, but... I've fallen in love with her, Noah."

"How does she feel about you?"

Flynn took a moment to recall the way they'd parted. "Before I found that file, I was sure we had something going on between us. Now I'm not so sure."

"I take it things got ugly," Noah mused.

"You could say that." Flynn's expression was so grim Noah looked alarmed.

"You didn't…?"

"No! Of course not! I've never taken my hand to a woman in my life! But I was shocked and angry and confused. I felt like the ground had shifted beneath me. I wanted answers."

"What happened?"

Flynn's lips twisted in another grimace. "She threw me out. We haven't spoken since." He scrubbed a hand through his hair. "I wish I could say that was it for me. That I was done. But I'm not. I still have feelings for her. Strong feelings. What kind of fool does that make me?"

Noah took another sip from his beer. Flynn looked over at him, feeling a little anxious.

"Are you okay with that, Noah? I mean, I know how you feel about her. You're in love with her. I didn't mean to like her. I tried to stay out of your way. I really did."

"It's cool, bro," Noah said.

Flynn sat forward in his seat. "I wish it didn't happen, Noah. She was your girl."

Noah smiled sadly. "She was never my girl, Flynn. I wish you all the best."

Flynn looked at his brother. Noah appeared to be genuine. Flynn sighed heavily. "Thanks, bro. For what it's worth. I appreciate you bowing out so gracefully."

Emotion flared behind Noah's eyes. "Just make sure you treat her right. If you hurt her, you'll answer to me. Got it?"

Flynn held his brother's gaze. "Got it."

Flynn went to bed that night thinking of Jayde. He was glad he'd made his peace with Noah. Flynn always felt his life was off-balance when he'd had a disagreement or he wasn't talking to one of his brothers. It didn't happen often, but when it did, it was always a relief when they reconciled.

Family was important to him. The death of his mother had devastated all of them, including Archie. And even when Flynn had tormented his father with the suggestion Flynn's mother had been having an affair with Henry, neither Archie nor Flynn had believed it for a second.

Janelle Craigdon had been sweet and warm and gentle. She'd always been there for her boys. An encouraging word, a sympathetic ear, a soft shoulder to cry on. She'd loved them unreservedly and they'd loved her back the same. It had been a tragic loss for all of them when she was taken way too soon.

He still couldn't work out what Jayde might have to gain by telling him his uncle had been drunk the night his mom had died. It didn't make sense for her to make up something like that. The only other possibility was that she'd been telling the truth and right now, that was something he couldn't deal with. He had too much of his own shit going on.

What he'd told Noah was correct. He liked Jayde a whole lot. But something was holding him back. He'd wracked his brain as to why she might have been spying on them and still hadn't come up with an acceptable explanation. There was no way she was involved in her father's illegal drug business.

Then what else is she hiding? Why won't she come right out and tell me?

Her refusal to offer him an explanation made him uneasy. He'd fallen in love with her and he was pretty sure she felt the same way. If they were ever to have a chance together, they had to be honest about their past. No secrets. That's the only way it could work.

He had to see her, talk to her, try and make her understand. First thing in the morning, he'd go and see her. If he got to the bar early enough, he could still make it to work on time. Decision made, he fell into a restless sleep.

Jayde didn't think she'd ever been more nervous. Late the evening before, Brian had given her final instructions about the raid. Jayde had tossed and turned all night, thinking over what was about to go down.

A surprise arrest always brought with it inherent dangers. It was impossible to cover every possible scenario. She thought about all the things that could go wrong. Various grim scenarios passed through her head, each one worse than the last. She wondered if her father had any idea this was his last night of freedom. Her only hope was that no one was hurt during the takedown.

She was already up and dressed before the sun rose. She'd gone downstairs and started the jobs she did every morning before opening time. She switched on the lights around the bar. She pulled the chairs off the tables and stood them on the floor. She wiped over counters, checked the fridges, checked the gas lines that ran to the kegs. She was about to refill the ice containers when she heard a knock at the door.

Her gaze turned immediately to the clock on the wall opposite the bar. *Seven-forty-five.* Strange. It couldn't be her father. Not only was it too early for him, he didn't usually knock. It couldn't be the police, either. They weren't due until after eight. And only then when she'd given the signal to confirm her father was on the premises.

The knock came again, a little louder. Jayde crossed the floor and peered through the glass. Her heart skipped a beat. *Flynn.*

Oh, God. What the hell is he doing here? Her father would arrive any minute, followed swiftly by heavily armed police. And then all hell would break loose. She had to get rid of him. Fast.

Releasing the lock, she flung open the door and tried her best to appear normal. "Flynn! What are you doing here?"

He was dressed for work in a suit and tie and looking more gorgeous than any man had a right to. That aside, he needed to leave. Now. She took him by the arm and began to lead him down the steps, away from the bar. Despite putting in all her efforts to keep him moving, he stopped. His superior size and weight meant there was nothing she could do.

Clueless about her motivation, he shot her a panicked look. "Jayde! I just want to talk to you! I promise I won't shout. Finding that file… It surprised me, set me aback. And I'll admit I was angry. Especially when you refused to explain. And then you threw me out. I was furious. It felt like a betrayal. I didn't know what to think. Who to trust. But I've had time to think, time to calm down. Despite everything, I love you. I didn't plan for it to happen, but it did. I love you, Jayde. If there's a chance of something between us, we need to clear the air. Explain what's going on. I'm here because I want to hear you out."

She blinked in shock.

Did he just say he's in love with me?

She wanted to dwell on the giddy feeling of joy that rushed through her. She wanted to throw herself in his arms and say the words right back to him. But time was running out. She grabbed him by the arm again and renewed her efforts to get rid of him.

To her chagrin, once again he dug in his heels. "Did you just hear what I said? Don't you care that I love you?"

She gritted her teeth and flashed him a brilliant smile. "Of course I care. It's just that… I'm a bit busy this morning and I don't have time to think about what you just said. There's plenty we need to talk about before we get into declarations of love. Besides, I'm sure you need to get to work."

"You're right," he said and deliberately shrugged off her hold and began walking back toward the bar. "I'm due in court this morning, but I wanted to see you first. I can't spend another minute with this misunderstanding between us. I haven't been able to concentrate on anything. It's been driving me mad. I want to have this out right here, right now. Okay?"

By then he was all the way back inside and her panic ratcheted up a notch. So much planning had gone into the next few moments… So many officers involved… She couldn't be the reason it failed.

"No, Flynn. It's not okay. Not now. Later."

"But—"

From the corner of her eye she caught sight of her father and her stress levels hit the roof. The time was upon them, only now she had Flynn to deal with. In all the wild scenarios she'd imagined the night before, none of them had included an unexpected visit from the man she loved. Though they'd parted in anger, she was confident they could resolve their differences later. But like she'd told him: Not here. Not now. Not with a raid about to happen.

"Good-morning, Dad! How are you?" She greeted her father with a tight smile.

He merely nodded, his attention focused on Flynn. "Who do we have here?"

Jayde reluctantly made the introductions. "Dad, this is Flynn Craigdon. Flynn, this is my father. John Hassad."

The two men shook hands. Her father eyed Flynn curiously. "Craigdon? Any relation to Henry?"

"Yes. He was my uncle."

"Your uncle, hey? How about that."

Jayde's panic continued to escalate. It was now after eight. The taskforce would be waiting. Tensions would be high.

She couldn't let them down. She had to make the call. Though the last thing she wanted was for Flynn to be caught up in it, she didn't have a choice. Slowly, she eased her phone out of the pocket of her jeans. With heart thumping and her breath coming fast, she hit the SEND button on the text she'd typed earlier.

It was done.

Chapter Twenty

Flynn stared at Jayde and tried to work out what was wrong with her. It wasn't just because her father had turned up, because she'd been acting strange before he'd arrived. Nervous and jumpy and odd. She should have been talking about how they'd parted and maybe offering him a long-overdue explanation.

He'd come there intent on clearing the air. He wasn't going to leave until she'd explained everything. Then he'd tell her how important it was not to keep secrets from each other. Important because he was in love with her and wanted to be with her forever.

It was heavy stuff and only a few weeks ago, he wouldn't have believed it were possible. Flynn Craigdon declaring undying love and wanting to make a commitment to just one woman? It was crazy! Madness! Anyone who knew him would think it were a joke. But it was true and now he'd told her, but she hadn't reacted the way he expected. In fact, she'd all but ignored his declaration. It was downright confusing and annoying.

What the hell's going on?

Jayde stood a short distance away. She looked tense and pale. On edge. There was an air of expectancy about her he just couldn't work out.

What the hell is the matter with her?

And then all hell broke loose.

All of a sudden, he was surrounded by heavily armed police. They charged toward him carrying hard plastic shields, guns and batons at the ready.

"Police! Don't move! Get on the ground!"

He stared around in bewilderment. An overzealous officer ran toward him and swung his baton across Flynn's shins. His legs crumpled under the assault and he fell to the floor, shocked and confused.

What the hell's happening? I've been caught up in some kind of raid…

His next thoughts were of Jayde. *Where is she? Is she okay? God, don't let them hurt her…*

He struggled to his feet. Through the mêlée, he saw John Hassad handcuffed and lying on the floor. It suddenly dawned on Flynn why the police were there.

It's a drug raid…

He found Jayde standing behind the bar. Though she looked grim and resigned, she didn't look surprised.

She'd known… That's why she was acting so weird. She knew…

The thought had barely formed when Flynn was grabbed roughly from behind. A few seconds later, he felt the hard cold steel of handcuffs close around his wrists.

"What the fuck?" he cried, shocked beyond belief.

He tried to twist out of the officer's hold, desperate to get to Jayde. He expected to see her cuffed, too. And then he saw her striding toward him, determination on her face. As she reached them, she pulled out a badge and flashed it at the arresting officer. His demeanor immediately changed.

"Detective. Is there a problem?" the officer asked.

Detective? What the fuck…?

"This man has nothing to do with my father. You need to let him go."

Flynn stared at her in shock as all the pieces suddenly fell into place.

She's a cop. Of course she is. That's why she was spying on us. She's one of them. She was setting us up. Searching for evidence to convict us… That's how she knew so much about Henry…and Mom…

The officer did as Jayde asked and released the cuffs from Flynn's hands.

Freed, he rubbed his wrists reflexively. All the time, he stared at Jayde. She averted her gaze and moved away, speaking quietly to some of the other officers. One by one, they left the bar, taking Jayde's father with them. John Hassad stared at his daughter with so much malevolence, Flynn felt an icy shiver run along his spine. And then it was just the two of them.

Flynn stood his ground, glaring at her as he waited for her to come to him. Finally, she did.

"Let's sit down," she said and indicated the booth closest to them.

Without taking his eyes off her, he took a seat. With a weary sigh, she sat down opposite.

"You must have lots of questions."

He nodded curtly.

She sighed again. "Let me start by saying I'm sorry. You were never meant to be caught up in that. I had no idea you'd drop by this morning. I didn't know what to do. It was too late to call off the raid and you didn't seem inclined to leave." She shot him a look that was filled with regret. "Like I said, I'm sorry."

"You're a cop," he stated flatly.

She nodded. "Yes. A detective. I've been working undercover in an effort to bring my father down. The taskforce had your uncle under surveillance even before he died. We didn't manage to put him away, but upon his death, we had to see if any of his relatives had taken over the reins."

Flynn stared at her. "That's why you had that file on us. That's why you were so interested in befriending my family!

Befriending *me*!" Realization dawned and his anger exploded.

"That's why you courted me, kissed me! Hell, you even let me make love to you! It was all part of your plan, getting me to lower my guard, say something incriminating. No doubt you hoped I'd let you in on some juicy family secrets you could use against me." He shook his head from side to side, unable to comprehend the extent of her deception. "All this time I thought you cared about me when all you cared about was putting me and my family in jail!"

She looked devastated. "No, Flynn! No! You have to believe me! It wasn't like that! In the beginning, I was just doing my job. Then I got to know you. I realized you couldn't be that person. You couldn't be involved with illegal drugs. I told my superior exactly that only last night. You and your family have been cleared of all suspicion. It was your uncle who was involved—and only him."

Flynn kept shaking his head. He refused to listen to any more of her lies. Lies, lies, lies. That's all it was. And to think he thought she'd cared for him.

Ha! What a joke!

As if she could read his mind, Jayde's expression turned frantic. She grabbed his arm. "Flynn! Please! You have to believe me," she implored.

He looked at her coldly. "No, Jayde. That's where you're wrong. You've proved beyond a shadow of a doubt that you aren't capable of honesty. I don't have to believe a word you say."

Her face fell. Tears flooded her eyes. He couldn't stand to sit there a moment longer. He slid out of the booth.

"Flynn!" she cried in desperation. "Please! I love you! Please, don't go!"

Her words gave him pause, but only momentarily. He desperately wanted to believe she loved him, but how could he? She'd told so many lies. And not told him enough earlier.

Her secrets were unforgivable. She was a cop and she'd been investigating him and his family for something as heinous as drug dealing. She said she loved him, but for her to have considered the possibility he was a criminal, showed she didn't know him at all.

Without another word, he turned and left her, blocking out the sound of her quiet sobs. He pushed open the door to the bar and left.

Jayde watched Flynn's retreating back and put her head down on the table and cried. She sobbed until she was weak with the effort of dealing with her distress. She'd known it would be tricky when it came to explaining who and what she was, but she'd never imagined he wouldn't believe her, or that he could look at her with such disdain.

A fresh wave of agony tore through her and she cried out from the pain of it. She was gutted. Completely and utterly devastated at the thought she might never patch things up with him.

Until now, her job had been the most important thing in her life. She'd given it her everything—heart and soul. She'd been proud of the part she played in keeping the people of Sydney safe. One less drug dealer on the streets was a great result for everyone.

Then she met Flynn and her priorities had changed. For the first time, her work wasn't everything. She found herself thinking about him when she should have been plotting her next move. He invaded her thoughts at all hours.

The more she'd gotten to know him, the more she liked him and the more she realized he was a good and decent man. He was nothing like her father, or his uncle. And that was a good thing.

She'd started to let herself dream about what it might be like to have a man in her life. Not just any man. Flynn. He was everything she could have wanted and he seemed to like her, too.

And now she'd gone and ruined everything by not being upfront with him.

But how was I supposed to do that? I'd never compromise an investigation, not even for the man I love…

And that was the sad truth: She loved him. With everything that she was. He'd left there hating her, despising her for what she'd done and for the secrets she'd kept from him. Her lies had destroyed the love he had for her and there was nothing she could do to fix that.

At Nick's request, the family had gathered for dinner at Craigdon Manor. Everyone had answered Nick's summons, all curious as to what could have catalyzed such a meeting. Though the family getting together for a meal from time to time wasn't unusual, what was out of the ordinary was that every single member of the Craigdon family, excluding the children and Christopher, was present. Even the honey-mooners had returned from Fiji.

Flynn sat between Logan and Noah, relieved he'd cleared the air between him and his brother. It made for a much more enjoyable get together than it might have been. It was also good to catch up with Logan. Flynn hadn't seen him since the wedding. He couldn't help but notice the flush on Logan's cheeks as he sank yet another Scotch.

His father and Aunt Elizabeth sat side by side at the head of the table. It appeared the two of them had reconciled. Flynn still hadn't talked to his father about the cheating. He'd had too much drama going on in his own life. Neither had he thought that much about Sophia. Knowing she was his half-sister didn't change the way he felt about her. The two of them had always been close.

Flynn was pleased to see Sophia and Jarrod were seated close to Archie and Elizabeth. The last time they'd been in the same room together, Sophia had distanced herself as much as she could. Now when he looked at his half-sister he saw she was more relaxed, chatty, laughing. Her scrapes and bruises had faded and she looked more like her old self. He hoped that meant she'd reconciled with her mother. He hated it when his family were at odds. As much as he hated that he and Jayde still hadn't reunited.

He swallowed a sigh. On that front, things had remained stagnant. Jayde had called and left several messages. He'd ignored all of them. Right now they were at a stalemate. He was trying hard to come to terms with the fact she was a cop and had lied to him all this time. At the same time, he yearned to be with her, to lose himself in her arms. It was a dilemma for which, right now, he didn't see a solution, though a part of him hoped like hell they sorted everything out.

The meal had been eaten and the plates cleared away when Nick stood and tapped his spoon on a wine glass, seeking everyone's attention. The conversation around the room petered out and eventually silence fell. All sets of eyes were glued on Flynn's cousin.

"I want to thank everyone for coming tonight. With crazy schedules, shiftwork and kids—even honeymoons— I appreciate it can't have been easy, especially on such short notice."

There was a murmur of agreement. Then Nick spoke again.

"I hope my request for you to join me hasn't caused any undue distress. That wasn't my intention. But something has recently come to light and I wanted to be the one to tell you. That way, everyone has the same information and there can be no conjecture, no misunderstanding."

"Just get on with it," Joel mumbled.

Flynn looked at him and realized Joel already knew what Nick was about to say. Joel was a cop. The implications were unsettling. A pit of dread formed in his stomach. He braced himself for whatever was coming.

"Some of you might remember, a few months ago, I found a strange list of names and dates locked away in Dad's safe. At the time, I couldn't work out what it meant. But, as most of you know, I like to solve puzzles…" There was a general murmur of laughter. Nick waited for it to die down before he continued.

"I wasn't prepared to let this one get the better of me. So, I started making enquires." Once again, he paused. He looked down at Harper, who smiled her encouragement. No doubt Nick had already filled her in on what he was about to say.

"There's no easy way to say this and I suspect it's going to come as a shock to all of you. The thing is, Dad was more than a successful property developer; he was also a drug dealer."

There was an audible gasp from many of them gathered around the table. Of course, Flynn and Noah weren't surprised.

"I didn't want to believe it, but there's no denying it's true," Nick continued. "Dad was paying drug dealers under the guise of legitimate company employees. The proceeds of crime were filtered back through the company's books."

"He was effectively laundering drug money through Craigdon Enterprises," Joel said dryly.

Sophia looked appalled. "How could he?"

"Why would he do that?" Isabella asked, looking equally stunned.

"I don't know," Nick replied. "The company was plenty profitable. It made Dad a lot of money over the years."

"Are you sure about this?" Callum asked quietly. Grace reached over and squeezed his hand.

Nick nodded, his expression grave. "Yes. I ended up tracking down some of those 'supposed laborers.' I spoke to them, asked them how they came to be employed by Craigdon Enterprises. It was quite obvious they were unskilled. Every one of them admitted they'd been dealers for Dad. He supplied them with drugs and they sold them on the streets. In return, they drew a wage from the company."

"What about the monetary amounts that were listed along with the names?" Logan asked.

Nick acknowledged Logan's question with a nod. "It's my guess these were the actual amounts Dad owed his dealers. The weekly wages paid to these men were commensurate with their awards. If Dad had paid them the large amounts they were owed, it would have raised suspicion in the human resources department. He was smarter than that. In fact, if he hadn't kept that list, no one would have been the wiser."

"So they're still owed money," Logan stated flatly.

"Yes," Nick replied, "but I don't think we have to worry about them coming after us."

"Where are these men now? Please don't tell me they're still employed by Craigdon," Jett commented.

"No," Nick replied. "All but one left our employ on Dad's death. I guessed they figured their gig was up. After all, it was Dad who'd supplied them with the gear. Now that he was dead—"

"It was a fair assumption the access to drugs had died with him," Jett finished, looking grim.

"Yes," Nick replied.

"You said all but one has left our employ. Are they still on the books?" Logan asked.

"As of yesterday, there's no one," Nick replied. "Igor Petrov had been with Dad for years as a head foreman. He was also the leader of Dad's gang of dealers. He'd been flying under the radar all this time because Petrov actually came to Dad as a qualified concreter. It was only some time later he and Dad got involved with selling drugs." Nicholas looked at Logan. "I confronted Petrov with my findings. He denied all knowledge. I hope it's okay with you, but I fired him yesterday."

Logan nodded decisively. "Hell, yeah."

"Nick asked me to look into Petrov," Joel said, taking up the narrative. "I spoke to a mate in the DEA. He confirmed Petrov has links to the Russian mafia. The police are still investigating him."

Once again, there was a shocked silence as everyone digested this latest development. Flynn looked around the room. Though none of them needed any more bad news, he might as well get it all out there now.

"There's something else," he said. Several pairs of eyes turned in his direction. He looked at Noah.

"Some of you met Jayde Hassad at Callum's wedding."

There were various nods from those gathered around the table.

"I thought she was lovely," Elizabeth said.

"Didn't she come with you, Noah?" Nick asked.

"Yes," Noah mumbled.

Flynn cleared his throat to regain their attention. "Anyway, I recently discovered Jayde's an undercover cop."

Noah gasped. "You can't be serious!"

Flynn regarded him with a grim expression. "I'm afraid it's true."

"But… What about the bar? She works there. I've seen her! Many times!" Noah protested.

"You're right. She does work there, but all of that was part of her cover."

Noah looked bewildered. "That explains the file you found, but…why?"

Flynn sighed. "She was conducting covert surveillance on her father. His name's John Hassad. Apparently he's a bigwig drug supplier. Jayde was also well aware of Uncle Henry's involvement in the drug industry." He paused and then added, "That's why she's been investigating all of us for months. She wanted to know whether any of us had taken up where Henry left off."

There was another round of shocked gasps. Family members turned to each other and shook their heads, stunned into silence.

"She was investigating us?" Logan cried.

"Yes. It was part of her assignment," Flynn replied.

"I had no idea," Elizabeth said, looking bewildered.

Archie squeezed her hand. "None of us did, Lizzie."

Once again, Flynn cleared his throat. "The one bit of good news about all of this is Jayde discovered Uncle Henry was acting alone."

"So we're in the clear?" Isabella asked with a hopeful expression on her face.

"Yes," Flynn replied. "We're in the clear."

There were general murmurs of relief. Flynn regained his seat. Noah nudged him with his elbow. He looked both bewildered and resigned. "Where is she?"

Flynn looked away. "I don't know."

"What do you mean, you don't know. I thought you liked her. I thought you liked her a lot?"

Flynn shrugged. He kept his face averted.

"Have you spoken to her since the bust up?"

"No."

"You can't blame her, Flynn. You said so yourself. She was only doing her job," Noah said quietly.

Flynn refused to respond. An irrational surge of anger flooded through him. It was all right for Noah to say that. He wasn't the one who'd been blindsided by her deception. Flynn turned his back on Noah and dropped his final bombshell on the family.

"Jayde told me something else. She was convinced Uncle Henry was drunk when Mom was killed."

This time, the loudest gasp came from Flynn's father. Archie looked pale and shaken. He shook his head from side to side. "No, it can't be true. Please, God. Don't let it be true."

"According to Jayde, her father knew Mom and Uncle Henry," Flynn continued. "Jayde's father told her the night of the car accident, they'd met up in a bar at the Hunter Valley. Uncle Henry was drinking heavily."

Flynn sighed wearily. "The whole tragic event has been difficult for all of us to comprehend. One minute our mother was here. The next she was gone. Just like that. There are too many questions without answers. We'll probably never know the truth."

"The police would have breath-tested Dad at the scene," Joel protested. "There's no way he could have been drunk."

"Joel's right," Jett added. "I don't believe that for an instant."

Flynn shrugged. He was done arguing. "Take from it what you will. I'm certainly not backing up Jayde's information. All I'm doing is passing it on. But I'm sure I'm not the only one who's wondered what the hell the two of them were doing together so far from home and so late at night."

Noah and Logan stared at the table. Archie looked equally dazed. Flynn's shoulders slumped. He hadn't meant to dredge up old, sad memories, but it appeared that was the case. Still, at least his conscience was clear. He'd given them all the information he had. What they did with it—whether they believed him—was up to them.

"I'm going to talk to my supervisor about opening an investigation," Noah said quietly.

There was a round of loud protests.

"You're best to leave things well alone!" Joel cried.

"She's been gone ten years! What difference would an investigation make?" Jett asked.

"Nothing's going to bring her back," Isabella said softly.

Noah stared them all down, his expression fierce. "I want answers. Flynn's right. There's so much we don't know. I'm going to push for an investigation." His words held a degree of finality that nobody dared challenge.

Flynn looked at his brother with admiration. "Good for you, bro," he said in a low voice.

The conversation once again resumed around the table. Flynn remembered one last thing. He got to his feet again.

"One last thing, I had a call from Christopher last night. He wanted me to let you know he's amended the terms of his lawsuit."

"Oh, don't tell me he's actually decided to withdraw it," Elizabeth said hopefully.

Flynn shook his head. "No such luck. No, he wanted to tell us he's reduced his claim from one hundred million dollars to eighty-five million."

As Flynn expected, there was an immediate outcry.

"What the hell?"

"No way!"

"He's got to be joking!"

Elizabeth merely sighed. "I thought he might have seen sense. Not to worry. It looks like we have no choice but to let the courts work it out."

Chapter Twenty One

It was New Year's Eve. Jayde sat alone on her couch, sipping wine and feeling morose. Ordinarily, she enjoyed the last day of the year. There was so much excitement, so much possibility looking down the barrel of a new year. But this year was different. In fact, it was scarily similar to the New Year's Eve she'd spent the year before—a couple of weeks after her mother had died.

She hadn't spoken to Flynn since the raid. She couldn't get out of her mind the way he'd looked at her in the moments before he'd walked out: shocked, disappointed, full of disbelief. Gone was any sign of the tenderness they'd shared. She was horribly afraid she'd never see that in his eyes again.

He'd been adamant about how important honesty was to him. He'd told her plainly how much he hated the fact he was surrounded by liars. His clients, the lawyers, even sometimes the kids. Everyone had an agenda and it most often resulted in lies. Now she had proven herself to be the biggest liar of all.

How will he be ever be able to trust me again? I'm no different than his clients...

No! She refused to accept that. The truth was, she'd had no choice but to maintain the façade. A long-term criminal investigation and people's lives were on the line. Surely he could understand that? It was nothing personal. She'd worked undercover on and off over the course of her career. She'd thought nothing of it. It was a necessary part of policing.

She'd never told her father she was a cop. Even back then, a year earlier, she'd been thinking about how she could gather enough evidence to bring him down. Then Junior had died and her resolve had hardened into an impenetrable goal. She wouldn't rest until John Hassad was in jail.

It hadn't affected her one little bit that she'd deceived her father all this time. As far as she was concerned, the ends justified the means. It was the same with Flynn. Only, Flynn hadn't done anything wrong. He and his family had been cleared of all suspicion. The thing was, she didn't know at the outset that would be the case. The subterfuge was necessary in order to find out.

The irony of the situation didn't escape her, but she was terribly afraid Flynn wouldn't see it that way. She wanted to call him, to try and explain, but she didn't know if he'd speak to her.

Coward.

The accusation echoed in her mind. She frowned and took another sip from her wine.

Is that it? Am I too scared to talk to him? Am I afraid he'll still be cold and dismissive?

She sighed. Ordinarily, she considered herself as brave as the next person. Maybe braver. After all, she didn't flinch at flying bullets or facing down a drug-addicted madman. She'd been in both situations in the past and though she hoped she wasn't ever put in situations like those again, she knew she could handle it.

So why am I so fearful about calling Flynn Craigdon again? It's not like I haven't already left him a heap of messages. So what if he's ignored me? Am I just going to give up? I've faced much more dangerous foes with more gumption…

Foe? Flynn wasn't a foe. She loved him. More than she'd thought possible. After all, they hardly knew each other. But she knew enough that mattered: He was good and decent and kind. He volunteered at soup kitchens, gave his money to the poor. He cared about people, even those who lied to him in order to get what they wanted.

Can he find it in his heart to forgive me?

All of a sudden, she felt brave enough to find out. But first she had to get his number. Though they'd been as intimate as two people could be, she still didn't have that. Before she could change her mind, she picked up her phone from the coffee table and dialed Noah's number.

Flynn swallowed another mouthful of beer and tried to forget it was New Year's Eve. With his elbows resting on the top railing of his balcony, he had a clear view of the crowds of revelers who'd flocked to Manly beach. There was music and laughter and shouting and every now and then there were catcalls. He stared sourly at the thousands of people all having fun, wishing they'd go back to where they'd come from.

He'd been in a mood ever since the raid on Beaches bar. It still upset him every time he thought about it. He'd opened his heart to Jayde. He'd told her about how serious he felt about honesty and how glad he was he could trust her. And all the while she'd been deceiving him.

No doubt she'd been laughing her head off as he'd gone on and on about how depressing it was to be surrounded in his workplace by liars. She'd looked at him with those big blue eyes filled with understanding and compassion and all along she'd known full well she was one big fat liar herself.

A surge of guilt went through him. He wasn't being fair. Like Noah had said, she was only doing her job. Though he'd never asked either of his cousins, no doubt as senior officers,

Jett and Joel had also conducted covert operations at some point in their careers. Flynn didn't judge them for it or think any less of them, or accuse them of the worst kind of deception…

So why am I so hard on Jayde?

It wasn't as if she could have told him what was going on. She was in the middle of an investigation—one that had apparently been going on for some time. It was only natural she jumped at the chance to get closer to his family. In her position and charged with the same assignment, he would have done the same. It made good sense to get to know the people she had in her sights. The better she knew them, the more accurately she could observe.

Still, it made him uncomfortable knowing she'd been spying on them—gathering information on him and his family. She'd denied his accusation that she'd only slept with him in order to gather intelligence, but how could he know for sure?

And then he dismissed the possibility. Jayde was a good and decent person. Before this, he would have described her as honest. She'd given him no indication he couldn't trust her.

So why am I feeling so gutted?

Because she'd lied about who she was. It all came back to that.

But she was only doing her job.

Just like that, the arguments went round and round again…

The sound of his phone ringing interrupted his depressing thoughts. He turned and picked it up from the small table attached to one of the loungers. He checked the screen. The number was blocked.

He frowned. Ordinarily, he ignored calls like that. Then again, it might be a client. Though he didn't usually hand out his mobile phone number to them, there were a select few who were in the middle of messy divorces who had it. With a sigh, he answered.

"Hello?"

"Flynn?"

At the sound of Jayde's voice, his heart skipped a beat and then took off at a wild gallop. With an effort, he managed to speak.

"Jayde? Is that you?"

"Yes."

"How did you get my number?"

"Noah gave it to me."

Flynn cursed silently beneath his breath, but another part of him was glad. "What can I do for you?" he asked, his tone stiff and formal.

There was a moment of silence on the other end of the phone. "Can we talk?"

Flynn swallowed at her hesitant tone, like she was uncertain about his reaction. He understood her reticence. Before they'd parted, he'd made sure she felt the full force of his anger and disappointment.

"Flynn?" Her soft voice came to him once again.

Oh, God.

Flynn was torn. He wanted so much to see her, to put everything behind him, but what about the lies, the deception? Could he forgive her for that?

She was only doing her job…

Noah's words reverberated through his mind and suddenly he accepted the truth of them.

"Where are you?" he asked.

"I'm at home. At Beaches."

He acknowledged her response with a nod. It was probably fitting they have this out at the place where it had all begun.

"I'll see you in fifteen minutes." With that, he ended the call.

While she waited on tenterhooks for him to arrive, Jayde paced the confines of her modest apartment. The last time Flynn had been there, they'd made love. She wondered if the memories of them together were as fresh in his mind as they were in hers.

The fact he'd agreed to see her was a good thing. At least she'd be given the opportunity to explain face to face. It was all she could ask for. After that, it was up to him. She just hoped she could convince him to give her another chance. To that end, she sent a silent, fervent prayer heavenward. With five minutes to go before he was due, she went downstairs and unlocked the main door. She stepped outside and stood on the top step. All she had to do now was wait.

All the way over to Beaches, Flynn ran through his conversation with Jayde in his mind. He didn't know how he'd react to her explanation, but he did know he wanted to try to patch things up. There was something special between them, something magical that didn't come by every day. In his gut he knew it was something worth fighting for.

That hope was the reason he was on his way over, to clear the air once and for all. He hoped against hope they could resolve things and move forward. Despite his hurt and disappointment, it's what he wanted. He hoped she wanted it, too.

And then he thought about all she'd been through and all of a sudden he felt like a prick. She'd been brave enough to spy on her own father, knowing full well that the intelligence she gathered against him would see him go to jail. She'd done that because it was the right thing to do, and yet it meant turning on the man who'd help to give her life. The only father she had.

Flynn felt a surge of admiration for the woman he loved.

At the same time, he was filled with shame. He'd treated her so badly, said some awful things. She hadn't deserved them. He prayed she'd find it in her heart to forgive him.

He turned into the parking lot of Beaches and spied her standing on the front step. She stood illuminated by the lamplights fixed to the wall behind her. She wore denim cutoffs and a T-shirt, but she could have been dressed in rags for all he cared. She was beautiful, inside and out, and he loved her.

The uncertainty on her face as he walked toward her hit him in the gut. He was the reason she looked so tentative, so scared, so uncertain… Keen to put her at ease, he smiled softly.

"Hey," he said, drawing close.

Her eyes flared wide with surprise. She gave him a hesitant smile. "Hey."

"It's good to see you."

"You, too."

They stood awkwardly outside the bar. Flynn was reminded all too clearly what had gone down there the last time he'd been there. He pushed the memories from his mind and focused on the present.

Jayde.

She shot him another uncertain look. "Shall we go inside?"

"Sure."

He stood back and waited for her to enter and then followed. Most of the lights inside were still switched off, leaving the room almost dark. One light had been left on outside the internal staircase. It illuminated their way. Flynn ascended behind her, his mind on what was to come.

"Can I get you a drink?" she asked.

"No, thanks."

She looked nervous. Edgy. Unsure. It broke his heart. Though this wasn't all his fault, he wanted to set her at ease.

See her smile again. He opened his mouth to speak, but she beat him to it.

"I'm so sorry for deceiving you, Flynn. At the time I didn't think much of it. Running covert operations, even undercover, has always been part of the job. And it wouldn't have mattered this time, except…"

She paused and looked even more uncertain.

"Except what?"

She drew in a deep breath and eased it out. As if gathering her courage together, she looked him directly in the face.

"Except that this time I fell in love with you and everything changed."

He blinked in surprise. "So it's true? You really do love me?"

"Yes. All of a sudden my deception mattered. It mattered a whole darn lot. By then I was stuck. I didn't know what to do. I certainly couldn't come clean. It would have jeopardized the entire investigation and that's one thing I couldn't do." She looked away and twisted the ends of her T-shirt.

The agonized expression on her face was the final straw. He took a step toward her and pulled her into his arms. She tensed momentarily, but then relaxed against him with a sigh. She tilted her head to look up at him, a question in her eyes.

"Flynn?"

He answered the question by kissing her, long and deep —and passionately. He kissed her until they were both breathless. The chemistry between them was extraordinary. It had been right from the beginning. When at last he lifted his head, she looked as dazed as he felt.

"Wow," she said shakily.

He regarded her somberly. "I won't deny I was shocked and hurt when I first found out, but after I'd had time to cool down and think about it, I understood why you did what you did. You were in an impossible position. There was no way you could blow your cover. Not even for me. After all, I was part of your investigation."

"Flynn—"

He held up his hand to halt her. "No, let me finish. I reacted badly to your confession and I'm not proud of that. I shouldn't have said the things I said and I sure as hell shouldn't have walked out on you. It won't happen again. I promise."

The tiniest glimmer of hope appeared in her eyes. A smile turned up her lips. "Does this mean what I think it does?"

Once again, he took her in his arms and held her close. "Yes. I love you, Jayde. I don't know how or when it happened. It snuck up on me and took me completely by surprise. I've never been one to hang around for the long term. In fact, I've never been in love."

His arms tightened around her. "There's something special about you, Jayde. You touched me deep inside. I want you; I need you; I love you. I'm yours, if you'll have me."

"Oh, Flynn!" she cried and threw her arms around his neck. They kissed like they couldn't get enough.

Walking her backwards, Flynn bent and lifted her in his arms. He didn't need directions to her bedroom. Lowering her gently to the mattress, he followed her down and covered her body with his. He kissed her mouth, her nose, her cheeks. He nibbled on the sensitive flesh of her ears. She moaned and moved restlessly beneath him, but he didn't let up.

He kissed his way down her neck to her breasts and cupped them in his hands. Lowering his head, he nuzzled her soft flesh and then took one of her nipples in his mouth. Licking and sucking, he drove her wild and filled himself with need. Hot and throbbing, his cock pressed against her stomach.

And then she pushed against him and they rolled together until he lay on his back. Jayde climbed on top and straddled him. A grin tugged at her lips.

"My turn to drive you crazy," she murmured.

Bending low, she flicked at his nipples with her tongue. The small nubs pebbled beneath her touch. She raked her fingers across his chest, combing through the light covering of brown hair. She squeezed his pectorals, stroked across his flat stomach and then finally circled his cock with hand.

The feel of her strong hand around him sent a surge of blood rushing to his groin. She squeezed and stroked and clenched and unclenched. It was so good he thought he might die. And then she wiggled lower and bent her head and took him in her mouth and his desire grew to fever pitch.

Her lips surrounded him, her tongue caressed him, the rhythmic pressure of her hand drove him insane. He buried his fingers in her hair and held her head against him. She stroked and sucked and licked and touched. In a frenzy of need, his hips bucked hard against her. She merely chuckled and continued her sensual onslaught.

"Jayde!" he gasped. "You're killing me! I'm going to come if you keep that up."

Once again, she smiled, but slowly leveraged her way up. Over his legs, up his chest until she was once again straddling his body. She leaned over toward the bedside drawer. Her breasts swung into his face. Unable to help himself, he reached for the full globe and brought her nipple back to his mouth. Opening his lips and suckling her, he smiled in satisfaction at the sound of her swift intake of breath.

Finally she found what she was looking for and sheathed him with a condom. Moments later, she lowered herself onto his cock.

"Oh, Flynn! You feel so good!"

He murmured his response, intent on the feeling of her warmth and heat enveloping him. She lifted her hips and settled herself more fully upon him and then moved in a rhythm that set him on fire. Her eyes closed and her head fell back. Her mouth came open on a cry.

Faster and faster she moved, pressing herself against him. Her breath came fast, her chest rose and fell and then finally she was there. At the precipice. Ready to fly.

Her eyes came open and she stared down at him, her gaze filled with love and wonder. He reached up and pulled her down on top of him. As he did so, her climax overcame her and he captured her cry in his mouth. With their lips fused together, he held her close, savoring the shudders of release that went through her body.

When she'd quieted, he rolled her over, taking care to keep them joined. Surging forward, he filled her, each thrust more powerful than the last. It didn't take long for him to reach his climax and he gasped as he reached the peak. With a final surge he orgasmed and emptied himself inside her.

Afterward, they lay together side by side, limbs entwined, exhausted and replete.

"I love you," Jayde whispered.

"I love you, too."

Flynn pressed a soft kiss against her lips. In the distance they heard the sound of fireworks exploding. They turned to each other and smiled.

"Happy New Year!"

Note to Readers

I do hope you have enjoyed reading Flynn and Jayde's story. If you've enjoyed this book, I would really appreciate it if you could leave a review at Goodreads and your favorite digital retailer. Every review increases visibility and helps other readers to find books they enjoy.

Receive a free book when you sign up for my newsletter if you like to receive news on upcoming stories, release dates, book launches and other snippets. I love to receive feedback from my readers. Please feel free to contact me at chris@christaylorauthor.com.au.

Noah is the next book in the Craigdon Family Dynasty series.

Keep reading below for a sneak peek at Noah:

Excerpt from

Noah

The Craigdon Family Dynasty

Book Seven

CHRIS TAYLOR

Chapter One

oah Craigdon felt the heavy beat of the house music thumping from the DJ's speakers deep inside his chest. In deference to the fact it was Friday night, he'd dragged his younger brother out to a night club in the city. The Pit was exactly the kind of place Noah usually avoided. He was quiet and shy—some would say reserved—and the noisy, crowded night club was completely outside his comfort zone.

But that was the point. On the advice of a girl he'd once thought he was in love with, he was determined to get out more and meet women, prospective partners. It was like Jayde had suggested: It was a numbers game. The more women he met, the more chance he had of meeting his soulmate.

The nightclub was popular with cops and other first responders. Paramedics, doctors, nurses, firemen—they all seemed to gravitate to The Pit. Loud music, dim lighting, the press of bodies. The beer flowed, wine glasses tinkled, catching the overhead lights.

The pool table out the back was well-used. Every now and then an argument would ensue that was quickly stifled. The patrons were slick and well groomed. Women with loose flowing hair, artfully applied makeup; guys with loose collarless shirts and designer jeans. There was a frantic sort of energy permeating the room that came from the fact the majority of the crowd were enjoying some downtime from stressful, difficult jobs.

Noah had talked Logan into coming with him. His brother had never had a problem with women. They flocked to him like teenagers flocked to Snapchat. It had always been that way. Logan and Flynn were very alike in that way. It was Noah, the middle brother, who'd always been the odd one out. It usually took every ounce of courage he had to even look a girl in the eye, let alone start up a conversation.

The only place he was confident in a social setting was on the dance floor. Which didn't make a lick of sense, seeing it was the one place where even the most confident of people could come unstuck. But Noah had always had perfect rhythm and the music transported to him to another place, somewhere far away from his usual awkwardness.

They found a spot at the far end of the bar, away from the noise of the music. They climbed onto bar stools and Logan got the first round of drinks. Noah took a sip of his cold beer and sighed.

"Oh, yeah. That tastes good," he said and then grinned.

Logan managed a brief smile. It was about as jovial as he got these days. What seemed like a lifetime earlier, Logan had been a competitive sailor, racing yachts. But a bad accident had resulted in serious injuries. He suffered fractures to his femur, his tibia and his fibula in several places and unfortunately, some of the broken bones hadn't set very well. He'd been left with a permanent limp and was no longer lithe enough to race competitively. He now designed and built super yachts for the family company, still headed by their father, Archie, but three years down the track, Logan was still down on everything. To make matters worse, his fiancée had also recently jilted him at the altar.

Noah swallowed a sigh and took another sip from his beer. "How's work?" he asked.

Logan shrugged. "The same as always. Dad's still pressuring me to take up a more managerial role in the company."

"Would it be so bad? You love Craigdon Super Yachts."

Logan response was swift and passionate. "I love being at the coal face, designing them, building them from the ground up. Not managing employees, paying bills, fighting with contractors. I don't want to be stuck in an office all day! That's the reason I put Nicholas in charge of Craigdon Enterprises. I'm not cut out for that kind of thing." He paused and then added in a bewildered tone. "I still don't have a clue why Uncle Henry left his company to me."

Noah considered his response. His cop instincts were telling him there was a chance Logan might have been the product of an affair between their uncle and their mother. He had no evidence to base his suspicions on and so he remained quiet. Instead, he responded by saying, "We've opened an investigation into mom's death."

Logan compressed his lips and nodded. "I still can't believe Uncle Henry was drunk behind the wheel when they crashed. I mean, WTF? How come we've only just found out about this? And why the hell were they driving together that late at night anyway? Where had they been? Did anyone bother to ask?"

Noah shrugged. He had all of those questions and more filling his head, but as yet had no answers. He was determined to get to the bottom of what had happened and bring to justice those involved in covering it up. If that's what had happened. The jury was still out on that.

He sighed and took another sip from his glass. "You heard from Flynn lately?" he asked, referring to their oldest brother.

"No. Ever since he and Jayde hooked up he's never

around. I left a couple of messages for him. He still hasn't called me back."

Noah refrained from commenting and chuffed down the rest of his beer. Logan eyed him speculatively.

"Didn't you bring her to Callum's wedding?"

Noah pretended confusion. "Who?"

Logan rolled his eyes. "Jayde."

"Oh, Jayde. Yeah."

"And?"

"And what?"

Logan continued to regard him steadily. Noah grimaced. "There's nothing to tell, Logan. Yes, I liked her, but she didn't like me. At least, not in that way, and that's okay. You can't help who you fall in love with."

"You're right. But who's looking to fall in love?" Logan's face twisted with bitterness. "Been there, done that. It didn't work out so well. In fact, she ran off with her best friend, remember? So from now on, I'm done with love. A little lust works just fine for me."

Noah felt a moment's sympathy for the shabby way his brother's long-term girlfriend, Virginia Maxwell, had treated him, but already Logan was looking meaningfully toward a couple of attractive, twenty-somethings women who stood together a little further down the bar. Noticing the attention, the girls smiled and waved. A moment later, they moved closer to the brothers and regarded them with friendly smiles.

"Hi, I'm Amy," said the blond, zeroing in on Logan.

Reluctantly, Noah turned his attention to the brunette and forced a smile.

"Hi, I'm Brittany," she said, flashing a set of perfect white teeth.

"Noah," he mumbled. Logan nudged him with his elbow. Noah ignored the subtle intrusion and managed another weak grin. "Um, can I get you a drink?"

Brittany moved closer. Her generous breasts brushed against his arm. Embarrassed, he quickly turned away and flagged down the bartender. He ordered another beer and ascertained from Brittany that she was drinking gin.

"Plus soda water, and don't forget the lime," she added with a wink.

Noah tried to rustle up some interest at the frank promise in her eyes, but it wasn't forthcoming. Swallowing a sigh, he ordered their drinks and wondered how soon he could call it a night.

Logan leaned toward him and wiggled his eyebrows. "Having fun, bro?"

Noah grimaced. "Sure."

Logan gave him a wry smile. A moment later, he grabbed Amy by the hand and despite his permanent limp, started heading toward the dance floor.

"Come on, Noah. Brittany wants to dance," Logan threw over his shoulder.

The brunette stood there with an expectant look on her face, batting her false eyelashes. Noah groaned beneath his breath. He was going to kill his brother. The last thing he wanted was to spend any more time in Brittany's company. She was pretty enough, but she wasn't doing it for him and that wasn't anybody's fault. Before he could get away with a mumbled excuse, Brittany had taken his hand, her face lighting up with enthusiasm.

"Yes! Let's dance! I looove to dance!"

With reluctance dogging his every step, Noah allowed himself to be led out onto the dance floor. The music was loud and fast with a rhythmic techno beat. Before he realized it, his body began to move—his feet, his hips, his legs. It was like he had no control over them. With a sigh, he relaxed and gave himself up to the music.

Brittany was a terrible dancer, but what she lacked in style, she made up for in enthusiasm. She draped her arms around his neck and pressed herself against him. She wiggled and jiggled and spun around, laughing as she stumbled and would have fallen if he hadn't reached out to catch her. He wished she was the kind of girl he could get into. There was plenty to like. But the only quickening of his pulse when he looked at her was from the exertion of the dance.

Simple, rhythmical, mesmerizing. He moved with effortless grace. People moved out of the way to give him room and to watch him, a mixture of envy, disbelief and enjoyment on their faces. Noah was mostly oblivious to all of them, caught up in the beat of the music. Sweat gathered on his forehead and ran down the sides of his face. He distractedly pulled off his glasses and swiped at the perspiration with the back of his hand.

Logan leaned over and said something in his ear, but Noah couldn't hear over the music. He shrugged and Logan mimicked getting a drink and Noah gave him a thumbs up. Logan's dance partner went with him and Brittany quickly followed. Feeling a little foolish out there on the dance floor alone, he same to a sudden stop.

And then another woman materialized before him. She was so beautiful, his breath caught in his throat. Her long dark hair blazed blue-black in the spotlights. She wore a sparkly crop top covered in beads that dangled low across her taut stomach. A tiny glittery skirt that barely covered her butt made up the rest of her clothing. Four-inch black heels that almost looked dangerous elevated her to just below his shoulder.

Her toned legs were long and tanned. She took his hand and put her other hand on his shoulder. His hand automatically came to rest just above her hip. The music changed to a tango and before he knew it, they were carving up the dance floor with a swishing of skirts and a flash of feet.

His heart pounded, both from the exertion and the exotic woman he held in his arms.

Who is she and where did she come from?

It was obvious she was a dancer. An instructor, perhaps? Or maybe she'd just been born doing it. Her dark coloring hinted at South American heritage, or maybe Spanish. It was hard to tell in the dimness, but there was no mistaking her beauty or the aura of confidence that surrounded her and sparkled in her dark brown eyes.

Noah lost all sense of time and place, like he usually did when he got caught up in a dance. The woman continued to match his every step, lithe and rhythmical in his arms. At last the music came to an end and they both stopped and stood staring at each other, breathless. Applause broke out around them. When Noah could finally speak without gasping, he held out his hand.

"Noah Craigdon."

"Ayla Rodriguez."

They smiled at each other. The warmth in Ayla's gaze flustered Noah and he quickly looked away. She turned and made her way off the dance floor. He sighed in relief and after a moment's hesitation, followed her. She came to a halt near an empty table and sat down, looking up at him expectantly. Nerves swirled in his gut. He swallowed hard and surreptitiously swiped sweaty hands down his jeans before perching on the seat opposite her.

"So, Noah Craigdon, do you come here often?"

Her eyes sparkled with good humor. He sucked in a breath and did his best to sound normal.

"Not really. This," he waved a hand around the crowded room, "isn't really my thing."

Her eyes widened in surprise. "You could have fooled me. I won't believe you learned to dance like that by watching videos on YouTube."

He laughed. Her relaxed attitude eased a little of his tension. "You're right. I took dance lessons for years. Jazz, tap, rock 'n roll. I pulled on my first pair of dance shoes when I was four."

She looked at him in admiration. "No wonder you're so good. So, do you dance professionally?"

He laughed and shook his head. "No. Not even close. I stopped lessons when I got to high school. It wasn't cool for a teenager to be attending dance classes. Especially not a teenage boy."

"Too bad. You're very talented."

He blushed with pleasure. When he was young, his mother had often praised his dance ability, but she was his mother. It was her job to ensure he had a healthy ego. Coming from this beautiful stranger, it really meant something. "Thank you. You're not so bad yourself."

It was her turn to duck her head in embarrassment. "Thanks. I'm no Solange Acosta, but I enjoy it."

He eyed her quizzically. "Solanage Acosta? I don't think I've heard of her."

"She and her partner, Max van de Voord, won the Tango World Championships in 2011. They're from Argentina."

"You know a lot about it."

She shrugged. "What can I say? I like to tango." Once again, laughter glinted in her eyes.

Noah's pulse rate picked up its pace. He swallowed against another rush of nerves. "Where did you learn to dance?"

"My parents are from Uruguay. They migrated to Australia when I was eight. I'd already spent enough time in my home country to feel the rhythm of the tango in my blood. My mom and dad love to dance and they've always loved the tango. They were happy to teach me. I fell in love with it, too."

"Is it hard to find dance partners?" he asked, curious.

"Sometimes, although there are a couple of fantastic

Central American dance clubs in the city that are as mad about the tango as I am. I go there fairly often. I can usually find someone who wants to dance. Who knows? I might even convince you to join me."

She smiled and his heart skipped a beat. *Oh, God. This is ridiculous. We've only just met and I'm in love. What if she has a boyfriend? Oh, hell, she might even be married.*

His gaze slid to her hands. *No rings. Okay then, hopefully not married. What the hell am I doing? We've only just met! Get a grip!*

Noah cleared his throat in an effort to get control over his wayward thoughts. "So, what do you do for a living?"

"I'm a cop."

He started in surprise. "Really?"

"Yeah. Why, do you have a problem with cops?"

"No, of course not. I'm a cop, too."

Now it was her turn to blink in surprise. "Really? I would never have pegged you as a cop."

"Why not?" he asked, curious.

She shrugged. "I don't know. You seem too…normal. Not hardened enough."

He gave a half-laugh. "I guess that's a compliment. The truth is, I haven't spent much of my career out on the street. I spent the first few years in general duties, but now I work for the Law Enforcement Conduct Commission. I'm a detective on the investigative team."

Her expression sobered. "The LECC?"

"Yes. The newest version of Internal Affairs."

"Wow. Investigating fellow officers isn't everyone's idea of fun."

He kept his expression carefully neutral. "I enjoy it."

"Good on you."

"So you don't have a problem with it?"

She shook her head. "No, of course not. You guys have a job to do, just like the rest of us."

He pulled a wry face. "Not all cops see it that way."

"You're right. A lot of them see you as traitors."

He tensed. "If cops didn't do the wrong thing, there'd be no need for us to investigate their behavior," he protested.

She held her hands up in a sign of surrender. "Hey, you'll get no argument from me, but it's not always as clear cut as that, is it? Our job isn't always black and white."

"It is in my world. There are rules. They're there for a reason. If you break them, you should expect to be punished. That's the society we live in."

"I wish I had the faith you seem to have in the system," she said softly.

He stared at her. She sounded so…disillusioned. He opened his mouth to question her further, but she merely waved him away and laughed. It sounded forced.

"Look at the two of us! It's Friday night! Who wants to talk about work? We're meant to be having a good time."

Noah let the subject slide even though he was keen to know more about the shadows that had crossed her face when she talked about the system they'd both devoted their lives to.

"Would you like a drink?" he asked instead.

"Thank you, but no. It's getting late. I should go." With that she pushed back her seat and stood. She held out her hand. "It was really nice meeting you, Noah."

He stood and shook her hand. She had a sure, firm grip. "You, too, Ayla." He wanted to say more, maybe even ask for her number, but by the time he found the courage, she'd slipped her hand out of his and had disappeared into the crowd. He was left to silently curse his cowardice and wonder if he'd ever see her again.

Chapter Two

Noah arrived at work the following Monday morning with a spring in his step. Though he hadn't made any effort to return to The Pit or otherwise track down the beautiful Ayla over the weekend, she'd consumed his thoughts for more hours than he cared to admit. All sorts of wonderful fantasies had gone through his head and though he wasn't sure if he'd ever see her again, their time together had been fun and had left him feeling hopeful for the future for the first time since he'd been overthrown by Jayde for his brother, Flynn.

To be fair to Jayde, they were never a couple. They'd attended his cousin's wedding together and Noah had hoped she felt as strongly about him as he did her. But it wasn't to be. Her heart belonged to Flynn. Now that Noah had been given time to come to terms with her rejection, he was okay with it and wished his brother much happiness. Now that he'd met Ayla, he felt far more positive that his soulmate was still out there and that maybe, just maybe he'd find his dream woman someday.

Tossing his briefcase on his desk, he hung up his jacket in the locker that stood in one corner of his office and then went searching for caffeine. He found his partner, Declan Munro, standing before the coffee machine, mug in hand.

Declan turned and greeted him with a friendly smile. "Craigdon! Good of you to drag your sorry ass in here."

Noah merely gave him the finger. Declan chuckled, taking the rude gesture in the spirit it was offered.

At forty, Declan Munro had started to gray at the temples, but he still stood shoulder to shoulder with Noah and was as fit as any of the investigators in their team. Six years earlier, Declan had worked as a detective for the Australian Federal Police in Canberra. His career had fallen apart when he'd been investigated by their internal affairs department for police corruption. Fortunately, he'd managed to clear his name and not surprisingly, he'd requested a transfer. He'd ended up in Sydney at the LECC a few years before Noah. They'd been partnered together and over time had become firm friends.

Declan wasn't into dancing, but he loved something else Noah enjoyed—fast motorbikes. Declan owned a Ducati 1199 panigale. A beast of a machine that went like the wind. With his million dollar inheritance, Noah had recently treated himself to a cherry-red Honda Fireblade. He couldn't wait to find the time to take it out on the motorway and open up the throttle.

Noah filled his cup and wandered toward his office. Declan followed him and threw himself down on the chair that stood opposite Declan's desk. Though his office was situated in the middle of his floor and had no windows, the décor was nice enough—especially for government digs. The carpet was new and pleasant to look at. The furniture was predictable, but comfortable and clean. The best thing about it was he had the office to himself. A luxury that was largely unheard of for the average cop.

Declan sipped at his coffee and then cleared his throat. "Where are we up to with your mother's case?"

Noah took the seat behind his desk. He'd brought the case

to his superior in the hope the LECC would decide to open an investigation. Fortunately, after providing them with the scant details he had, they agreed it was worth looking into.

"At this stage, we only have the word of a known criminal—John Hassad—that my uncle was drunk behind the wheel when he crashed the car in the accident that killed my mother. I've put in a request for the old police file. We need to head over to the records department to collect it. Do you want to ride with me?"

Declan grinned. "Beats sitting around here. Let's go."

The Corporate Records & Logistics department was in Parramatta. All of the New South Wales police records relating to archived cases were kept there on site. As Declan started the ignition of the unmarked police vehicle and entered the stream of traffic heading west, Noah pulled out his phone and called ahead to let them know they were on their way.

Traffic was slow as people made their way to work and did the school run. Pulled up a set of lights, Declan sighed with impatience. He tapped his fingers on the steering wheel. He scratched his nose. Finally, he turned to Noah.

"So, what did you get up to on the weekend? Anything exciting?"

"I went out clubbing with my brother. The Pit."

Declan looked at him without comprehension. "It's in the city," Noah added.

Declan shook his head. "Never heard of it. I'm a married man, remember? Three kids under six. I can't remember the last time I went to a nightclub."

Noah shot him a look of sympathy. "Poor old man."

"Hey! Steady on the old! I'm only forty."

"So, what did you get up to on the weekend? Twister?" Noah grinned.

"Ha, ha. Smartass. In fact, I took the twins to the park and played soccer. Ran off a bit of their energy."

Noah kept his expression somber. "Sounds super exciting. How old are they?"

"Three. And my daughter is five."

Noah pulled a face. "Ouch."

Declan smiled with amusement. "That's exactly how I felt when I was your age."

"How long have you been married?"

"Nearly six years."

"You sound…happy about it."

"I *am* happy about it. Chloe's the love of my life. I couldn't imagine what it would be like to live without her. God, did I just say that? I'm such a sap. Chloe would fall over herself laughing if she heard me."

"She sounds like one hell of a woman."

"She is. One in a lifetime. You got a girlfriend?"

"No."

"Boyfriend?"

"Hell, no. I like women well enough. It's just that…" His voice petered off. He flushed with embarrassment.

Declan shot him a look. "It's just what?"

Noah's embarrassment deepened. Declan continued to throw him expectant looks. Noah shrugged. "I get tongue tied whenever I get near them. Especially one I like."

Declan grinned. "Man, you need to get out and meet more of them. Practice, if you like. It gets easier the more times you do it. It's even easier if you practice with girls you're not into."

"So you're suggesting I go up to some random female and start up a conversation?"

"Why not?"

"Because it's weird."

"Why? You're in a nightclub. People who go to nightclubs are looking for a mate. Everyone knows that."

"Maybe I just like to dance."

Declan rolled his eyes. "Puhlease! Are you *sure* you're not into guys?"

Noah's cheeks heated. His thoughts immediately went to Ayla. "No, I'm definitely not into guys."

"So what did you do at The Pit?"

"I hung out with my brother, Logan. Had a few drinks. Danced."

"With a woman?"

"Of course."

"Well, that's good. It's a start. Did you share any conversation?"

"Yes. We did. In fact, she was really easy to talk to."

"So I take it you weren't into her?"

Noah flushed again. "To the contrary. I was very into her."

"And yet you were able to carry on a conversation with her?"

"Yes."

"So sometimes you can manage it," Declan replied, his brow creasing in thought. The lights turned green and he hit the accelerator. The car leaped forward. He shot Noah a measured look. "Maybe you overthink things, mate? Get yourself into a panic? The thing is, talking to a woman all comes down to practice. Like I was telling you."

Noah nodded in agreement. Declan was the second person to encourage him to put himself out there and meet as many women as he could. Perhaps it was good advice, after all. Heading out to The Pit last Friday night had resulted in him meeting Ayla and that was a good thing. Too bad he hadn't asked for her number. Still, she knew he worked for the LECC and she'd told him she was a cop. It shouldn't be too hard for her to track him down if she wanted to. That was the question. Did she want to? Was she as into him as he'd been into her? He wished he knew.

An hour later, they arrived at the records department. An

attractive young woman in her twenties sat in a chair behind the counter. She had blond hair, blue eyes and a tidy figure. Declan took one look at her and turned and gave Noah a meaningful look of encouragement, followed by a wink.

Noah was immediately filled with nerves. His palms turned sweaty. His cheeks flooded with heat. Declan stood back, forcing Noah to approach the woman behind the desk.

"G-good-morning. I'm D-detective Craigdon. This is Detective Munro. I called earlier. We're here about the C-craigdon file."

While Noah blushed furiously, Declan stepped forward and shook the woman's hand. She glanced at Noah. "I was the one you spoke to. I took the liberty of locating the file. I have it here." She handed a file across the counter. Noah took it from her. It was much thinner than he expected for an investigation that had resulted in someone's death.

"Th-thank you," he mumbled.

Declan rolled his eyes. Noah steadfastly ignored him. He tucked the file under his arm and bid the woman a muttered farewell. The bright morning sunshine hit him full in the face as he walked out of the building and headed toward the carpark.

"What the hell was that all about?" Declan asked, chuckling.

Noah pretended innocence. "What?"

"That. In there. Didn't you listen to anything I said? There was a gorgeous woman in there. You had every opportunity to flirt with her and you failed miserably. You looked like you were about to face your executioner, not engage in casual conversation with an attractive female." Declan shook his head slowly from side to side, his expression somber. "Boy. You sure weren't joking when you said women tie you up in knots. You need more practice than I thought."

And then he gave him a friendly slap on the back. "Never mind. There'll be plenty of other opportunities. Lucky you have me. I haven't met a woman I couldn't charm. Just ask my wife. We met while she was investigating me for police corruption."

Noah smiled in surprise and shook his head.

Declan winked. "It's all in your manner, mate. There's an art to approaching women. One I happened to perfect. Trust me, you're going to be able to observe and learn from the best."

The two men laughed. With that, they climbed into their car and headed back the way they'd come.

Commander Ayla Rodriguez sat at her desk in the police executive offices that were located in the heart of the city and dealt with the pile of emails that had come in over the course of the weekend. In her position as chief of staff for Police Commissioner Kevin Beechwood, it was her responsibility to deal with any emergency that might arise in relation to her boss. Given Kevin's flagrant disregard for the rules, it was no easy task.

Right now she was formulating a response to an enquiring journalist who appeared to have way more information about the commissioner's personal life than she should. Ayla wondered about the woman's source. Then again, maybe the journalist had been following him. It wasn't hard to do, given Kevin's flamboyance and desire to see and be seen. It was the bane of Ayla's existence keeping his name out of the papers.

And then she thought about her Friday night. The way she'd spent it clubbing with her friends, and in particular, her time at The Pit. At the thought of Noah Craigdon, her cheeks grew warm. He was a cop, so he understood the job like lay people couldn't. He was also nice. And cute. And he loved to dance. Not only loved it, he was good at it. Such a contradiction. Sweet and shy, but amazing on the dance floor. So confident, so sexy. A heady combination.

The door to the commissioner's office opened and Kevin strode out. In his mid-fifties, he was of average height and average build. His gray hair was cut military short. A soft paunch spilled over the top of his trousers. Today he was clean-shaven, but he went through periods where he grew a beard. It always made him look decades older. Ayla could never work out why he did it.

He came up to her and tossed a file on her desk. "I heard whispers the LECC might be looking into the motor vehicle accident involving Henry Craigdon," he said without preamble.

Ayla's stomach lurched at the mention of the Craigdon name, but she forced herself to keep her expression blank. "Really? Why would they be interested in a case that happened more than ten years ago?"

His lip curled up in disgust. "Who knows? They must have plenty of time on their hands. Or a limitless budget. Frankly, either scenario is plausible. This new LECC is a joke. They think they're going to identify every single case of serious police misconduct in this state. Ha! They're babes in the wood. The Police Integrity Commission couldn't keep a handle on it. What makes them think they'll be any different?" He paused and gave her a pointed look. "You haven't…?"

She flushed and briefly lowered her gaze. "No, of course not."

His gaze remained hard. "You're happy in your position as my chief of staff, aren't you?"

"Absolutely. It's a dream job."

He nodded, his lips compressed. "Yes, it is. And it can disappear in a heartbeat. Life's like that. You can never take it for granted. Don't you forget that."

With that, he turned on his heel and left, leaving Ayla staring after him, confused and shaken. Dread formed in the pit of her stomach.

What the hell was that all about?

Chapter Three

There were scant few pieces of paper that made up the decade-old investigation into Henry Craigdon's motor vehicle accident. Noah and Declan had the entire contents of the file spread across Declan's desk. Declan picked up the police report made at the time of the incident. He scanned the opening lines and then frowned.

"Kevin Beechwood was the officer in charge of the investigation."

Noah looked at him in surprise. "The same Kevin Beechwood who's the current Police Commissioner?"

"Yep."

"You're kidding!"

"Nope."

"Great. That complicates things. Now what do we do?"

Declan shrugged. "We do what we always do. We examine the evidence, see what we come up with. You already indicated there's no guarantee Hassad was telling the truth."

"Yeah, but I understand the conversation in question occurred with Hassad's daughter. It was nothing more than casual talk. She didn't know about the events he spoke of. She didn't know the people involved. There was no motivation for him to lie to her. The way I see it, he was merely passing on information in the course of an idle conversation and therefore, it's more likely he told the truth."

Declan looked unconvinced. "Yeah, maybe." He scanned the report again. "It says here Sergeant Joseph Bettino was Beechwood's 2IC. What do we know about him?"

Noah reached for another piece of paper. "I did some digging into his background—thirty-four years of age, divorced, father of two. He's the non-custodial parent. Lives in Cronulla. He's currently on paid stress leave from the police service."

Declan nodded and looked at the police report again. "According to this, the accident occurred at 11.18pm on Saturday, 10 April, 2010 on McDonalds Road, Polkobin." He looked at Noah. "It's an area in the Hunter Valley famous for its wineries. About two-and-a-half hours' drive north of Sydney. Nice place to stay for the weekend."

"I'll take your word for it," Noah replied.

Declan flicked through the other papers on his desk. "Let's see what else we have here. Statements from Beechwood as the OIC, Bettino as the 2IC, a report from the police mechanic…" He scanned the contents. "No mechanical fault with the vehicle. Then there's a draftsman's drawing of the scene of the accident to scale, including a handful of photos of the scene. We also have a report from a Dr Richard Mitchell of Maitland Hospital pronouncing Janelle Mary Craigdon dead on arrival."

He looked up. "I'm sorry. I hope this doesn't stir up bad memories."

Noah bit his lip and shook his head. "It happened a long time ago. I still miss her, of course, but the pain of that day has faded with time. I must admit, this has brought things back again, but I need to know what happened. All these years, I believed my mother died in a tragic accident. My uncle insisted that was the case. Now I'm not so sure. For better or worse, it's time to expose the truth, once and for all."

"What were they doing out there together?" Declan asked. "Were they on a business trip? Did your mother work for him?"

"No. She didn't work for him. We were shocked when we were told where she was killed and that she was with Uncle Henry in his car. We still have no idea why she was with him. She'd told my father she was staying with a girlfriend for the weekend. Harriet Young was a good friend of my mother's and had apparently been recently released from hospital after surgery. My mother said she was going to look after her for a couple of days until the woman's daughter could fly down from Brisbane. Dad didn't think too much of it. He knew Harriet had undergone surgery for "women's problems" as he put it. The only thing, Harriet lived in Northbridge, a long way from the Hunter Valley."

"Did anyone speak to her afterward to find out why your mother wasn't there?"

"No. Not as far as I know. We were all too traumatized from her death. None of us were thinking straight. I was only eighteen. We were in shock. Plus, we believed Uncle Henry. He'd never given us a reason not to."

"Were any of you interviewed by the police at the time?"

"No. Except Dad. He was the one they informed about Mom's death. Dad was the one who told the rest of us."

"How many of you are there?"

"I have an older brother and a younger brother. And I just found out I have a half-sister."

Declan merely raised a single dark eyebrow. Noah flushed. "S-Sophia. She's… She's my dad's daughter to…Elizabeth Craigdon." He finished in a rush and stared hard at the floor, willing his embarrassment to cease.

Declan frowned. "Elizabeth Craigdon? Isn't she…?"

"Yes. My aunt. Married to Henry Craigdon."

Declan responded with a low whistle. "Wow. And I thought my family was complicated!" He grinned and Noah slowly grinned back, relieved the awkward moment was over.

Declan returned his attention to the police report. "According to this, your mother wasn't wearing a seatbelt. She was thrown through the windscreen and died from severe head trauma at the scene."

"Is that supported by the autopsy report?" Noah asked.

Declan flicked through the papers and came up with nothing. "It isn't here."

Noah frowned. "The matter would have been automatically referred to the coroner because of the death. There would have been an autopsy."

"I'm not saying there wasn't one. I'm only saying it hasn't been included in the police file."

"I'm going to request a copy of the autopsy report. I want to get a clearer picture of how my mother died."

"Fair enough."

Once again, Declan referred to the police report. "It says here that mandatory drug and alcohol tests were performed on the driver at the Maitland Police Station. The results were negative."

Noah felt a surge of relief. At the same time, he wondered why John Hassad had lied to his daughter.

"So it appears John Hassad wasn't telling the truth after all," Declan mused, voicing Noah's thoughts.

"Seems so," Noah agreed. "The negative test results explain why we were never told my uncle was drunk. John Hassad lied. The question is, why? What did he have to gain?"

Just another mystery I have to unravel…

Declan continued with the report. "Apparently the driver indicated he'd swerved to miss a kangaroo. He lost control and hit a tree."

Noah frowned. "Swerving to avoid an animal is contrary to traffic laws and involves criminality. Why weren't any charges laid?"

Declan shrugged. "It looks like the matter was deemed to be an accident where no fault was attributable to the driver and the case was closed. There's no indication whether a civil suit was instigated by the family of the deceased. Do you have any information on that?"

"No. The family didn't sue."

And that was that.

Declan gathered the scattered papers into a pile and replaced them in the file. "Where to from here?" he asked.

Noah looked at him grimly. "Might as well start with the man at the top.'

"Beechwood?"

"Of course."

Declan groaned. "I thought you'd say that. Beechwood has a reputation for being a bit of a dick with an ego the size of Sydney Harbour. He's not going to welcome our intrusion."

Noah grinned, filled with anticipation. "Just the kind of interview I like to do."

"And yet you look like you couldn't even swat a fly," Declan mused.

Noah winked. "You're a decorated police officer. You should know better than to judge a book by its cover."

"I'll call and set up an appointment," Declan muttered, reaching for the phone.

As Ayla tackled the huge pile of letters in her in-tray, her thoughts kept returning to Noah. It had been five days since she'd met the sexy cop and she couldn't seem to get him off her mind. She still hadn't decided if she wanted to track him down. They hadn't exchanged numbers, but he wouldn't be hard to find. After all, he'd told her he worked for the LECC. They only had one head office in Sydney and it was a short cab ride down the street.

Did she want to track him down?

It would most certainly indicate her level of interest. Did she want to show her hand like that? But how else would she get to see him again? And she did want to see him again.

At twenty-nine, she was well past the impulsiveness of youth, and she was also mature enough that she was past playing games. She liked him, was attracted to him. She enjoyed spending time with him. She wanted to get to know him better. That should be all that mattered.

Decision made, she reached for the phone. At the same time, she tapped the keys on her keyboard and opened a search engine. She typed in the words "LECC" and was rewarded with their contact details. Before she could put her plan into action, the receptionist appeared before her, an expectant look on her face.

"Ayla, there are two investigators from the LECC waiting outside. They don't have an appointment, but they asked to see the commissioner."

Ayla stared up at the woman and her heart skipped a beat. *No, it can't be. Just a coincidence. That's all.*

Gathering her wits, she gave the receptionist a smile. "Send them in, Sarah. I'll see them now."

A few moments later, Sarah returned to Ayla's office. Behind her followed Noah Craigdon and another man, equally tall and broad-shouldered. Both men had that somber look about them that told her they meant business. This was no idle meet and greet.

With an effort, she got her pulse rate under control and offered them a bland smile. "Gentlemen. What can I do for you?"

It was the unfamiliar officer who replied. "I'm Inspector Declan Munro. This is Detective Noah Craigdon. We're here to see the commissioner."

"What about?"

Noah cleared his throat. "We're looking into a traffic accident involving the death of Janelle Craigdon that happened ten years ago. The commissioner was the officer in charge of the investigation at the time."

His words echoed through her head. She was still trying to come to terms that the man who'd filled her thoughts since the previous Friday night was now standing before her. Then the import of what he'd said registered.

All of a sudden, she felt lightheaded. She recalled her boss mentioning the rumor that the LECC had started looking into the Craigdon MVA, but after her initial surprise, she'd completely dismissed the conversation from her mind. Now two stern-faced investigators from the internal affairs department stood before her asking to see her boss. She blinked hard and did her best to hide her discomfort.

"Ten years ago? Why the sudden interest?"

"Do you mind letting the commissioner know we're here?" Noah asked, neatly sidestepping her question. He gave her a level look. They both knew he had no obligation to reveal anything about an LECC investigation.

"O-of course."

Seeing him here, in his professional capacity, threw her off balance. Her normally unruffled demeanor deserted her. It was all she could do to remain calm and unaffected. She could see Noah was also struggling. He lowered his gaze and shuffled his feet and then looked at her again.

Their gazes caught and held for what seemed like an eternity. She saw the questions in Noah's eyes, but was helpless to answer them. When he finally looked away, she felt shaken, embarrassed, confused.

"I-I'll let him know you're here." With that she turned and headed straight for her boss' office.

As they waited for Ayla to return, Noah shot a surreptitious glance in Declan's direction, hoping his partner wouldn't notice the temporary shock that had surged through Noah the moment he spotted Ayla. She'd told him she was a cop. She hadn't told him she worked for the Police Commissioner. He took a moment to adjust.

She looked different to the vivacious woman with the long flowing hair and sparkly, barely-there outfit he'd met the previous Friday night. Instead she wore a tailored designer suit. The pale pink jacket was fitted. The matching skirt fell to just above her knees.

All perfectly sophisticated and proper. Nothing like the spontaneous, wild firecracker he'd danced with. Of course, her grace and poise were just as evident in the suit as it had in the nightclub, but that's where the similarity ended. Instead of her long hair loose and flowing, it was tucked into a neat bun that sat on the back of her neck and secured with pins. There wasn't a hair out of place.

When Ayla returned, her expression looked decidedly strained. Noah couldn't help but wonder what effect news of their arrival had had on the commissioner. Surely he had to wonder why the LECC had chosen to investigate such an old case. No doubt he'd plie them with questions.

"Commissioner Beechwood will see you now," Ayla said tightly and then turned and led the way back to Beechwood's office.

She opened the door and stepped back to allow them to enter. She pulled the door closed behind them. The office was large and airy. It was fitted out with rich wood paneling and stained glass windows. Sunshine poured through the window behind the commissioner's head.

The walls were decorated with several paintings in gilded frames. Next to them were similarly framed citations and awards, including one where the commissioner had been delivered the keys to the city. A floor-to-ceiling bookcase overflowed with books and smaller framed pictures and other nick knacks and collectibles lined the shelves.

Beechwood greeted them with forced civility, but they had expected that. No one wanted a visit from the LECC, particularly when it involved opening an investigation into one of their old cases. The commissioner indicated they take a seat on the studded leather couch that matched the same style of the seat behind his desk. Noah and Declan did as they were asked.

"Gentlemen, Ms Rodriguez tells me you're here about the Craigdon investigation."

Declan nodded. "Yes."

The commissioner nodded. "I must say, I'm surprised. What would you want with that old matter? It was an open and shut case."

"So you remember it?" Noah asked.

Beechwood shrugged. "Not in any great detail, but I remember enough to know there was nothing to it."

Noah and Declan shared a glance, but neither man commented. Instead, Noah asked, "Do you remember who worked that investigation with you?"

The commissioner screwed up his face in thought. "I think it was Joe Bettino. He was a young sergeant, still wet behind the ears. If I recall correctly, Maitland was his first country posting." He smiled fondly.

"Where can we find him?" Declan asked.

Beechwood paused. "I'm not sure. We lost touch some time ago. Let me make some calls, see what I can do."

The commissioner stood and moved around his desk. "Well, it was sure nice meeting the two of you. I'll let you know how I go with Bettini, but I'm not making any promises. I haven't seen the man for almost a decade."

It was obvious they were being dismissed. Noah and

Declan stood. Noah pulled out a business card and offered it to Beechwood.

"If you remember anything you think might help us, give us a call."

The commissioner merely offered him a tight smile. On the way out, Noah couldn't help but look toward Ayla. She sat upright behind her desk, her gaze fixed on the computer screen in front of her. He tried to catch her eye, offered her a brief wave but she either didn't see him or deliberately ignored him. The stab of disappointment was almost overwhelming.

Ayla stared at her screen and pretended to tap away at her keyboard until Noah and his partner had left. She was trembling with fear. Two officers from the LECC had arrived on her doorstep. Albeit, they appeared to have the Commissioner in their sights, but what if they dug deeper? Discovered the truth? It would be the end of her. She couldn't believe her past was coming back to haunt her. She'd worked so hard to keep it buried. She thought it would stay that way forever.

Most people assumed she'd slept her way to the top. She was the youngest chief of staff ever. Most people were in their late-thirties—even older—before they could be considered for such a lofty position.

She couldn't care less what people thought of her morals. How she got to where she was now was so much worse than performing sexual favors for her superiors. She dreaded anyone finding out the truth.

NOAH is available for preorder at all of the digital retailers. It will be released on 18 April, 2021.

About the Author

Chris Taylor grew up on a farm in north-west New South Wales, Australia. She always had a thirst for stories and recalls writing her first book at the ripe old age of eight. Always a lover of romance and happily-ever-afters, a career in criminal law sparked her interest in intrigue and suspense. For Chris to be able to combine romance with suspense in her books is a dream come true.

Chris is married to Linden and is the mother of five children. If not behind her computer, you can find her doing the school run, taxiing children to swimming lessons, football, ballet and cricket. In her spare time, Chris loves to read her favorite authors who include Richard North Patterson, Sandra Brown, Kathleen E Woodiwiss and Jude Devereaux.

You can find out more about Chris and sign up for her newsletter at her website:

http://www.christaylorauthor.com.au

www.ingramcontent.com/pod-product-compliance
Lightning Source LLC
Chambersburg PA
CBHW060802190726
48285CB00002B/525